A LAW FOR THE LION

"Mr. Auchincloss, with surprise and invention, wit and knowledge of the field, keeps you reading."

The New York Times

"Light, sophisticated, yet heartwarming."

Library Journal

Louis Auchincloss

A Law
For
The Lion

 AVON PUBLISHERS OF BARD, CAMELOT, DISCUS AND EQUINOX BOOKS

AVON BOOKS
A division of
The Hearst Corporation
959 Eighth Avenue
New York, New York 10019

First Avon Printing, October, 1971

AVON TRADEMARK REG. U.S. PAT. OFF. AND
FOREIGN COUNTRIES, REGISTERED TRADEMARK—
MARCA REGISTRADA, HECHO EN CHICAGO, U.S.A.

Printed in the U.S.A.

"One law for the lion and ox is oppression."

WILLIAM BLAKE

Part One

1

ELOISE DILWORTH, without going so far as to attribute the various personal events that altered her life in the fall and early winter of 1949 to her mother's visit in the preceding August, was quite sure that she was right in dating them from that time. Until then, it sometimes seemed to her, she had lived her life in a single tone, a mild tone of light grey, the perfect cover for a subdued but continuing anxiety. Afterwards the tone had changed with the situations.

She and her husband had rented a house for the summer, an old house of weather-beaten shingle with a crazy tower and banging screen doors, on the dunes of the south shore of Long Island. Storey Beach was a small and sober summer community of lawyers and bankers; its only really impressive house was the big, white, clean cottage of her uncle, Gerald Hunt, half a mile down the dunes from her own. Uncle Gerald, who was her husband's senior law partner, was quite the most magnificent creature that her family had produced, a bland, polished, hearty gentleman whose eye was unfailingly cheerful and whose heart unfailingly realistic. George, her husband, would have preferred to have spent his summers in Southampton, which offered greater social advantages, but he was not yet sufficiently sure of himself to give up the encircling protection of Gerald's avuncular arm.

It was precisely because of its quietness and sobriety

that Eloise had wanted her mother to visit her in Storey Beach. Irene, as everyone, including Eloise's little girls, called her mother, had recently come back from Paris, after long years of expatriation and remittances, for an operation. This had been performed successfully, and she was staying in a hotel in New York, much recuperated, where all the family, particularly Eloise, had been to see her. It was definitely not felt, however, that Irene would like Storey Beach or even, more importantly, that Storey Beach would like Irene, and in this respect Eloise had been obliged to listen to the kind of arguments to which her family always resorted on such occasions.

George Dilworth placed his opposition squarely on moral grounds. Irene was disreputable, he maintained; it was as simple as that. The example of her life, to say nothing of the sophistication of her conversation and occasional intemperance of her drinking habits, would hardly be an example for their two little girls or even for Eloise herself. George, who at forty-seven was fourteen years older than his wife, felt entitled to advise her in such matters. Like many lawyers he derived a definite satisfaction from selecting a word like "disreputable," a word out of fashion even with his own generation, and using it, deliberately and emphatically, even antagonistically, to underline his conscious self-identification with an earlier day of more rigid principles. He regarded this identification entirely as an intellectual rather than a reactionary process. He was never, he always maintained, a stuffy man. The stuffy man was he who accepted old values out of his emotional need without having thought them through. Yet Eloise knew perfectly well that his moral code was almost confessedly tied up with his simple American goal of getting ahead, a goal in which he had an absolute faith, less from hardness of character on his part than from a näive and literal acceptance of what he thought he had been taught as a child in a New Hampshire rectory.

"The thing about your mother is that she's thrown away everything she's ever had," he pointed out to her one Sunday morning while they were sitting on the beach. "Her money, her only child, two out of her three husbands. Her life has been a figurative strip-tease."

"I don't think I like that, George."

"You may not like it, my dear, but you'll have to admit there's more than a grain of truth in it."

"More than a grain?" she protested. "But I *want* more than a grain. Don't you?"

He shrugged his shoulders.

"You want a lot."

She looked at him critically. George was the kind of man who in a business suit seemed too well built to have anything to gain from clothes; one had to see his white, hirsute, rather lumbering body at the beach to realize their importance to him. Then the whole dignified and severe effect of his smooth black hair, almost free of grey, his small thick firm nose and grey eyes, the round cheeks and cleft oval chin which were dark with the thickness of his closely razored beard was diminished to something more stubborn, almost pouting.

"Your mother and I form a rather interesting contrast if you can see it that way," he continued. "We started out on opposite sides of the fence. She's spent her life jettisoning her cargo. I've spent mine accumulating one."

"I wonder if it isn't fundamentally the same thing."

"Really, Eloise! I don't see that at all."

No, she reflected thoughtfully, you wouldn't. George believed too implicitly in the validity of his goal. When people recognized this in him, when they appreciated the quality of his sincerity, they could become quite fond of him, but when this was not the case, when they failed to see it as ingenuousness, they were apt to

11

dislike him. Most of the persons in the latter category were those whom he had outgrown socially. For it seemed perfectly obvious and proper to George that one should change one's friends in life as one got ahead, as inevitably as one paid a higher income tax, lost more hair or put on weight. It was difficult for him even to understand that such things should be resented.

"I'm always nice about *your* mother," she pointed out.

"But that's an entirely different thing," he answered in the same willfully patient semi-exasperated tone that he used with the little girls. George treated children and adults in exactly the same fashion. "My mother never abandoned me to the care of an uncle while she gallivanted around Europe. She worked for us and loved us. And it was no easy job, either, let me tell you, being a minister's widow with six children to raise."

"I know your mother's a good woman, George," she said stubbornly. "But she's your mother, that's the point. Not mine."

"I fail to see what that has to do with it."

"It has everything to do with it!"

"You mean Irene can do no wrong? Because she's your mother?"

"No. I mean that no one but me has the right to criticize her. No one but me was hurt."

"I must say, Eloise," he said shaking his head and frowning, "I've rarely seen you in such a contrary mood."

Uncle Gerald's objections were simpler. He had always deplored Irene, not so much for the life she had led as for the trouble it had caused him. Although he could usually be prevailed on to help out when it was absolutely necessary, he saw no reason why the tranquillity of Storey Beach, which he regarded as peculiarly his own, should be shattered by the presence of a controversial younger sister who had enjoyed all the

12

beaches of Europe, many of them at his expense. Gerald had the amiable imperturbability of one who has been early and continually successful, who had never really doubted that he would succeed his late father, the Judge, as senior partner of Hunt & Livermore. He did his duty as he saw it in a bland, unfussing manner that seemed to imply that life was complicated not so much by the undutiful as by the confused. There was little question in his mind that Irene was one of the latter.

"I want to talk to you, my dear," he told Eloise later that same morning when he found her watching her two daughters having their swimming lesson in the pool of the tiny bath club of which, needless to say, he was president. Straight and thin at seventy, he made the rounds of the pool and terrace every Sunday after lunch in a straw hat, a blue coat and tightly pressed, closely fitting, yellowing flannels.

"George tells me you want to have your mother down here," he continued, steering her along the side of the pool by her elbow. "Now let me make one thing entirely clear. I *like* that in you, Eloise. I expect it of you. You've always shown complete loyalty. And I think a mother deserves loyalty, no matter what she may have done." He held up a hand to stop her as she was about to speak. Gerald rarely expected to argue; his technique was to anticipate contrary argument, to overwhelm one with approval until opposition seemed churlish, to triumph in a single monologue. "Now wait, my dear. What you perhaps don't entirely appreciate is that Irene is more the responsibility of my generation than yours. We're a good deal older and a good bit tougher, too. I think I understand her pretty well, even if she is ten years my junior. I think I can safely predict that she will be bored down here with the children and George and me and—you know." He frowned and shrugged his shoulders as if, with his sym-

13

pathy and understanding, he could even put himself in Irene's alien shoes.

"I'd try to amuse her, Uncle Gerald," she protested.

"Of course, you would, my dear! No one would try harder. But you can't get away from the fact that it just isn't your mother's cup of tea. Now leave it to me, Eloise. I'll have it all fixed. When she's feeling a bit better I'll see to it that she has a trip to Saratoga or Southampton. Much more in her line, you know, with bridge and cocktail parties and things like that."

"Uncle Gerald, if you don't mind," she said desperately, "I think I know what's best for Irene. I've asked her down here, and she's coming. That's the way it is."

She stopped and had to take a breath, her heart beating very fast. She had always, since her childhood, hated being praised by Uncle Gerald. It only made what she regarded as his inevitable disillusionment the more painful.

"I see," he said, obviously taken aback, but nodding his head. "Well, if that's the way it is, then we must make the best of it, mustn't we?"

That was how Uncle Gerald differed from George. He would never waste energy over an accomplished fact. Grateful, she felt dependent again.

"Will you ask George to be nice about it, Uncle Gerald?" she begged. "As long as he's spoken to you about it anyway?"

He gave her elbow a little squeeze.

"George be nice about it? Why, of course, he'll be nice about it! The only person we're really thinking of is you, my dear."

Eloise smiled without in the least believing him. It never occurred to her that older members of the family should not be hypocrites.

When she met her mother at the train the following week, she was struck by her thinness. Irene had always

14

been pale and thin, but she seemed actually gaunt as she descended slowly from the car, looking carefully down at each step as she took it, one hand on the railing and the other held out to balance herself. Yet when she finally glanced up and saw Eloise and smiled, she was the old Irene again. It was a smile of such charming surprise, a surprise that expressed pleasure but not asonishment that Eloise should be there to meet her and at the same time, without in any way diminishing her welcome, somehow indicating that if she hadn't been, then she, Irene, could still have managed for herself. Oh, yes, Irene had charm, Eloise reflected as she waved back to her, charm in the truest sense of that overused word, charm that was her only discipline and had to make up, in its easy solitude, for the lack of so many others. There was not a spot or a wrinkle on her white summer dress, even after her long trip, not a bead of perspiration on her high, white powdered brow or on her long bony fingers with all the big rings. Only the black circles under her large dark eyes and the row of moisture on her upper lip, touching the rouge and making it glisten, gave any indicaion of her exhaustion or the heat. "There, my dear," she said when Eloise had kissed her, "it's a bit hot for that, don't you think? Do take care of my love birds, child. They're in with the baggage in a frame covered with brown wrapping paper. Do you think they'll like the sea air?"

Eloise pointed out changes in the neighborhood in a rather nervous way during the short drive from the station, but Irene only nodded, smiling enigmatically and not really looking at anything. When they got to the house they found Peggy and Jo, Eloise's two daughters, waiting for them on the porch before the front door. Peggy was twelve; she was tall and thin and liked to stand demurely in front of older people, her heels together, her large hazel eyes discreetly fixed on the

15

floor. Jo, a year younger, was fatter and bolder; her blond hair was cut in an uncompromising bang.

"Mummy, can we ask Irene a question?" Peggy inquired.

"If it's a nice question, dear."

They both turned immediately to their grandmother.

"Will you show us your scar, Irene?" Jo demanded.

"The scar from your operation," Peggy explained.

"But you mustn't ask a thing like that," Irene reproved them.

"Why not?"

"Because, as your mother would say, it's not a nice question."

"Why isn't it?"

"It doesn't matter why. Some questions are nice and some aren't. You have to learn which are which, that's all."

"That sounds silly."

"It *is* silly," Irene conceded. "Lots of important things are silly."

"Children," Eloise broke in, "Irene is tired. She wants to go up to her room now."

When she was sitting on the porch later, staring out at the ocean and waiting for her mother to come down for tea, she reflected how little Irene liked children, yet how entirely at ease she was with them. Eloise loved her daughters, but she could still be a little bit envious of Irene's unconcern at her own maternal deficiency. Life was so simple for people like that. The screen door behind her banged, and Irene came out. She went slowly over to the railing and stood with her hands on it, gazing down the dunes.

"The same old beach," she said, shaking her head with a rather mocking air of melancholy. "Is it any wonder that if a child is brought up here the way I was, with her nose stuck into the Atlantic, she'll want to cross it rather than drown?" She smiled and shrugged her shoulders as she pointed down the beach to her brother's house. "I see Gerald's white box is just as it was. Would I have been happier, do you suppose, child, if I'd stayed in New York and Storey Beach and married a man who could set me up in a big white house like Gerald's? Maybe." She became almost serious as she gazed down the beach. "Maybe indeed I would have."

"Now, Irene," Eloise protested quickly, knowing how close to boredom this mood of her mother's could be, "you forget. Sentiment doesn't become you. If you go on that way I'll get you a long black dress and a white cap. Like Whistler's Mother. Say something sharp, dear. To clear the air."

Irene turned around with a little smile, taking her in, obviously, for the first time that day.

"Something sharp, you say?" she asked, coming over and sitting in a wicker armchair by Eloise. She turned and looked at her again, carefully, critically. "You're not really a Renoir, you know, as some people say. You could be, but you need something. I don't quite know what. Till then, anyway, you're a Puvis de Chavannes."

Eloise smiled, determined to take it all even more lighly than Irene.

"And what are you?" she demanded, handing her her tea. "What is someone pale and thin and angular? Dark-eyed and mysterious? With a big aquamarine on a lean finger? You're a Dali, Irene. That's what you are. An early Dali."

"And what is George? A Grant Wood?"

Eloise smiled again, this time a touch less freely.

"That does it," she said. "I guess the air is quite clear again."

"You must keep me informed," Irene said dryly. "Most people, I find, prefer a mild mist."

There was a slight but awkward pause.

17

"We're giving a dinner party for you on Saturday night!" Eloise exclaimed, with a rather forced gaiety. "All the local gentry and Uncle Gerald and Aunt Gladys. I hope you'll survive it."

Irene sniffed.

"Well, do it all at once and get it over with, I suppose that's best," she said. "But I'm surprised. I wouldn't have thought George would want to feature me so."

"Oh, George is terribly fond of you, Irene. He really is."

Her mother gave her an oblique look.

"It's really very bad manners to tell fibs to people like me, child," she pointed out. "It insults our intelligence. I know perfectly well that George doesn't give a hoot about me, and I couldn't care less. But that's not the point. Does he give a hoot about anyone? Does he give a hoot about you?"

Eloise stared.

"Of course, he does, Irene. What a funny question."

"It's not a funny question at all. Does he love you? That's what I'm driving at. The way he should?"

"How should he love me, Irene? Is there a particular way?"

"Of course! Passionately!"

Eloise put her glass down on the table.

"There's a great deal said about passion first and last," she remarked. "A bit too much, don't you think?"

But Irene only laughed at her.

"Do you know this is the first time I've seen you irritated since I've been back? Let it come out, child! It won't kill you."

"Do you think it's *always* good, Irene, to let things out?"

Her mother shrugged her shoulders.

"Why not? I'm a very irritating woman. What you really want to tell me is that I've lived so long in Europe, I've forgotten what good clean American married love can be. Then *say* so!"

"I don't want to say that at all, Irene," Eloise answered, making an effort to control herself. "I know that you have very high standards about what love should be. They may be right for you. I don't presume to doubt them. But that doesn't mean that they have to be the only ones—"

She stopped. How could she go on like this under Irene's mocking eyes? Besides, it was not at all the kind of discussion that she had wanted to have with her. She folded her hands in her lap in a gesture of giving up.

Irene lit a cigarette and wagged the burning match slowly back and forth until it went out. She didn't take her eyes off her daughter.

"You don't see what I mean, darling," she said. "You haven't from the beginning. Let me try it another way. Does George snore?"

"Snore?" Eloise felt her cheeks beginning to redden. "No, what on earth makes you think so?"

"Well, I was taking a little peek around while I was upstairs, and I couldn't help noticing that you had different rooms."

Eloise looked quickly away from her, over the beach, feeling suddenly sick. When the Atlantic had been between herself and Irene she had enjoyed imagining the congeniality that she had hoped to achieve with her, a congeniality that was to have been sophisticated without being hard, warm without being too close, a mutual sympathy that in its light comfortableness was to have had nothing to do with George or the children or Uncle Gerald or Aunt Gladys.

"George sleeps better in a room by himself," she explained self-consciously. "And that, for George, is very important. You know how hard he works. Of

19

course, it doesn't mean that we aren't—that we don't
—"

"That you can't visit," Irene finished for her with an impatient shrug. "No, of course not. But it certainly means the honeymoon is over."

"Honeymoon! After thirteen years, Irene!"

"Well, my dear," her mother said, leaning back and looking at her in the half-commending, half-critical way that she had when she was making up for her tongue, "if I had hair as blond as yours and skin as light, I wouldn't expect my husband to be worried about his sleep. And if he was, I'm sure I'd let him sleep his head off. While I looked for someone who was more rested!"

"Oh, Irene." Eloise glanced quickly at her watch and jumped up. "Good heavens, I must meet George!" She leaned down to kiss her mother as casually as she could, to make as light of it as she knew how. "You're incorrigible, darling. You're just trying to make me think you're as wicked as you pretend to be!"

Wicked, Irene reflected, as she sat alone watching the flat August sea curl into sharp little breakers that rolled over and fell with a staccato bark. It was a word they had always been very fond of in Storey Beach.

2

ELOISE had grown up virtually without parents. Her father, barely remembered now even by Irene whose first husband he had been, a dark-eyed smiling boy in a photograph, dressed in football clothes and sitting on the Yale fence, had been killed in the first war when

Eloise had been only a year old. Reduced to a single parent she had really been reduced to none, for Irene, all during her childhood, had been less a mother to her than a rare and somewhat exotic possession of which she had to take particular care, a possession which other people, especially sensible, practical people like Uncle Gerald and, much later, George, were apt to find too European, too sophisticated for someone as simple and impressionable as herself. Eloise had never thought of her mother as belonging to an older generation, or, for that matter, to any generation. To her Irene had been the essence of the gay, the beautiful, the faintly malicious, the way she had been the last summer that Eloise had lived with her in Dinard, when she was twelve, in the hotel with the big windows that looked out over the beach and the red and yellow umbrellas. Irene and Pierre had scolded her because she had been ashamed to wear the French bathing suit they had brought her. She had secretly put mercurochrome on her tongue, believing it was poison, and pretended afterwards that she was too sick to go in the sea, but Irene had found out and simply made fun of her, as if she had been just another girl herself, a slightly older girl. And if ever Eloise reproached her, as she had then, begged her for more attention or sympathy, implored her to be like other mothers, Irene would only smile and face her as she was later to face the others, Uncle Gerald and Aunt Gladys and even George, ultimately, with the flat, final argument that if one was prepared to take the consequences of what one was, what more could be said? It had been this way even after Pierre had shot himself and Aunt Gladys, tight-lipped and dry-eyed, had come over to Paris to fetch Eloise back from an apparently consenting, still smiling Irene, all through the years in New York and Storey Beach with the Hunts, the still orderly years of being a young niece to an aunt whose fussiness was meant to make up for

21

love and an uncle whose decorous politeness was meted out to her exactly as it was meted out to everyone else. Yet there was always the image of Irene, so different and obviously, by all accepted standards so impossible, roving from Paris to Rome, from Rome to Paris, in a white Renault, wearing a long veil and a hat with a wide brim and perhaps casting an occasional mildly curious, semi-amused glance across the tossing Atlantic to where her daughter was sitting quietly at table in the sea-green dining room at Storey Beach. And thinking of her mother's rare visits to New York Eloise could still feel the thrill of coming back from school into the dark, armor-gleaming hall of Uncle Gerald's town house and hearing Irene's sharp, clear tones bouncing down the stairway from the drawing room where she was talking to Aunt Gladys, and rushing up the stairs and leaping into her arms and hugging her and dragging her up to her bedroom so that she might have her alone, all to herself, between four walls where just for the moment, anyway, it wouldn't matter, even to Uncle Gerald, that Irene was not as other people. But when the first rapturous moments had passed, when she had lovingly fingered all of her mother's big, semi-precious jewels and had heard what play or plays Irene might take her to, and when she had settled down to pouring out to her the passionate things that went on at Miss Heely's School, the teacher she had a crush on and the girls who made fun of her because she never understood jokes of a certain kind, she would see, after a moment, the abstracted look in Irene's eyes and know with a dead tired feeling that Irene was bored.

"Well, I suppose your mother found it thoroughly dead here," Aunt Gladys would say after each of these visits, shaking her head so that the tall grey hair over her brown forehead wiggled. She disapproved entirely of her sister-in-law and made little effort to hide it from Eloise. "But if anyone expects me to turn this house

22

into a three-ring circus every time she comes, they're very much mistaken!"

She grew up, of course, to resent her aunt. It was only to be expected after such remarks. But she never for a conscious moment forgot that her resentment was basically unjustified, that it was she who had been thrust upon Aunt Gladys, not Aunt Gladys upon her. Her uncle and aunt never asked her for gratitude and to do them justice they never really expected it, but she always felt that she owed it to them, whether they wanted it or not, and she was careful to express it on appropriate occasions. She was surrounded by a disinterested kindness, a formal benevolence, that she knew was generally supposed to be a better thing than her mother's indifference, but she never really believed this and she clung, guiltily but firmly, to her secret disbelief. It may have been this reservation, this concealed dissidence that through her maturing years refined her good manners into docility, her gentleness almost to fatuity, that found its reflection in her motions and gestures, begun with such grace, yet somehow held back before completion, truncated, as though the performer had lost his nerve, so that the final effect was jerky instead of integrated, hurried instead of whole. Whatever it was, it even marred her looks which lacked the boldness or the frankness to stand out at the parties to which her aunt dutifully sent her, and at seventeen, at the small tea dance at which she came out, it was generally considered that she was little more than passably good looking. And yet, as she sometimes dared to ask herself, in sudden fits of boldness when alone before her mirror she would stare at herself, posing dramatically, had there ever been such eyes? Large and a light, clear blue tinged with grey, they seemed incapable, she would insist to herself, of any sort of malice, incapable of seeing, finely intelligent as they were, anything but the loveliest things in people. And her nose,

23

turning upward, her wide pale forehead and firm chin, the whole heart-shaped, high-cheekboned face, mightn't those who remembered say it was as pretty as Irene's? But no, not really, she would admit suddenly, her mood collapsing, not with her hair. Its very blondness, she would tell herself in quick humility, made her face seem doll-like.

"Uncle Gerald, would it be all right if I went to college?" she asked at breakfast one morning. "I don't mean anything expensive where I couldn't live at home. I mean Barnard."

"Barnard?" Aunt Gladys intervened. "Don't you want to go to Vassar or Bryn Mawr with the other girls from Miss Heely's?"

"Oh, Aunt Gladys, I think not. Please!"

"And *I* think that Eloise is old enough to make up her own mind," her uncle interrupted. He was by no means a stingy man, but as long as she had expressed a preference for a college where she could also live at home, he saw no reason to argue against it. Besides, he was fond of Eloise and liked having her in the house now that his own sons were married. "I never did see why it was important for girls to get their education away from home. Home should be their vocation. And a most important one it is," he added, nodding across the table with silencing approval at his wife.

Whatever her vocation, she felt at home, for the first time, at Barnard. She had less of a sense of being an imposter with her classmates than with the girls at Miss Heeley's; they came from different backgrounds, and they didn't have fathers like Uncle Gerald. One of them, Lorna Hughes, who wrote poetry without punctuation and professed to be a communist, became her first truly close friend and made her read authors like Veblen and Dos Passos whom she had never even heard mentioned by her uncle or aunt or by the English teacher at Miss Heely's. She was never fully convinced,

24

however, despite all Lorna's rather caustic arguments, that there was anything really wrong with Uncle Gerald or his friends; she developed instead, as a defense against the violence of the two extremes between which she was caught, a picture of the world as a series of smaller worlds that could exist, quite properly and easily, despite what people might say, side by side, if only they were not mingled. There was Uncle Gerald's world, for example, and Lorna's; neither could possibly be expected to like or understand the other, but was that any reason that she, Eloise, should be expected not to like or understand both? Lorna pointed out that she was simply afraid of offending either, but Eloise was impervious to such remarks. She never took her Barnard friends home or asked them to stay with her in the summer; this was a life of her own, and she saw no reason to share it with her aunt and uncle who wouldn't, in any event, have been interested. Uncle Gerald assumed that all of Columbia was red, but he assumed at the same time, with the comfortable assurance of a mind that had never opened, that any relative of his was fundamentally incorruptible. Oh, true, they might go through a slight pinkish stage, but that was like scarlet fever or the measles, perhaps even desirable as once cured one was cured forever. Aunt Gladys, for her part, was glad to have Eloise so busy and occupied; she hardly had to think of her at all. Of course, it seemed a pity that she showed so little interest in nice young people of her own sort, and it was certainly not a good idea for a girl to be too bookish, but when one thought of her mother's life, well, perhaps it was a good thing on the whole that she was leaning in the opposite direction.

There was one ambition that Eloise had always nursed when she thought of the future, the only concrete thought among the fantasies of being an actress, a singer, a great painter, of bursting like a bird of paradise from her quiet corner. This was her ambition, when she was twenty-one and in control of the tiny trust fund which Uncle Gerald had managed to save from Irene's depredations, to bid a polite but firm farewell to her aunt and uncle and sail away to Paris to join her mother. Whatever Irene's world turned out to be like, she felt quite sure that she would be more a part of it than Uncle Gerald's. And when just before her birthday, which almost coincided with her graduation, she received a cable from Paris, she hardly dared open it, wondering excitedly if Irene had really remembered to congratulate her on her impending *magna,* or even if Irene—impossible thought—were going to suggest the visit herself. But no. Of course not. The cable simply announced her marriage to Henry Bleecker and impending departure to India. The door was banged in her eager face, and Eloise could only turn wearily back for another long summer at Storey Beach, to eat and sleep and wander through the large, still, cool rooms with the shades half lowered, a book in hand, restlessly aware of the heat outside, of the perfect, ordered garden and the buzz of big insects against the window screens.

"Bleecker?" her aunt would repeat at almost every meal. "India? This time we don't even know his nationality!"

But so much stillness could not last, particularly when one was twenty-one, and that was the summer of George Dilworth. He had just been made a partner in Uncle Gerald's firm, Hunt & Livermore, at only thirty-four, and he had also just lost his wife. The Hunts had asked him to spend his vacation with them at Storey Beach and to bring his little daughter, Hilda, a child of seven. As he was in mourning, very little was provided for his diversion, and he and Eloise, thrown constantly together, soon became good friends. No man of Uncle Gerald's world had ever taken her so seriously. He

26

listened to her when she told him about her economics courses at Barnard and argued firmly but never irritably when he found her, which was frequently, "unsound." He knew a million times more about it than she did, and she gave in, as he evidently expected her to, like a convinced pupil. He taught her to play golf in the same grave, methodical but essentially encouraging way, and in the evenings while Aunt Gladys knitted and Uncle Gerald played chess with a neighbor they would sit out on the dark veranda overlooking the sea, and George, with a naïveté that she found very winning, would tell her about his late wife and their moderately happy life together and his long hard pull to get where he had got in her uncle's frim. There was something rather alarming, but at the same time not unlovable in the quality of his honesty. It was as if George could not tell anything but the truth because he lacked the imagination to understand what it was in others that made them palliate it.

"Hilda was a good girl," he said one night of his wife, his grey eyes looking into hers in the semi-darkness. "But we married too young. She would have been a better wife for the kind of man my father was. She'd have loved a small New England parsonage. New York always bewildered her. She never understood people like your aunt and uncle."

Listening to him Eloise felt a slight shudder, as though poor Hilda had been consigned to an early grave because of her inability to keep step socially with her rising husband, but even as she felt it, she knew how unfair it was and that if Hilda had lived, George would have been faithful, even kind, in his unvarying manner. She began to identify herself with Hilda, wondering if she, too, had derived a sensation of smothered pleasure at being told what to do and when to do it by this man of such remarkable assurance. When he was out fishing with Uncle Gerald, an occupation that the latter would never share with women, she spent her time with little Hilda, a serious child with long auburn hair and George's eyes, whose affection she tried hard but unsuccessfully to gain.

"Why do you always kiss me?" the girl would ask her gravely. "Mrs. Hunt doesn't kiss me. I don't like to be kissed, except by Daddy and Mummy."

When George left, taking Hilda with him, he had not said a word that she could construe as sentimental, but there was a directness about him that partially communicated what he left unsaid. When she received, a week later, a two-page letter in his rough neat handwriting asking her to be his wife, she was less surprised than she dared admit to herself.

"I know I'm a bit older, but I'm also more settled and dependable," he argued soberly in the letter, "and fundamentally I believe I'm an easy person to live with. Come and look after me and Hilda, Eloise. We'll do our best to look after you."

"Has anything happened to upset you, dear?" Aunt Gladys asked as she watched her staring blankly at the letter, minute after minute.

Eloise looked up suddenly and stared at her.

"I've just made up my mind, Aunt Gladys," she said, with a tremor in her voice, "this very minute. I'm going to marry George Dilworth."

Uncle Gerald and Aunt Gladys were, of course, delighted. A cable was duly dispatched to Irene who sent a cynical answer about the advantages of keeping Hunt & Livermore in the family. Uncle Gerald thought it in the poorest taste which indeed it was. Eloise, however, having decided that she was very happy and very much in love, minded nothing.

"George," she wrote to Lorna Hughes, "is perhaps not the kind of man whom you would find particularly exciting, but he's a man who is going to accomplish a

28

lot of things, and I think important ones. I hope I shall be able to help him."

They were married in a small chapel with only George's mother and the Hunts present, because of the short interval since Hilda's death, and took up their residence in George's house in Scarsdale. George wanted only two more children, and two were duly born, both girls, in the first two years of their marriage. He did not seem in the least to mind that neither was a boy. Children, after all, were children. Eloise made efforts to establish a relationship with her step-daughter, knowing only too well what a motherless life could be, but little Hilda, without being overtly hostile, always held herself in reserve. She continued in a rather sullen fashion to recognize no authority but her father's, and whenever Eloise asked her to do something she would look silently first to George, if he was there, for confirmation. But George was not apt to be there, that was the point. What congeniality Eloise and Hilda managed to develop through the years lay in great part in their common recognition of the fact that they each would have to be content with what was left over of George from his law practice. For he was almost terrifyingly industrious. Eloise never knew when to expect him for dinner or when he might go off on a sudden trip, to Chicago, to London, to Tokyo. He took it entirely for granted that she should accept his schedule, just as she should accept his increasing absorption in it and his almost compulsive habit of jacking his standards higher and higher as each immediate goal was reached. The bedroom arrangement that Irene had observed in Storey Beach had started a few years after their marriage at a time when he was coming home very late from the office and said he did not want to disturb her. It gradually became a habit, and in time even the "visiting" to which Irene had referred as a possibility was largely discontinued. George after forty was infrequently amorous. On a Saturday night, after a party and several drinks, he would sometimes go to her room instead of his own, but more often, with his radiating if rather silent self-assurance, he managed to convey the impression, without in any way expressing it, that such things were all very well for younger-marrieds, but could hardly be expected to play a large role in the lives of active, middle-aged citizens. Eloise could only feel, in a rather shame-faced way, that she ought to agree with him.

His industry did not go unrewarded. He rose in the firm until he was just under the small group of senior partners of whom Uncle Gerald was number one. They moved from the suburbs to the city, first to one apartment and then to a larger. Eloise had to entertain clients and other lawyers, and she had to do it often. She tried to keep in touch with her college friends, but they lived mostly in a different world and, with the exception of Lorna, she found her social life largely restricted to Hunt & Livermore. Lorna had married a poet and lived in Greenwich Village, and Eloise sometimes went there, but when she did she felt stuffy and out of place and inarticulate, even when they were jabbering about books that she had read. George said they were a lot of phonies, and it was possible that George was right, although she still harbored much of her old feeling that all ways of life were equally valid if only kept separate. Which was perhaps, she sometimes speculated, only another way of saying that she believed in none of them. She read more and more and kept her reactions increasingly to herself. She read particularly novels, novels about war and persecution and suffering, about tortured people in occupied countries and brave people in undergrounds, about raids over Germany and undersea warfare, about nightmares. She felt increasingly guilty at all the painful things in the world that she had escaped. She thought of this whenever she caught herself thinking of the pleasures that she might have missed.

But although she conformed conscientiously to George's pattern and to the pattern of his lawyer's world, she came more and more, as time went by, to fear the obliteration of herself in it. It was what she strove for and yet at the same time what she stubbornly held back from, reserving a little corner of herself to which she could more and more retreat and from which she could smile out with her shining, rather empty smile at a world that was somehow sinister behind its welcome, that seemed to scrutinize her and to nod only in semi-satisfaction, reserving a doubt as to whether she were really a true part, whether she could, in the last analysis, absolutely be counted on, no matter how well, even how charmingly she appeared to play her role. For wasn't it a role? Wasn't that, fundamentally, what people could see? And what was it, really, but an extension of the role she had played when she was little, the role of being a child to the Hunts converted into the role of being a wife to George? Was there any real she? These were the doubts and questions that she could try to drown in fiction or in fantasies, burningly erotic and attended with dreadful punishment, but they were doubts and questions that could never be submerged for long. It was their solution that she really sought, without daring to articulate it, from Irene. For Irene, bad as she had been, disapproved of as she was by Hunts and Dilworths alike, was nonetheless the source of memories and reflections that had nothing to do with the rest of Eloise's life. If Irene was what she had always been punished for, Irene at least had had rewards that she had never had. Irene represented the one small hope, a hope that the actual presence of Irene, ironically enough, was apt to smother, that there was something more in a family weekend than wet

31

bathing suits and tennis lessons, something more in a party than listening to Uncle Gerald, something more in a summer than Storey Beach.

3

ON SATURDAY NIGHT, before the first guests had arrived, Irene sat alone on the porch, dressed in black with sequins, and balefully contemplated the sea. She was not in the least looking forward to the party or to the prospect of being inspected by the curious eyes of any community as small-minded as she assumed Storey Beach to be. She had taken two more Luminal tablets than her prescription allowed and had almost been caught in the act by Eloise bursting into her room uninvited to help her pin up her dress. Now she felt slightly feverish and tense, not at all in the euphoric state that she had counted on to get her through the evening. She would be lucky, she reflected, if she managed to sneak in more than one cocktail while Eloise was not looking, and she wouldn't even put it past her to refuse her a glass of wine at dinner. But what good did wine really do, especially when it was passed as stingily as it was at George's who had some vulgar notion that it should be saved for special occasions and that guests, when they heard the pop of a cork, should smile broadly and rub their choppy hands and ask what they were celebrating?

There was a rustle behind her, and Eloise leaned down to give her a brief peck on the cheek.

"Hello, darling, you're looking wonderful," she said, and passed on to the wicker table where she deposited a small bowl of yellow flowers. "There." She turned back, plumping out her white tulle skirt, and gave Irene a bright smile. "All set for the party? Or are you simply dreading it? Poor Irene, we must seem so poky after Paris."

"Oh, I'll survive," Irene said grumpily. "Never fear."

"I've got a surprise for you," Eloise continued cheerfully, putting her hands on her knees and leaning down towards her mother. "Guess."

"Don't tell me. We're doing tableaux."

Eloise laughed too appreciatively, too much like the movie version of the grown-up daughter, sophisticated, assured, congenial.

"Aren't you mean? No. The doctor says you can have a cocktail now. A whole beautiful stinging martini. Super dry. And maybe even a dividend. If you're good."

Irene's scanty store of patience ran out at this.

"If that's your way of asking me not to get squiffed in front of Gerald and Gladys," she retorted angrily, "I wish you'd come out and say so. I can't stand your indirection, Eloise."

It gave her a fierce little pleasure, almost sharpened for just a moment by the quick stab of remorse, to see Eloise straighten up and turn pale.

"But I never meant that, Irene," she said softly. "I'm sorry, darling. It must be so trying to get used to me."

"Don't stifle me, child! *Please!*"

Eloise turned away quickly and moved about the porch, putting down packages of cigarettes and matches in handy corners, very pale and tense and humming a little tune. Irene, watching her uneasily now, could only try to persuade herself that her daughter's kindness was self-dramatization, her patience self-pity. For if Eloise was truly humble, truly sincere, where did it leave a mother who took favors and took them so ungraciously?

33

There was the sound of a car on the drive below, then another; people were prompt in Storey Beach. Then came the banging of a screen door from the front hall and George's voice, hearty but perfunctory, in greeting and the brief picture of Eloise assuming her party smile. And there, of course, Irene observed gloomily, was her brother Gerald, with his little arriving cough, coming across the porch to greet her, dominating the scene with the same easy air of superiority that he had worn so comfortably ever since her childhood, the same pleasant, politic little smile on his lips, the same neat white mustache above it. Why of all people should he at seventy have been privileged to keep every one of his steel-grey, wavy hairs, to have guarded his slimness, to look so well, so prosperous, his square neat face and light blue thoughtless eyes carefully expressing sympathy as he caught her attention? Oh, yes, he would be solicitous about her health, as solicitous as if there had never been a breach between them, as bland as if they were total strangers.

"You're looking very fit, I must say, Irene," he told her. "I suppose you're beginning to think already about getting back to your beloved France."

"I would, Gerald, if I had any money."

"Oh, come, come, things can't be that bad."

And if they were, she reflected sourly, he wouldn't want to hear about them. She had always resented his assurance that everyone was after his money and his even greater assurance that no one was going to get it.

"Well, it so happens they are," she insisted. "Not only as bad as that, but worse."

"Nothing I'm sure that your young people can't take care of. You're very lucky, you know, Irene, to have a son-in-law like George. I have the utmost confidence in that boy."

"Boy! My God, Gerald, he's forty-seven!"

"Well, that's a boy to me," he said imperturbably.

"I wonder if he seems exactly ancient even to you, Irene."

She snorted.

"Maybe he is one, at that. There's certainly something of the little girl in Eloise. In fact, I might go so far as to say there's a bit of the nursery in most of your Storey Beachers."

She watched his brow pucker with a perverse satisfaction.

"You haven't lost your sharp tongue, I see, Irene," he said reprovingly. "I hope you will confine its use to your tough old brother. Eloise, you know, is a gentle creature."

"You haven't lost your talent for sermonizing, Gerald," she retorted. "But you forget. I don't have to listen to you now. It's George I have to listen to."

He made a little bow of concession.

"I trust you find him more instructive."

"Not in the least. But he's earned the right to be listened to. That's the point."

He nodded, still maintaining his pose of mock gravity.

"And how is that right earned, may I ask?"

"By direct financial support, of course. Why else, in the name of God, would anyone listen to a sermon from a relative?"

But he only laughed, putting his head back, his booming, mirthless laugh. She had never been able even to touch him, much less hurt him.

"Dear Irene," he said, putting his hands on his knees, about to rise, "you never change, do you?"

He stood up to leave her and as he moved across the porch she took advantage of the coverage of his tall figure to snatch an old-fashioned from the tray passed by a disapproving maid, one undoubtedly warned by Eloise, and secrete her empty glass under the couch. The porch was beginning to fill now, with large,

35

healthy-looking men of George's age who rubbed their hands together as they came up the steps followed by their quieter and plainer wives. Two of the latter were appealingly pregnant, large with belated additions to already established families, the final mark of middle-aged success and security. Irene was sure that everyone there had been sailing all day; they had that air of having "earned" their drinks. She looked down at her long white hand with its delicate blue veins and wondered what it had to do with Storey Beach.

"Irene, dear." Eloise was whispering to her, glancing at the cocktail and evidently sensing it was not her first. "Do you think you *should?* I mean, after your operation and all?"

"I think I'm the best judge of that," she said dryly.

"Well, of course, if you are," Eloise murmured dubiously. *"If* you are. Be an angel, darling, will you, and talk to Hilda for a moment? She's come all the way down from New York to spend the night and meet you, and she's so shy with older people."

Irene had not seen Eloise's stepdaughter since she was a child. Now she was twenty-one and had graduated from Vassar.

"Is that she?" she asked, glancing over at the auburn-haired girl talking to George. With her healthy clean skin and regularity of feature she might have been the model of the Eastern college girl, the same medium sized, semi-athletic figure, the same broad shoulders. Yet there was something distinguished about her, too; it might have been in the pronounced firmness of her jaw or even in the quiet concentration with which she listened to her father. "Oh, of course. A Dilworth to the bone. But you know, Eloise, she'd be *lovely* if she had more life. Bring her over and let's see if we can't put some life in her."

"Now, don't tease her, Irene. Please."

Eloise went over and came back with Hilda, who

shook hands with Irene, fixing her calm brown eyes on her.

"I'm glad to see you, Mrs. Bleecker."

"You can call me Irene if you like. Peggy and Jo do."

"But that's different," the girl pointed out. "You're their real grandmother." And then, evidently, feeling that she might have been rude, but still unwilling to concede her point, she carefully changed the subject. "I hope you're not tired after your trip down here," she continued gravely. "It must have been hard after your siege in the hospital."

Irene gave her a quick, critical glance.

"Oh, I survived," she said casually. "I'm an indestructible old bag, you know."

There was a pause.

"Hilda's got a new job," Eloise said hastily. "Entirely on her own, too. George didn't have to lift a finger. She's a receptionist in a law firm."

"That sounds frightfully serious," Irene remarked, looking Hilda over more carefully. She could see that the girl resented Eloise's gushing, and she almost liked her for it. "But then I guess Hilda *is* serious. Are you very serious, my dear?"

Hilda flushed.

"A lot of my friends are serious, Mrs. Bleecker. We find it a serious world."

Irene tried for a moment to picture her own life and past as this girl would see it. Basking on red and yellow rubber floats no doubt, on the Riviera. Drinking gin with Elinor Glyn.

"And here I was thinking you were all bobby-soxers," she said, smiling as if to apologize. "That's all one reads in the American papers. It sounds so gay, too."

"Hilda was talking about college girls, darling," Eloise interjected quickly. "Weren't you, Hilda?"

"Oh, I don't mean to imply that we're all blue-stockings, Mrs. Bleecker," Hilda protested, ignoring her stepmother's assistance. "But most of the girls in my class at Vassar felt they ought to be able to earn their own living. A girl can't get along any more just by chitchatting on the dance floor."

Irene simply laughed, as she had laughed at Peggy and Jo.

"Don't you think, my dear, every generation of women cares pretty much for the same thing?"

"And what is that, Mrs. Bleecker?"

"What is that? Why, men, of course!"

Irene watched the scorn in the girl's eyes, her restless shrug of the shoulders.

"Don't mind her, Hilda," Eloise said lightly. "She doesn't mean a word of it."

"Of course, I mean it!" Irene retorted irritably. "Why must you keep insisting, Eloise, that I don't mean the things I say?"

Eloise only nodded, in a rather frightened way, and took Hilda off to talk to Gladys Hunt. Irene was not simply bored now; she was angry. They were screening her, George and Gerald and Eloise; they were keeping her from the others in fear that she would do something terrible. Well, they would see. If they wanted a show they would get one. She got up, a bit unsteadily, feeling the Luminal and the whiskey, and poured herself a real drink at the table where the drinks were. Looking around she saw Eloise, who had been watching her, nervously trying to get the people to go into the dining room. She turned away.

"Darling," came Eloise's troubled voice, a moment later, from behind her. *"Please!"*

Irene refused to look at her.

"I was only getting one to take in," she said at last, and followed the others into the dining room. It would not do to see Eloise's eyes. They were unsettling, those eyes, like the eyes of a trapped deer.

"Don't you think trapped animals should be shot at once or else liberated?" she asked the startled old gentleman on her right, a retired judge who lived the year round at Storey Beach. "Don't you think it's cruel to keep them in captivity?"

"Are there any trapped animals down here, Mrs. Bleecker?"

Irene looked significantly down the table at her daughter and shrugged her shoulders. She glanced down at the matted floor and then up at the big black lithograph of a Landseer dog and sighed.

"More than you think, Judge."

"I wonder if I quite understand you, Mrs. Bleecker," he said blinking his eyes. "I very much doubt—"

"But that's it!" she interrupted rather incoherently. "You doubt! Look at my brother Gerald. He's never had a doubt in his life! That's why he looks so young. Look at George, too. Doubt ages, Judge. Doubt and fear." She smiled at the waitress who was passing the wine and reached to bring her glass nearer, but the latter, misinterpreting this as a sign of refusal and moving on to the next place, had to be plucked back by a gesture that was observed around the table. "A perfectly closed mind," she continued, jealousy watching the flow of wine into her glass, "acts as a preservative." She closed her eyes and shook her head several times to emphasize her point. "Now you and I, Judge, are doubters. We're scared about the future, about war—"

"I beg your pardon, Mrs. Bleecker, but I never said I was scared."

She felt hazy and warm now and looked at him affectionately.

"It doesn't matter," she said vaguely. "I like you, anyway."

He pretended in his alarm to be suddenly interested

39

in what her sister-in-law, Gladys, was saying across the table. Gladys' comfortable grey pompadour wiggled as she chatted, somehow chaperoning the quiet, amiable features beneath. She was talking, as usual, about her sons.

"Young Gerald, of course, is a partner in the firm now," she was saying. "But big Gerald tells me he had nothing to do with it. In fact, he says that being the senior partner's son may actually have stood in young Gerald's way. Made people expect more of him, don't you know?"

"Naturally people expect more of a partner's son, Gladys," Irene broke in suddenly. "They expect him to be made a partner."

Well, that stopped her, she reflected, as her sister-in-law turned coolly away. That did it. But there was no point in this eternal being nice to people, covering up, patching up, like Eloise. She felt suddenly dizzy and placed both her hands on the table. Watch it, Irene. Perhaps it *had* been a mistake to start this, perhaps one less drink would have made her less obviously and more effectively rude, perhaps—but, oh, what the hell, and there was George glaring at her and Eloise sending timid, frightened looks down the table and the chances were ten to one she wouldn't get another glass of wine, much less a whiskey after dinner or even a brandy, but maybe she could slip up to her room when the ladies were out and get another tablet if Eloise hadn't hidden them. . . .

Eloise had only to nod her head as her Uncle Gerald maintained his monologue about Hunt & Livermore. She tried not to look in her mother's direction, but nothing could keep her from hearing, at sudden jarring moments between her uncle's elaborate little anecdotes of long deceased partners, odd snatches of Irene's more lively conversation. She saw George's face at the other end of the table getting darker and darker; she saw, too, the meaning glances that he received from Aunt Gladys. She even found herself wondering if Uncle Gerald, who rarely bothered to talk to her at such length, was not in his diplomatic fashion trying to shield her from the scandal of her mother's behavior. They would all, of course, be embarrassed for her; it was *her* mother; it had been *her* idea to bring her down there, *her* responsibility. But however intensely they felt the identification she felt it more intensely still; it was as if she and her mother were two faces of the same individual, two masks, Irene a grinning comedy mask, grinning wider for every finger that was pointed and every brow that was bent, unassailable, blatant, brash, and she herself a mask of frozen propriety, without other expression than a smirk, a doll's mask covering the same face over the same guilty body. Perhaps this was why she felt in her heart that she could foresee what Irene would do before she did it, why she knew now that Irene would get even worse, why she had known it from the beginning, why, as she now dimly saw, she had brought her there. It was to have it over with, wasn't it, to show people the other mask and ease the sense of hyprocrisy, to suffer as she suffered in her fantasies when she was brought out on deck, a captured princess on a pirate ship, and stripped and whipped before a jeering crew? The image of her punishment loomed so vividly that she put down her fork and held her forehead suddenly.

"Are you all right, my dear?"

She started and looked into the inquiring, faintly surprised eyes of her uncle.

"Oh yes, Uncle Gerald, I'm fine, thank you. It was only that I suddenly thought of something."

"Nothing bad, I hope."

"Oh, nothing at all."

She wondered if people like Uncle Gerald and Aunt

41

Gladys had fantasies like hers, if they ever thought of themselves as naked in public, as exposed at a men's dinner party, standing on the table in a ring of black ties. But no, one had only to look at them to see they didn't: Aunt Gladys' fantasies, if any, were all of Uncle Gerald, and his—well, his might be gayer than hers, but they wouldn't be like her own. Never that. And if they knew what her thoughts were, what would they think of her—or *did* they know?

"As I was saying," Gerald continued, "it's perfectly true there are several partners senior to him, but it still wouldn't surprise me a bit if he ended up in my spot one day." He was speaking, of course, about George. "He's got drive, that George of yours. Great drive. You know the first question he asked me when he applied for a job in the office? When he was nothing, mind you, but a shavetail just out of Harvard Law?"

Did she know? Had there ever been a time when she hadn't known? She stole a quick look down the table at Irene and noticed that her expression was becoming glazed. Gerald proceeded inexorably into his well-known tale.

" 'Mr. Hunt,' " he said, in a rather poor imitation of George's voice, " 'I wonder if you could tell me how soon, if I take this job, I could reasonably expect to become a member of the firm?' " Here he guffawed pleasantly. "It wasn't exactly what I'd call a conventional question, but it showed the right spirit. Yes sir, it's that kind of spirit—Eloise, are you sure your mother's all right?"

His last words sounded faint and far away for she had suddenly looked around and caught her mother's eye, and although she had looked away immediately as if afraid that any communication between them might lead Irene on to worse things, it was too late. A startled silence fell upon the table, and when she turned again she saw Irene on her feet, leaning heavily against the table and holding up her empty wineglass in her direction.

"I'd like to drink a toast to a daughter," she began in a tense, rather shrill voice, "who has taken in her poor old battered mother after many years. You probably shouldn't have done it, my child. Certainly no mother ever deserved less of a daughter." There was a terrible silence, as she put her glass down, knocking it over, and leaned forward both hands now on the table. "But don't anyone think," she continued, explosively, tossing her head in a gesture of defiance, "that I'm sorry! I despise remorse! If I had my life to do over again, I'd do all the same things. If my purse were replenished, I'd scatter it to the winds." She paused, stretching out an arm, and described with a sad dignity a slow arc in the air, her fingers twitching as though she were scattering largesse. "I would never embarrass Eloise with apology. I marvel, indeed, at my own serenity. Perhaps I may turn into one of those white-haired old ladies you see in modern plays. The kind who have learned from folly and shettle down, after the final lover has departed, to advishe youth in the ways of love."

Eloise sat absolutely silent and still until her muscles seemed to contract, her veins to go cold, her whole body to harden into an impenetrable cast around her beating heart. Yet at least this impenetrability walled out the others, the hostile, horrified others. She jumped up when she saw Irene begin to sway and hurried down the table to take her by the arm.

"You poor dear, it's all my fault," she said soothingly. "I should never have let you do so much so soon after the hospital. Come, darling, we'll go upstairs."

And putting her arm around her shoulders she led her slowly into the hall and up the stairs while behind her, from the dining room, she could hear Gerald, the saver of scenes, raising his voice in a distracting anecdote. Irene was quite docile now; she ambled along to

43

her room murmuring derogatory remarks about Gerald and Gladys and went fast asleep on the bed while her daughter was trying to undress her.

When Eloise came down, an hour later, the Hunts were already leaving. Aunt Gladys said good night to her in a hurried, nervous way, pecking her on the cheek, and Gerald gave her a little wink as he took her hand.

"I wouldn't have your mother's head tomorrow for the world," he whispered to her. "But don't worry, my dear. It's an old story with Irene."

She did not even look at George until the others had left and Hilda had gone to bed, but she could feel his brooding all during the rest of the evening. When she turned back from the front door after bidding good night to the last guest and switched off the porch light she saw that he was waiting for her at the foot of the stairs. He had a fresh drink that he was stirring with his finger, staring into it as he did so.

"Well, that's it, that does it," he began with a slow, bitter emphasis. He did not look at her. "That's the end. She goes back to town tomorrow or as soon as she's well enough. I'll get her rooms in a hotel. Anywhere she wants. I'll be glad to pay. But I won't have her under my roof. I won't have her corrupting my children."

She wondered if it was the sound of the surf that was pounding in her ears or the beating of her own heart. She looked at his face in the dim light of the hall and made out the familiar pink and blue tints of his anger.

"She's sick, George," she protested in a low voice. "It wasn't her fault."

"Sick, my eye," he retorted. "She was plastered. Fried. Stinko. That's her gratitude to you for looking after her! That's all she cares. And what a mischief-maker, too, my God! Why in the name of Heaven did she have to pick the evening that Gerald was here?"

44

She shook her head slowly.

"You're making it worse than it was, George. Uncle Gerald understands."

"Well, Gerald or no Gerald, I don't relish being made an ass of in my own house, Eloise. I don't relish it a bit."

"I didn't think you were made an ass of." She turned to the stairs, trying to get away before his decision was irrevocable. "But it won't happen again, George. I promise you that. Something got into Irene tonight. She's never been that bad before."

"Eloise, you're a child!" he exclaimed impatiently. "You have no concept of the sort of woman your mother is! It'll happen again and again. But one thing I promise you. It won't happen again here."

She paused, one hand on the bannister, without looking around.

"Then we won't have any more guests while she's here, George," she conceded in a nervous tone. "Irene won't care. She didn't like them anyway."

"You don't understand me, Eloise," he said, exasperated. "I want her to go back to town. Tomorrow morning. Or no later than the afternoon. Is that clear enough?"

She turned around, her eyes wide with dismay.

"But, George, we can't! I asked her here."

"Of course, you asked her here. I said she was a drunk, not a trespasser."

She saw that he meant it this time, that there would be no budging him. She clasped her hands, suddenly sick.

"I won't tell her, George. I can't!"

"Then I will. Would you rather it that way?"

"George!" She went over to him and took him by the hands, staring up at him. "George, you wouldn't do that to me? You wouldn't really?"

"Not to you, of course not. But I'd most certainly do

45

it to your mother. A woman whom you owe nothing and I less."

"George!" she repeated frantically. "Suppose I go with her?"

"That's up to you, my dear," he said in a dry, suddenly hard tone. "If you wish to leave your husband and children for such a pretext I can hardly stop you."

She stared at him incredulously for a moment and then breaking away she fell on the window seat by the coat closet and began to sob. Never in their life together could she remember so breaking down before him. There was almost a satisfaction in the very abandonment of it, even while she resented his bewilderment and continued implacability. He simply stood there and watched her. She might have been a naughty child.

"Oh, I'm so sorry!" she heard a voice suddenly from the stairs, and she jumped up, one hand on her forehead. It was Hilda in her wrapper and nightgown, peering down at them in shocked amazement. "I thought if I took an early train tomorrow I might miss you both, and I wanted to thank you for the party."

"Don't be silly, dear." She dabbed her eyes quickly with a handkerchief, suddenly controlled. "I wish you could stay longer. But don't go in by train. Irene may be going in tomorrow with Uncle Gerald's chauffeur. She can take you. Good night, dear."

She hurried upstairs, not even stopping as she passed her stepdaughter to kiss her good night. She could not bear to have Hilda see her weep. It would have been too much to give them both in a single evening.

"What is it, Daddy?" Hilda asked, coming quickly down. "Was it about Mrs. Bleecker? Oh, Daddy, I felt so terribly for you. It was awful. I tried to warn Eloise, but she wouldn't listen to me. I could tell by the way Mrs. Bleecker was talking that she was in no condition to go to dinner."

"Hilda, will you go to bed, please?" George said

sharply, and then turning impatiently and catching sight of her stricken countenance he closed his lips tightly for a second. "I'm sorry, dear," he forced himself to say, "I'm a bit upset. I didn't mean to be short with you. I want to be alone, that's all."

"Can't I help you turn out the lights, Daddy, and clean up?"

George passed his fingers quickly over his brow.

"No, dear, really. Go to bed. Get some sleep."

He didn't look around until he heard her reluctant footsteps on the landing above. Then he moved slowly about the living room to empty the ash trays and put away the glasses, the kind of thing he never left to others. It had unsettled him to see Eloise weeping. He had wanted to go over to her and put his hand on her hair and tell her that she could keep Irene as long as she wanted. Yet he had been held back by an unexpected and rather shocking little satisfaction at the very pain that he was causing her. It was because she was being unreasonable, he argued to himself, hastily and irritably, as he tried to fit all the glasses on one tray. Obviously it was unreasonable of her to want a woman like Irene staying in the house with two impressionable youngsters like Peggy and Jo and with so many of his and Gerald's friends in the neighborhood just dying to know every minute what was going on. Eloise would admit it herself once she had thought it over. She had always been reasonable about taking his advice, and why not, after all? Hadn't it usually turned out to be right? Oh, of course, people might argue that she ought to be given her way now, just for once, even if she *was* being unreasonable, but he couldn't see it. One had to be firm, he decided, as he switched off the lights and climbed the stairs to his room. Women had no idea what it took to build up a life and reputation such as his. He was at least now in sight, even if distantly, of the day when he could boast, in addition to

47

his apartment in the city and this crazy rented house on the dunes, the handsome red brick Georgian house with the wide lawn on the north shore of Long Island that would definitely establish him as a "three place" man. After his step, the distinguishing one, all the rest would come almost as a matter of course, the fishing camp in Canada, the box at the opera for alternate Monday nights, even the small yacht. It was not a scheme, he resolved, as he got to his room and laid his gold watch, chain and pencil carefully beside the photograph of Eloise in the silver frame with his initials on it, in which he was going to tolerate any interference by Irene.

4

THE NEXT MORNING Eloise went to her mother's room while she was having breakfast and sat, looking rather mournful at the end of her bed.

"Did you sleep well, dear?"

Irene looked up sharply from her coffee cup.

"Say what you mean, child. The answer to the question you meant is no. I don't have a hangover. But you look terrible yourself. Did those people keep you up late?"

"No. I couldn't sleep."

Irene grunted.

"I suppose I embarrassed you. Yes, of course, I must have. But don't expect apologies from me. I never apologize, you know. To me there's nothing cheaper than remorse."

Eloise, recognizing her speech of the night before, said nothing.

"You don't agree?" Irene pursued, taking in her daughter's averted gaze. "Well, why should you? Though I can't think last night could have been as embarrassing for you as all that. Those people all have ideas about me. They'd probably have felt cheated if I hadn't acted up."

"Please, Irene. Don't say that."

"It's true, and you know it." But as she looked up again from her coffee she saw the tears in Eloise's eyes, and her expression slightly softened. "Why, my poor child, you're really upset. George was furious, I suppose?"

"Well ... he didn't like it. You know how he is about the firm and Gerald."

She wouldn't put the blame on George. She could see now, as she rubbed her eyes, that the fault was hers, in not standing up to him. If he was hard, she was weak, and it was worse to be weak.

Irene was watching her thoughtfully.

"Maybe this visit of mine wasn't such a good idea," she said. "I can see it must be a strain on you. I'm a million times better now, and it might be for the best all around if I slipped back to town. The season's almost over, anyway. What do you think, dear?"

There was a long pause. Eloise simply stared at the floor.

"Don't overwhelm me with objections," Irene said dryly.

"Oh, Irene, dearest, forgive me."

She fell forward on the bed, pressing her head against her mother's thin legs under the cover. It was all she had wanted, she told herself, a chance to look after her. But there was no hand on her back or shoulders to console her; she could feel Irene's stiffening in the rigidity of her limbs.

"You needn't take on so about it," Irene said coldly. "It's your house and your life, and I don't wish to

49

outstay my welcome. But I can't help observing that if you and George are so upset by a sick woman with a slight bun, you must be on very insecure grounds indeed. In fact, I think you're behaving like a couple of children."

Somehow Eloise got through the weekend and sent Irene off with Hilda, on Sunday afternoon, in the chauffeur-driven town car which Uncle Gerald, under the circumstances, had been only too glad to loan her. There had been very little conversation around the house, prior to the departure: Irene had been calm, distant and injured, George had sulked and Eloise had hurried about, making arrangements, calling the Stafford Hotel every hour with questions and suggestions about the preparation of her mother's rooms. By Monday morning, when George had gone into town for the week, she felt listless and played out. The prospect of taking the children to the beach club was for once too much for her, and she called her friend Lorna Sterne, in Mogue.

"Can I come over for the afternoon?"

"And the night if you want," the brisk voice came back. "Bringing the little girls?"

"No. Really not. That's the reason."

"You don't hear me begging for them, do you?"

Lorna, who had been Lorna Hughes, Eloise's radical Barnard friend, now worked as fiction editor of a fashion magazine to support her husband who was a poet. She was a large, big-bosomed, big-featured girl with messy long hair over which she was apt to wear a net and a smiling, amiable expression that could become very mean when she was crossed. She was a direct and forceful person, with humor about everything but her own liberalism and her husband's verse; she deplored the magazine for which she was glad enough to work but hotly defended the caliber of its fiction against the sneers of her husband's friends whose more advanced prose and poetry appeared only in quarterlies or in the *Partisan Review*. She made no secret of what she thought of Eloise's "trapped life." She and Henry, her husband, had a small shingle shack for the summer on the dunes of Mogue connected with the patch-work of other small cottages by a winding boardwalk that ended up in front of the building that served the summer community as a general store and night club. Mogue had the reputation of being an artists' community which meant that five per cent of the colony were artists. Its only sports were soft ball and swimming, and the couples who sauntered arm in arm on the beach were sometimes of different sexes and sometimes of the same. But there were no raised eyebrows at Mogue; taboos had been left by common consent to the ample territory of the city and the winter months.

Most people in Storey Beach had never been to Mogue, and some had never heard of it. To those who had, it was a boundary mark of iniquity, and Eloise never found it necessary to mention the fact when she disappeared to spend the day with Lorna on the beach. This Monday, however, she felt so strongly the need to get away that she wondered if even Uncle Gerald, with his all knowing and rather menacing smile, could have blocked her way. And when she had finally made her escape, when she was actually at Lorna's, leaning against a back rest on the sand, protected from the world by her colored glasses and even by her large straw hat, she could feel the tensions within her relax as she gazed out at the world as it could have been for anyone, apparently, but herself. For it was certainly not Storey Beach. It was gay, and it was warm, and it at least seemed undemanding. She watched a boy and girl jitterbugging on the sand to a hand radio. The boy, she could see, was a professional dancer, for his movements had an extraordinary grace, even on the sand; he wore tight gold bathing trunks and was almost too

51

wonderful to look at, too young, too tanned, too regular of feature. She felt a pain in her heart at the sight of him, at the very perfection of his bloom. Farther down the beach she saw a colored man sitting by the reclining figure of a white girl; to her right she heard the high giggles of three gesticulating young men whose argument, as it drifted in snatches to her across the sand, now very clear, now confused, had something to do with ballet. She thought now contemputously George would have dismissed the whole scene, and the thought angered her. All right, she said to his reproving image, so it was decadent. Full of queer people. Anything he wanted. But it's me, she almost cried aloud, it's *me!* It was all the beauty and laughter she had been punished for having or for not having, she was never sure which. Oh, when life could be so easy and so nice, she wondered—

"You're very quiet today," Lorna observed. "Is there something on your mind?"

"Only this." Eloise made a vague, inclusive gesture. "All this wonderfulness."

"It's the same beach and sky you have, isn't it?"

"Dear, no." Eloise shook her head. "Everything's special at Storey Beach. Even nature. Here you're—well you're more general."

"Don't start to romanticize us, Eloise," her friend warned her. "That's always the beginning of the end for the inhibited."

"And you don't think it's time I began?"

Lorna shook her head decisively.

"Not yet. Wait till George is a senior partner or on the supreme court. Then it'll make more splash."

Eloise smiled, but only in her usual fashion, to hide the gravity of what she was about to say.

"You've never taken me seriously, Lorna, have you?" she asked. "You've never really thought I was a bit too good for what I've got."

Lorna gave her a brief look.

"You like it, don't you?"

"Not all the time. Nobody likes anything all the time."

"What *do* you like?"

"I've told you. This." Again she made her vague gesture in the air.

Lorna looked at her more carefully. Her big, curious green eyes seemed almost ready to reappraise.

"Well, you're quite welcome to it," she said. "You know that, don't you? Why not stay over tonight? We're having a picnic. See if you can let yourself go and forget the children and George. Just for an evening."

Eloise instinctively shook her head.

"I'd love to, Lorna, but I'm afraid I must get back."

"Give me one good reason," Lorna persisted. "George is in town, and so is that sticky daughter of his. And as for the girls, it'll do them good to be alone with the nurse for a change. They've probably got a complex about being brought up by their mother. So unlike their little friends. And I've got that nice boy, Carl Landik, coming, you know, the one who wrote *Even for an Eggshell*, that you liked so much? He's shy, but so are you. You can be his date."

"Oh, Lorna!"

"Don't look so shocked. I'm not a procuress. I just want you to relax. Does George beat you if you don't stay home?"

"Oh, no. George is glad to have me go out." She hesitated, terribly tempted. Landik's book about marines on Iwo Jima had been the war novel that she had most liked. His name and the abrupt possibility of actually meeting him brought back his story in all its violence, and looking down the beach she pictured marines disembarking from landing craft, crouched over, running. She had a sudden memory of Uncle

53

Gerald, who read everything and liked nothing, saying: "But there's no excuse for his language, Eloise. It's perfectly inexcusable. Can nothing be left to the imagination?" Nothing, she had thought silently, as she had given way to his opinion. Nothing, she thought passionately now. Please, nothing!

"Let's go right up to the store and telephone your house," Lorna was saying briskly. "If they need you, you can always get home in half an hour."

When the call had been made and the nurse placated and Eloise herself convinced that there was nothing so terribly unusual in what she was doing, she went into the shack with Lorna and for the rest of the afternoon helped her to make sandwiches and salad. Later on, when she got out of her damp bathing suit and into her red dress and white sweater, she felt positively exuberant.

"I love a party," she told Henry Sterne, a tall, thin, rather sallow and taciturn man who only came to life with a very few friends and a great many drinks, "where I know I'm not going to know a soul."

"And why, pray?"

"Because she thinks she can do anything she likes," Lorna said coming out on the porch with a tray of cocktail glasses of different sizes and shapes. "But don't go too far, Eloise. Fundamentally, Henry and I are very respectable."

"Oh, I'll be good!" Eloise cried. "I promise you!"

It turned out that she was quite right about not knowing a soul. Not only had she never met any of the Sternes' guess, but with the exception of Carl Landik she had never heard of any of them before. They were a couple of poets and an abstract painter, two women from Lorna's magazine, and some others whom she never identified. They all seemed to know each other and to talk easily to each other, and although she was quite left out, she didn't mind, sitting on the porch rail near Henry, listening to him talk and drinking as many cocktails, for once, as she wanted. She watched Landik curiously; he was by far the youngest of the group, being only twenty-seven, and he seemed to be talking as little as she was. He was a determined, rather sour-looking young man, with wide cheekbones and cheeks curving sharply inwards, dropping to a pair of thin, set lips and a small chin. His black hair was thick and glossy; it made a truculent background for his dark eyes and low forehead. He was short but well built and stood with his feet apart holding his glass with both hands as he listened to the others talk. While she was watching him he suddenly turned and walked down the porch steps to the beach. He sat down, his back to them, looking at the sea.

"Well, don't just stare. Do something." It was Lorna, passing by with the shaker and refilling Eloise's glass. "He's your date for the evening. Remember."

Eloise looked at her in alarm.

"But what should I do?"

"Go and bring him back. Or amuse him. I don't care." Lorna was beginning to feel her own cocktails. "Leave him be, if you want. He's in one of his moods. These child authors. To hell with them."

"You don't think he'd mind if I went over and talked to him?"

Lorna shrugged her shoulders and passed on to the next group. Eloise took a long sip of her cocktail. She was not exactly drunk, but she had reached the point where she did not feel at all herself, the point that she had wanted to reach. The old Eloise was standing in the shadows, watching her with a grudging admiration. She saw her get up and walk lightly across the sand to where the young man was sitting.

"Mr. Landik?"

He turned around, and she saw, even in the dusk, that his eyes were not friendly.

"Lorna suggested that I come out and talk to you," she continued, feeling indifferent, all of a sudden, to his bad humor. "Can I sit down?" She laughed. "No, I shouldn't say that, should I? My uncle always used to answer: 'You *can*. Of course, you *can*.' So, *may* I sit down, please? I'm Eloise Dilworth."

He shrugged his shoulders.

"Why not?"

"You mean why not Eloise Dilworth?"

He gave her a steady, questioning gaze and then looked away.

"No. Why not sit down."

But Eloise had already seated herself.

"You know, I loved your book," she said, not even caring in the mellowness of her mood whether or not she bored him. "It meant more to me than anything I've read about the war. Oh, I can't criticize intelligently, I know, but I wonder if I even want to. If I feel it, isn't that enough?"

He was looking at her, again now, obviously irritated.

"What feeling could a woman like you get out of my book?" he asked crossly. "What do you know about marines on Iwo Jima? You don't talk their way, you don't feel their way. So far as they're concerned, you might as well have come from Mars!" He snorted. "Or, should I say Venus?"

She laughed. She felt reassured, now that he was being rude, as Lorna had told her he would be.

"Why shouldn't I feel what they feel?" she came back at him with a boldness that only gin could have given her. "Can't I imagine what it's like to be in battle? I think I can, because you describe it the way I picture it. Your world, in a funny way, is my world, not other people's." She paused a moment, feeling excited and confused, and the feeling that the book had given her flooded over her again, her sense of the binding, sus-

56

taining force of friendship in the midst of horror, of a world made easier than her own by the rolling back of inhibition so that sentimentality, yes, just plain sentimentality, could drip creditably over the plain of heat and blood, making love and tears without shame. "That's what other people don't see, critics and people like that," she continued rather incoherently. "Uncle Gerald, for example. He says your writing has no shadow."

"Oh, he does, does he? And who the hell is Uncle Gerald?"

She shook her head impatiently, as if to indicate that Uncle Gerald was beneath their notice.

"Don't get mad. It's really a compliment, the way I look at it. There's no shadow in my imagination, either. It's like the glare of an operating room. I *see* your men on Iwo Jima. I even see them being killed!"

He threw his hands up.

"What is this, anyway? A Joan of Arc complex? A Freudian death wish?"

"Do you treat all your admirers this way, Mr. Landik? Is it a crime to admire you?"

He ran his fingers nervously through his hair.

"Look," he protested. "I wasn't asking for trouble. I was just sitting here."

"You mean you want me to go away?"

He gave a little groan.

"Please, lady, will you stop? Let's talk about you then. I'd much rather talk about you." He faced her with a sigh of resignation. "Are you married?"

"Oh, yes."

"Are you happy?"

"I keep telling myself I am," she said eagerly. "And that I love my husband and children." She felt suddenly and unaccountably dejected. "But then we never know, I suppose. We never really know."

He rubbed his brow.

"Was your husband in the war?"

She was silent for a moment. He had changed the subject which could only mean that he was embarrassed. Even Mr. Landik. Embarrassed. She would have to pull herself together.

"Yes. He was in the war."

"He was an officer, of course?"

She even understood the sneer, because she understood the young man.

"He was a naval intelligence officer," she said distinctly. "On an aircraft carrier."

"That was the real war," he said with perfunctory bitterness. "Watching the show from a floating Union Club. All the thrills and no mud. Oh, you may get sunk, sure, but what the hell? Everybody dies."

"I remember you made that point in your book," she said, without stopping to think that he might not like this. "In the chapter about the officers' club in Guam. I showed it to my husband, and he said you'd obviously never been in an officers' club."

"I suppose you think they were all little gentlemen," he retorted, piqued. "Nice little gentlemen who played by the rules."

"It doesn't matter what I think," she said docilely. "I don't write books."

He looked at her in perplexity.

"I'll say one thing for women like you," he conceded. "You won't get mad till it suits you to get mad."

She stared.

"Women like me?"

"Society women. Women who trot down to Mogue to see the animals. With bright smiles and gay little resolutions not to be shocked."

She suddenly saw that to him there was no difference between a woman like herself and a woman like Aunt Gladys, and the realization gave her a feeling of extraordinary confidence. It made her sophisticated, almost superior to him in her knowledge of how the world really was.

"I wish you'd give me a chance to prove how wrong you are," she said. "I could if we were friends. I'd like so much for us to be friends. Oh, I know that sounds fatuous and foolish, but there you are. I *am* fatuous and foolish."

For the first time he almost smiled.

"What would there be in it for me?" he asked more easily. "In this friendship, I mean?"

She thought for a moment and then started to count on her fingers.

"You mean what can I offer? Well, let's see. I have a husband who's a very smart lawyer and two fairly nice little girls. I have a rather wonderful mother, quite wicked, whom you might like. I have some moderately amusing friends. And some who aren't amusing at all. So there you have it. You can take your pick."

"You mean I can tie a string around them and lead them away?"

She laughed.

"You're certainly putting me in my place, Mr. Landik," she said pleasantly. "And I certainly deserve it. Why, after all, should you want any part of it?"

With this she got lightly to her feet and went back to Lorna and Henry who, with the others, were frying hamburgers on the beach. She had no feeling, however, of being rebuffed. Her heart was too full of emotion. The summer was almost over; she could feel already the first chill of autumn in the darkening air. Soon she would be moving back to the city where she could see Irene, and the girls would go back to school. George, too, was always in a better mood when there was no commuting, and she looked forward to sitting in bed after he had gone to the office, her breakfast tray still on her knees, the sun pouring in the window from

59

Lexington Avenue as she read again that young man's novel in the light of an excitement which she had been almost able to articulate.

5

ON THE SUNDAY before Eloise went to Mogue her stepdaughter Hilda drove into New York with Irene in Gerald Hunt's town car. Hilda had been upset by the events of the night before and sat rather stiffly in her corner during the two-hour drive, responding to the older woman's comments as briefly as she could with any semblance of manners. She kept wondering uneasily what she would do if Irene suddenly asked the chauffeur to stop at one of the bars that lined their route to the city. Fortunately, however, this did not happen.

"I'll give you a tip, my dear," Irene told her as they pulled up before her hotel. "I know you haven't asked me, but that's just the beauty of it. The best tips in life are always unsolicited. I've noticed that you copy your father in everything. Now wait." She held up her hand as Hilda was about to protest. "I'm not saying a word against your father. He's perfectly all right, from his point of view. But how about from yours?"

Hilda stared.

"From mine?"

"He's a man, you little goose!" Irene exclaimed, getting out of the car. "Do you really want people," she asked, turning back to her, "to say you're like a successful, middle-aged man?"

Horrid old creature, Hilda reflected, as she threw

herself back in the seat to be driven on to the apartment on Fourth Street that she shared with two Vassar classmates. It was a relief to be back in the city and ready for work again.

The firm for which Hilda worked was not a large corporation law firm like Hunt & Livermore. It was what her father rather contemputously referred to as an "uptown" law firm, located in Radio City and having for clients mostly advertising agencies and public relations advisers, not to mention a lucrative side business in domestic discord. It was a small firm by downtown standards, having only four partners and three clerks, none of whom worked at night the way George so often did and all of whom called their secretaries by their first names. It was exactly, however, what Hilda wanted. Deeply as she admired her father she was very conscious of belonging to a different generation and was gravely determined to equip herself to deal with the coming world, however uncongenial she might find it. Television, for example, she would tell her friends with a resigned if deprecatory nod, was here to stay. Like Margaret Fuller, she could accept the universe. Then, too, the job had the advantage of coming to her on her own, without assistance from her father. Hilda believed so strongly one should get everything in life on one's own, that she was even bothered that her qualifications for the job were the results of an education not available to all. But this, she decided, could be carried too far. What, after all, about the brain itself? Didn't some people have better brains than others? The injustices of nature, like the universe, could only be accepted.

She was glad, she reflected the following morning, that she had started as a receptionist. Her desk was next to the door in the grey, modern entrance lobby, and surely there could be no better way of studying her new environment. After only two weeks she had developed a truly professional note in her "Name, please?"

and her "Are you expected?" Mr. Herbert, the head of the firm, had complimented her on her looks and manner, and she was already indulging herself with a little daydream in which she rose from one level to another to the position of a great woman executive, the head, say, of a vast department store . . . except, of course, she reminded herself quickly, she didn't really want that. What she really wanted was to marry and raise a family, keeping herself, naturally, at the same time, a vital, interested person, not letting herself slack like Eloise. Not that poor Eloise wasn't dear and sweet, a little too sweet for that matter, but what did she ever accomplish that was worth anything, what would Eloise ever be able to point to and say: "This *I* did"? Unless, Hilda conceded with a shrug, one gave her credit for meals on time and a habit of asking people rather tense questions about themselves that only betrayed her essential lack of curiosity.

She started at a loud whistle, almost in her ears, and looked up into the smiling face of a young man with very blond hair. He was leaning forward over her desk, gripping its edges with his hands.

"I'm sorry, but you were miles away," he said, straightening up. "How long have you been around?"

"This is my second week," she said, flustered. "Whom do you wish to see, please?"

He shook his head, still smiling.

"No one," he said. "No one at all. You see, I work here too. I've been off on a business trip. And I come back to find you. I'm Bobbie Chapin."

Hilda nodded gravely at him.

"I'm Hilda Dilworth. I'm the new receptionist."

"Ask and ye shall receive!" he exclaimed, spreading his arms. "Can you tell me one thing, Hilda? Is there any reason in the world we shouldn't be the best of friends?"

"Is there any work I can do for you, Mr. Chapin? I'm supposed to type, too."

"No, just sit there," he said, taking a step back and tilting his head to view her as if she were a painting. "Just sit there and be yourself. Your lovely self. Until twelve-thirty. And then perhaps you'll give me the great pleasure of having lunch with me."

Hilda murmured something that he took as an acceptance, and he disappeared into the office. She thought it might seem snobbish to refuse. When she asked one of the other girls later that morning, it seemed she had done the right thing. Bobbie was a junior partner and very much the office favorite. He had been a fighter pilot in the Pacific where he had won the Distinguished Flying Cross, and his friendliness of manner was considered irresistible. Hilda, however, was not one to prejudge people. She would wait and see for herself.

Promptly at half past twelve he picked her up and took her to a restaurant that seemed designed for anything but the quick meal that her father had always told her was in keeping with good business habits.

"Will you have something to drink?" he asked.

"Oh, nothing, thank you."

He leaned forward and winked at her.

"And you think people who drink before lunch are wicked. Am I right?"

"No, Mr. Chapin. I don't suppose they're wicked."

Still looking at her, he laughed. He laughed for rather a long time, but in a pleasant, contagious manner. Hilda glanced down at her plate. She had never met anyone quite like him before. He had long thick light hair and large blue eyes. His straight nose and clear, even features went well with his blondness. She had been told he was over thirty, but he seemed no more than twenty-five. He wore a gold identification disc on one wrist and a watch with a gold band on the other, and when they sat down at table she had seen him slip a small pocket comb through his hair. He was neatly, even fastidiously dressed, except for a tie with too much yellow in it, but his eyes, which he never seemed to take off her, had a steady, curious stare. They were most certainly not effeminate eyes, nor was his neatness an effeminate neatness.

"Let me tell you about myself," he said. "And then you can tell me about you. I go first, because I can see you're shy."

He went on to talk about himself as a lawyer and how he was handling a certain divorce case. He represented, as she felt immediately he always did, the wife. It was soon evident, from the time that he was taking, that they weren't going to get to Hilda at all, but it didn't matter. She had taken the job, after all, to learn. Only when he was describing, with seeming acceptance, the shady tactics of the husband's lawyer did she interrupt.

"But isn't that dishonest?" she asked. "Isn't it crooked?"

He shrugged his shoulders.

"He hasn't made a flat misstatement of fact. He's much too smart for that."

"Too smart?" she protested. "Couldn't he be disbarred?"

"Lord no. That's routine."

"But surely all lawyers don't do things like that?"

"They're only human, Hilda. Like you and me."

Hilda thought of her father and shook her head.

"I wouldn't do it."

He laughed again.

"Maybe you wouldn't. I guess you wouldn't at that. Well, I'm glad we're developing some moral tone in the office. We could use it."

"But I don't follow you," she protested, leaning forward. "Would *you* do a thing like that?"

"I might. Who knows? I never pretended to be a saint."

She looked at him soberly.

"Well, I don't think you would."

To her surprise she could see that he was pleased. He changed color slightly.

"Well, thanks!"

"The girls tell me you were a pilot in the war," she continued understandingly. "Maybe you're used to seeing people from up in the sky. Maybe that's why they seem small and buggy to you."

"But you don't seem small and buggy to me, Hilda," he said, leaning towards her with a grin. "What can I do to convince you that I don't find you in the least bit small or buggy?"

She gave him a level look.

"You can take me seriously," she said. "I mean the things I say."

He hesitated and then smiled again broadly.

"And will you do the same for me?"

"Certainly. I already have."

"Hilda, I think we're going to be friends!" he exclaimed, slapping the table. "I really think we are!"

By the time lunch was over he had convinced her that he meant this. And she had to admit that it was fun to have a friend in the office. Each time he passed her desk in the lobby he winked at her, and she felt a small tense excitement, however much she might tell herself it was nonsense, as if they were joint conspirators against the monotony of office routine. Two days later, after work, he took her to a cocktail party given by a radio announcer. Everybody there seemed to know everybody else and to know Bobbie; they were all in the radio or advertising business, and there was a lot of noise and loud laughter and a great deal of drinking. Hilda didn't really like the people; she stayed rather silently by Bobbie's side while he joked and laughed with them and reflected several times that it was all part of her new experience. When he took her out to dinner afterwards he was moderately drunk and told her war stories, about pilots and night club singers, pilots and nurses, pilots and Wacs. They were not the kind of stories that Hilda really liked, but there didn't seem to be any way of stopping him, so she let him go on. When he took her back to her apartment she was afraid that she might have trouble with him, but she didn't. He left her on her doorstep with a ceremonious little bow that took considerable concentration and suggested politely, after apologizing for the lateness of the hour, that if she was a bit late at the office the following morning, the world wasn't going to come to an end.

Hilda, however, did not take advantage of his suggestion; she was always on time. In the washroom she had a conversation with Miss Ranick, the kind, elderly lady who managed the office.

"You went out with Mr. Chapin last night, didn't you?" Miss Ranick asked, drying her hands carefully with the paper towel. "You needn't ask me how I know. He told me he had asked you. He tells me lots of things, for I'm just as fond of that boy as I can be. But that doesn't keep me from telling a nice, quiet girl like yourself that he's a very fast young man. You don't have to say a word, my dear," she said holding up her hand as Hilda was about to speak. "It's none of my business, I know. But it's the privilege of my years."

After picking up her glasses from the washstand she gave Hilda a dim, self-conscious little smile and departed. A week later, when Bobby asked her to another cocktail party, she brought this up.

"Miss Ranick tells me you're fast."

He gave a delighted laugh.

"One of these days we'll have to pension old Ranick or poor Bobbie won't be able to get himself a date. The woman's undermining me. And do you know why?"

He leaned down over her desk and spoke in a loud whisper.

"She's jealous."

"Of me?"

"Of everyone! She's got a passion for me, poor soul. We have to be kind to her. It's so unseemly, at her age."

"Please, Bobbie." She turned away from him to nod to the senior partner who was just then coming into the office. "Good morning, Mr. Herbert."

"I promise you I'm a changed man," Bobbie continued when Mr. Herbert had passed, crossing his heart. "Ranick has no idea what a quiet and sober citizen I've become. Or if she does, she's too spiteful to let people know."

She couldn't help smiling at this.

"Because she wants you all to herself?"

"Exactly! If you won't go out with me, you're throwing me into her arms."

"Which I suppose I mustn't do."

"Which, of course, you mustn't do!"

The party turned out to be almost a replica of the first one he had taken her to. There were the same people, the same noise, the same bachelor friends of Bobbie's, all over thirty and laughing boisterously at how drunk Sam had been on Saturday and what Phil and his boss's wife had been up to at Twenty-One. There was something rather desperate about the way they tried to spread the small coverlid of their college years over the expanding surface of life. Hilda's mood was not brightened by a conversation that she had in their host's bedroom, where the girls' coats were put, with a rather intoxicated blond fashion model called Elaine who seemed to know Bobbie very well.

"If you don't mind my saying so, you don't look Bobbie's type at all," the model said, sitting on the bed and looking at her in a bleary way. "Or maybe he's changed. Maybe he's tired of the old razzle-dazzle."

Hilda gave her a brief look.

"Maybe he's growing up."

Elaine considered this for a moment before deciding to take offense.

"You needn't be so damn snotty," she retorted. "I probably get more for one picture than you get in a year. And don't be so sure of Bobbiekins. I suppose you think he went right home the other night after he dropped you."

Hilda stared at her contemputously and put her coat on.

"I'm sure that's Bobbie's business," she said as she left the room. "Not mine."

She did not report this to Bobbie, as she had her conversation with Miss Ranick, but she did review the brief facts of their relationship that night after she had gone to bed. She admitted that she found him attractive. In fact, he was attractive enough to have upset already the equilibrium of her carefully balanced existence. But Hilda, like a true Dilworth, was equally careful to take note of the things that were less attractive about him: the fact that he drank too much and showed it, that he went to parties only to drink and meet more girls, that he knew nothing whatever of art, music or literature, to the appreciation of which she had so persistently, if somewhat deliberately, addressed her leisure hours. Bobbie could talk about law, about the war, about planes and infinitely about women, but he had hardly ever read a book or listened to a symphony, and he assumed, like so many Americans, that art was fundamentally a fraud. But worst of all, he made light of the moral values that she believed in. In this respect he did not even live up to their bargain.

"Do you think any of your friends are really happy?" she asked him the next day when they lunched

68

together. "Do they really enjoy that sort of thing, night after night?"

"They have fun," he said with a shrug. "What more do you expect?"

"You know what I expect."

"But you're so serious, Hilda," he said, shaking his head. "You're too serious. What do you really want out of life?"

She hesitated.

"If I tell you, you won't laugh?"

"Why should I?"

"I don't know. You might."

"Cross my heart," he said with an elaborate gesture across his chest. "Now. What do you want out of life?"

"I want to get married." She said it solemnly, so that he would have no occasion to take it personally. He blinked at her.

"But isn't that what every girl wants?" he asked. "What's so laughable about that?"

"Because I don't want it the way other girls want it. I want to choose it the way a man would choose his career. To me it's a life job. Something you have to train and train and *train* for."

He made a grimace.

"You make it sound so grim."

"But it's not grim!" she protested. "It's grim the other way. It's grim when people wrangle and divorce. When they stop loving each other!"

He looked at her for a moment in obvious perplexity.

"It takes two to make a marriage, Hilda," he pointed out, in a reasonable tone. "Where are you going to find the guy who's worth all this? You may know a lot about books and ideals, but I know something about men, married men too, and what they're usually up to. I'll bet you'd be surprised, Hilda. I bet you really would."

She shook her head sadly.

"You're so cynical, Bobbie. You're much too cynical. I suppose it was the war and all the terrible things you saw."

He snorted.

"War, hell. I knew these things long before the war. You've got to compromise, Hilda. That's life."

"But I don't have to!" she exclaimed heatedly. "Nobody *has* to. That's the point!"

He waved his hands impatiently.

"Okay, okay. So you don't have to. Have it your way."

She was really troubled now. When she came back from lunch she could only stare blankly at the unfinished letter in her typewriter and wonder if she was anything to him but a stubborn little girl whose perverse principles were simply amusing. The thing had decidedly gone too far. For here she was already building fantasies—yes, these things *had* to be faced— fantasies in which she convinced him of the sterility of his "razzle-dazzle," in which she played the role of patience, the woman in the *Sonnets from the Portuguese,* the loving and intellectual, the eventually loved— oh, Hilda! She flushed in mortification. For was this any way to be thinking of a man who, as far as she could make out, had no principles at all beyond a certain messy generosity of manner, probably only the mask of his need to feel liked? One thing at least was certain. If she was to continue to see him as frequently as she had been seeing him, he would have to meet her father. She had gone as far as she could go without that,

6

Two weeks after the Dilworths had moved back to the
city from Storey Beach Eloise was sitting in bed, having
put aside her breakfast tray, the telephone book lying
open in her lap. George had gone to the office, leaving
her with memorandum of instructions about the party
they were giving that afternoon. It was only a cocktail
party, but it was in honor of Arthur Irwin, the invest-
ment banker, to celebrate his purchase of a well-known
publishing house that had recently failed. George was
always nervous with Arthur Irwin. He was Uncle Gerald's principal client.

"I'll be uptown at four-thirty," he had told her, "and
the cocktails are already mixed. Don't forget to call up
that hired butler and remind him. And the flowers. I
guess that's all."

"Yes, George."

He had paused for a moment in her doorway.

"Are there any friends of yours you'd like to ask?
Now that Arthur's bought this new business it might be
a good idea to give the party a literary touch. What
about Lorna? Or that young writer you were telling me
about?"

"Landik? Oh, I don't really think it's his affair."

"No? Well, just as you say."

He was trying to be nice, she reflected afterwards
with a new, rather curious detachment. He had been
actually solicitious about her ever since what had happened at Storey Beach. Of course, he would never come
out directly and apologize. Oh, no. That was not

George's way. But he would try to make it up to her in small things, as when he had surreptitiously added Irene's name to the list of guests to be asked that afternoon. She had made no comment. To have thanked him would have been to refer, even indirectly, to the incident of the preceding August, and this she would never do. Until he did so himself. But this was beside the point. Should she ask Landik, as he had suggested? Did she dare? Her heart was beating faster at the very prospect of doing anything so bold; she tried to picture her living room as it would strike him, and the people in it: old Mr. Irwin, George, even Irene. But would they be anything but boring to him? Wouldn't he think it presuming of her to ask him? Henry Sterne, when she had met him in the street, had smiled his sardonic smile and congratulated her on "making a conquest of Carl," but was this anything more than Henry's usual hyperbole? Badly as she wanted to consult Lorna, she knew that she couldn't do so without asking her to the party, and she hated to give her any chance to sneer at George's friends. No, she would have to give it up, it was a ridiculous idea, it was folly—and yet. When would there be another excuse even as literary as Arthur Irwin?

The telephone book lay open on her lap, and she had marked his name, Landik Carl, 133 Grove Street. She would call and ask him quickly, matter-of-factly, as if it were the most usual thing in the world for her, an accustomed hostess, to add new recruits, casually met, to her circle. She put her hand on the telehone just as it rang, and she started. It was Hilda.

"Did I wake you, Eloise?" She felt the cool tone of the early riser. Hilda had probably been at her desk for an hour. "Do you think you and Daddy could go to the theatre with me some night next week? Say Tuesday? There's someone I'd like to have you meet."

"Oh? A man?"

There was a sudden silence at the other end of the phone, and she felt immediately that she had been too abrupt. She and Hilda did not ordinarily discuss such things.

"Well, yes. Sort of. Nothing special, you know."

"It's all right as far as I'm concerned, dear. But you know how your father is. If he has to work at the last minute—"

"Oh, can't you stop him?" Hilda begged. There was a new urgency in her tone. "Can't you please, Eloise? Just this once?"

She almost forgot Landik and the party in her surprise. She had sometimes been aware of impulses of affection from Hilda, even of love, but they had always been cut off at the last moment by what George rather sourly described as his daughter's "murky loyalties."

"Well, of course, I'll do my best."

"Thank you, Eloise. You're very sweet. I'm sorry to have bothered you."

She heard the click of the receiver and hung up, wearied by Hilda's constant assumption that Daddy's wife was not to be bothered, not to be interfered with, that Daddy's wife belonged to Daddy and couldn't be shared with others. And then, in a sudden spirit of determination, she turned quickly and dialed the number that she had marked in the book.

"Is Mr. Landik in?" she asked in a high, nervous tone when she heard his voice. "Oh, this is Mr. Landik? It's Eloise Dilworth. I wonder if you remember me—oh, you do. I'm afraid I made a terrible fool of myself that day. I don't know what got into me. But I saw Henry Sterne, and we happened to be talking about you, and when he told me that you really hadn't been offended, I thought what fun it would be to see you again, and *would* you be free at this late date to come in this afternoon for a cocktail?" She stopped, but only for breath, her pulses jumping, and caught sight of her startled face in the mirror. "We're back in town now, and Arthur Irwin will be coming. I thought it might amuse you."

"Why thanks. I'd like to very much."

"Oh, how nice. About six?"

When she rang off she sat up in bed and hugged her knees until, with a sudden sense of shame at her childishness, she got up quickly to dress and distract herself from the contemplation of her own temerity.

The reaction of her prospective guest was more complex. He sat for several moments quietly by the telephone asking himself, with unfeigned curiosity, if he, Carl Landik, knew what he was doing. To begin with, he had an absolute rule against "Park Avenue cocktail parties," and in the second place, who the hell was Arthur Irwin? Yet he had accepted instinctively. That was the startling thing. He could hardly go on now denying his preoccupation with the intense and admiring lady who had followed him out on the beach to discuss her rather individual reactions to his novel. He had thought of her, he had to admit, not once but many times in the past few weeks. Oh, true, he had dismissed her at first altogether as another cocktail party sentimentalist. But there had been something in the sincerity of her tone that kept coming back to him, something in the rather desperate appeal of her large worried eyes, in her paleness in the dusk that made him regret the rough way he had spoken to her. For what, after all, had she done but tell him that his book was important to her, and why in God's name had he written it if *that* was going to make him mad?

It was true, of course, that he was particularly prone just then to distracting influences. He had not yet found a theme for his next novel, and he was filling in his time with rather dreary short stories which his agent occasionally sold to magazines on the lingering reputation of *Even for an Eggshell*. He would sometimes sit for minutes on end, staring blankly at the abstract painting which Lorna had given him to put over his fireplace and wondering if his first book hadn't been a fluke, if he was anything more than a reporter whose single important story had been the invasion of a tiny island in the Pacific that most sensible people wanted to stop thinking about. For now that the money from it had been largely blown in a year of European travel, to the disgust of his father and brothers who owned a hardware store in White Plains that he had refused to go into, now that he couldn't see how to squeeze more education out of the G.I. bill, he was beginning seriously to wonder what would happen. He polished and repolished his short stories until twelve and took long walks in the afternoon. His friends in Greenwich Village, accustomed to his antisocial attitude, were surprised to find him dropping in for drinks in the early evening. He was particularly apt to go to Lorna whom he found brisk and encouraging. It was what he needed at the end of an anxious day.

One afternoon there, only a couple of days before the telephone call, he had brought up the subject of Eloise. They had been speaking of the summer in Mogue and the picnic that he had been to.

"And what was the name," he had asked, rather self-consciously, "of the beautiful woman who went to Barnard with you who pursued me out on the beach?"

Lorna was putting slices of cheese on the biscuits.

"Eloise Dilworth. Did you really think she was beautiful? She's rather a dear, of course. But not at her best on books. I suppose she bored you."

"Not at all. We didn't talk about books, anyway. We talked about the 'eggshell.'"

It was by this abbreviated title that he referred to his own novel. Lorna smiled.

"Ah, well, of course, that's different. I'm sure you had a lovely time. Did she tell you it was powerful and

75

moving, but if she could make just one small criticism, dear Mr. Landik, was it *absolutely* necessary to use all those terrible words?"

Carl frowned.

"I thought she showed real feeling about the book."

"Oh, Carl. Lady Bountiful says a few kind words. You don't have to fall on your face."

"I'm not falling on my face," he said irritably. "As a matter of fact, I was damn rude to her. But you just assume that a woman like her can't read. I doubt that, Lorna."

"Children, children."

This last was from Henry Sterne who was reading a French quarterly in the corner. Lorna was angry with herself for seeming to have denigrated a friend. It was true that she was fond of Eloise, but Lorna was possessive about her friends and jealous if they showed any interest in each other. What she really wanted was to have Carl admire the loyalty in herself that had made her include an old and rather boring classmate in a party of intellectuals.

"I don't know what you mean by a woman like that," she said sharply, determined now to go into this, at whatever cost to Eloise. "But if you mean the cautious American wife and mother whose husband protects her from everything but her own curiosity, then, yes, I do assume they can't read. Except, of course, for escape. And I think it was really nicer when escape meant milkmaids marrying dukes and not squads of marines being cut to ribbons."

"You're being most unfair, Lorna."

They argued for a while more, and when he left he was thoroughly irritated. It was a further inducement to his acceptance of the invitation which he received, shortly thereafter, from Eloise herself. When he arrived at the Dilworths' apartment, however, he again asked himself what he thought he was doing. Glancing distrustfully into the long living room as the maid helped him out of his coat, he could see that at least it was handsome and expensive and quite undistinguished, not, as he had feared, fussy and French and perfect. There were several people standing around the fireplace, but Eloise came right over to him and took his hand in both of hers.

"How sweet of you to come," she whispered. "Let me take you round."

She led him about and introduced him to everyone in the room, none of whom he had ever seen before. Then she took him over to a big table with a white cloth covered with glasses and plates of hors d'oeuvres where her husband was mixing cocktails.

"George, this is Carl Landik."

"How are you, Mr. Landik?"

He felt the impact of those distant, oddly curious eyes and the strength of his handshake. He glanced at Eloise and saw that she was already across the room to greet an arrival, and he felt a stab of jealousy.

"Eloise has been telling me about you," Mr. Dilworth was saying in a firm, hospitable tone as he stirred the contents of the big shaker. "She was terribly keen about your book. I'm ashamed to say I haven't read it. You know how it is, the practice of law doesn't leave much time for that sort of thing. But Eloise read some passages aloud to me which I thought were excellent. Although, if you don't mind my saying so, I thought you handled your soldiers better than you did your officers. I gather you were in the Pacific. No picnic, was it?"

Carl could only mutter assent to this. The strength and candor of the man were as overwhelming as his assumptions. He felt relegated immediately, with a friendly but firm push, to the category of Eloise's world, the world of uptown lunches, of shopping, of bridge and literature, of babies and music, a world severed from Mr. Dilworth's downtown by a gap so wide that even their joint membership in the great club of the Pacific war could not heal it. He drank two cocktails while Mr. Dilworth told him about life on Admiral Halsey's staff.

"There's a lot of bitterness about the war now," Mr. Dilworth was saying, "which is inevitable when you take several million young men who've never taken an order before in their lives and suddenly stuff them into uniform. Of course, they assume that everyone at headquarters is goofing off. The over-all planning is too big to be apparent to any one unit. But speaking for the staff I was on—"

The room was beginning to fill, and other people joined them to interrupt the flow of Mr. Dilworth's reminiscence. Carl was duly introduced to Mr. Irwin and told about his new publishing venture. He was immediately disgusted that Eloise should have held out this as bait to him, that she should have assumed, in a smug Wall Street way, that any author would be glad to meet Mr. Irwin. He turned away only to be caught again by the firm hand of Mr. Dilworth and taken over to be introduced to Mrs. Bleecker, a pale-faced lady in black with large, angular features. A Modigliani. The latter's eyes opened wide.

"But you're the writer," she said as Mr. Dilworth moved away. "I'm afraid I read only French novels, but I know about you, of course. What in the name of heaven are you doing here? Is this Irwin man going to publish you?"

"Lord no. Mrs. Dilworth asked me."

"Eloise?" Her stare became incredulous. "You mean, she wrote you a fan letter?"

"Of course not. I happen to know her. What's so odd about that?"

"Where did you meet?"

He laughed.

"Now just a minute, Mrs. Bleecker." He held up his hand. "Why are you entitled to know that? Can't the poor woman have any secrets from her friends?"

Mrs. Bleecker leaned closer to him and smiled conspiratorially.

"I hope she has, Mr. Landik," she said insinuatingly. "I hope there are lots of things about Eloise I don't know. For her sake, anyway. Pour a little of that drink of yours into mine, will you? That's a good boy. I'm on probation here. If George catches me taking more than one, he'll probably throw me out."

He tipped his glass into hers.

"Isn't that a bit rough?"

"Well, I won't say it's entirely without cause," she said, raising her replenished drink and winking at him. "Though George is stuffier than a cushion, I grant. Oh, they all are. It takes someone who has lived to see that. You must come and see me in my little apartment at the Stafford, Mr. Landik. I can give you lots of good material for your stories. Lots."

So she was a bore, too. He was tired of women who thought their own promiscuity was the staple of fiction. Hell, he wasn't exactly a virgin himself.

"What about Eloise? What could you tell me about her?"

She looked mysterious.

"I thought you were the one who knew her secrets, Mr. Landik."

"Me? No. I was only supposing that she had them. As a matter of fact, I should think there might be a whole novel in Eloise."

"A novel?" She considered it. "No, not a novel. Perhaps a series of pale, still sonnets. Lovely. And unread."

He felt suddenly irritated. Like Lorna, she would concede Eloise nothing.

"I'd read them," he said truculently.

"Well, don't be so defensive about it," she reproved him. "It's always tiresome when people go on the defensive. You think I'm criticizing Eloise. I'm not, really. I'm criticizing the life here. The whole stultified life on this side of the Atlantic. Now in Paris, Mr. Landik—"

Carl suddenly lost his temper. It was not so much at the ridiculous creature before him as at Eloise for exposing him to her. First he was expected to hear Mr. Dilworth on the Pacific, now Mrs. Bleecker on the Atlantic. And the excuse of it all was the privilege of meeting Arthur Irwin! He turned abruptly away from her and walked over to the door of the dining room. He caught Eloise coming back alone from the pantry.

"Are you having a nice time, Mr. Landik?"

"A nice time! What do you expect? Do you really think I want to stay here and listen to that old woman sneer at how uncultivated Americans are? I thought that had gone out with Henry James."

"Oh, dear. What old woman?"

He jerked his head towards the corner of the living room where Mrs. Bleecker was staring after him. Eloise gave a rather desperate laugh.

"Oh, you poor boy, of course you don't. I'm sorry. That's my mother. She's rather a dose, isn't she?"

"Oh." His temper collapsed. *"I'm* sorry. I had no idea she was your mother. God. Shall I go and apologize?"

"No, no, Mr. Landik, don't give it a thought," she said hastily but obviously meaning it, "Irene will survive. She may even like you for it. That's the way she is."

He looked at her blankly, at her nervous, smiling eyes.

"Why do you give these things, anyway?" he went on, exasperated at his own break and confusion. "Do you really like them?"

"George does. It's business."

"Why ask me, then? What am I supposed to do? Stand on my head?"

He saw that he had hurt her, but it only exasperated him the more.

"I wanted to ask you to the house," she explained sadly. "I thought you'd think it was stupid if it was just me."

"Try it sometime."

"Oh, do you mean it?" she asked, her eyes widening.

He turned away, impatient with her humility, with his own concession.

"Of course I mean it. Why shouldn't I? But can I go now? Please?"

"Dear boy, of course you can go." She turned and led him out into the hall. "But promise me one thing," she added as she opened the front door for him. "Promise that you won't lump me with all the rest in there." She indicated the living room. "Try to remember that I'm different. At least in one way."

"*Are* you different?" he asked. "How are you different?"

"I understand you." She was looking at him now in that peculiar way that he remembered from Mogue. "Don't you remember? But the others." She waved her hand again towards the room. "To them you're a writer. Your novel is a novel. It's like other things to them."

"Except none of them have read it."

"Would it be any better if they had?" She smiled as she said this and nodded. "Good night, Mr. Landik."

When she closed the front door behind him Eloise stood by herself for several moments in the dark vestibule, looking blankly at her own startled eyes in the mirror over the hall table. She couldn't go back to the party until she had calmed down. That was obvious. But what was more obvious still was that she didn't

81

want to calm down; she wanted, on the contrary, to be alone so that she could study and afterwards remember each symptom of this excitement that had caught her: the constriction around her heart, the breathlessness, the smothered impulse to justify the amazement in her eyes by opening her mouth and singing into the mirror. And it was even an excitement, she could concede, without in the least begrudging the concession, that might have been less intense had he not left when he had, had he lingered on, for example, to dissolve the impression that he had come to the party, not to see Arthur Irwin or George or any of the friends or even out of a writer's curiosity to see what they were like, but simply and purely to see her. *Her!* That had been the unbelievable thing, the moment when she had realized this, the moment that had proved that she had not, after all, made a complete ass of herself at Mogue, the moment when she had reached a timid hand through the mild mist in which, as Irene would have put it, she habitually lived, to touch, at long last, another human being.

Going to the living-room doorway she gazed more critically into the crowded room. How George loved that room. For it was certainly the most expensive thing they had ever done. One could relax, he used to say, in wicker furniture at Storey Beach, but in the city a standard had to be maintained. With its bright chintz and Chinese rug, with the open shelves in the built-in bookcases for the Wedgwood and the amber gleam of the Phyfe chairs, with all its sustained neatness and harmony it jumped at her every morning, bright and harmonious, as from a page in *House and Garden*. But now that Carl had been there and had filled it with himself and his characters, until then figures only of her fantasy, it seemed as soulless and unthreatening as a small, expensive cocktail suite rented for a business party at a large hotel. She even smiled as she caught sight of Irene huddled in a corner with the guest of honor, talking excitedly and gesticulating with her hands. Mr. Irwin was sitting quite still, listening to her with a reserved, slightly distrustful look, but she could still make out the curiosity in his cold green stare, that stare that showed the American accumulator behind the pink cheeks of what, at first meeting and before one had heard his graveled speech, might have struck one as an almost Pickwickian old gentleman. Oh, it was all right, she told herself, he was amused. And supposing he wasn't? Would the world come to an end? Wasn't it even all right if Irene, as she could hardly doubt, was only monopolizing him to irritate George?

"Eloise!" It was the tone of a headmaster on vacation, uncomfortably playful. "Eloise, you haven't addressed a word to me all afternoon! You haven't so much as conceded that I might even be here!"

She turned, with a forced smile, to the bulky figure of Harry Hamilton, standing alone, watching her, a whiskey drink in one hand and a cigar in the other. A little grin flickered under the great aquiline nose and the shining baldness of his round head.

"I am indeed remiss," she answered, falling, as she always did, into his habit of speech, more to appease him than to amuse herself. "I've been looking after the lesser lights."

Harry was the kind of fat man who made his weight formidable instead of grotesque. A bachelor partner of George's, he was also his greatest admirer and looked out for him with the sometimes patronizing, sometimes servile, but always fussing attention of the vain man who is not accustomed to emotional dependency. He took it as anxiomatic that he knew better than Eloise what was best for her husband, and he had always managed, without a hostile word and despite his rather cumbersome compliments, to make her feel that her timid overtures to him were basically unacceptable.

"You mean, perhaps, the lesser literary lights," he came back at her. "For I observe that the Dilworth salon has taken on a literary flavor. Not perhaps as yet bohemian, but we can hope, can't we?"

"You mean Mr. Irwin? Do you find him bohemian, Harry?"

"No, Eloise," he said with a patient, knowing smile, "I don't mean Arthur Irwin."

He had done it again, she thought with a mixed sensation of anger and fear. He had put her, as he always did, in the position of the recalcitrant child from whom the truth must be extracted by firm but gentle pulls. She gazed over his round bulging black eyes at his more vulnerable dome.

"Oh, you mean Mr. Landik," she said as casually as she could. "He's nice, isn't he? Did you meet him?"

"No, I did not meet him," Harry answered with a slow shake of his head; as though it was quite obvious that this, too, she must have known. "But I identified him. From the jacket cover of his book."

"Identified him, Harry? You make him sound like a criminal!"

"There may be those who would argue that the author of his last piece of pornography is neither more nor less," he said blandly, inserting his cigar carefully between his teeth. "But I pass that. I did not realize, Eloise, that you and George frequented the four-letter-word circles of the literary world."

"You know perfectly well we don't," she retorted, angry with herself for even denying it. "I happened to meet Mr. Landik this summer, that's all. And I liked him, Harry, as you would if you'd only—."

"This summer!" Harry exclaimed, his eyes widening. "In Storey Beach? I would have hardly thought it a community to attract a young man of his type. Is he a friend of your Uncle Gerald's?"

"No, Harry, of course not," she said impatiently. "It wasn't at Storey Beach at all."

"But you *did* spend the summer at Storey Beach?" he asked, dropping his voice and raising his eyebrows as he would in court with a difficult witness.

"Of course, I did. But that doesn't mean I was glued there. I met Mr. Landik at Mogue."

"In Mogue!" Henry pounced on it as if this was what he had been building up to. "I confess, my dear Eloise, that if it surprises me to think of Landik in Storey Beach, it surprises me even more to think of you in Mogue. Do you go there often?"

Her sense of the witness stand was suddenly intolerable.

"Oh, Harry, you're impossible!" she cried, slapping her hands together.

For a second they stared at each other, equally amazed at the violence of her outburst.

"Impossible, Eloise?" he asked with hurt, ponderous dignity. "You won't even permit me my little joke?"

So there she was again, a fool.

"I'm sorry, Harry," she said, turning away from him. "I seem to be nervous today."

It was uncanny what he could do to her. She was trembling all over as she crossed the room. Not only was her good mood quite gone, but she was worried again by the old things: whether or not Arthur Irwin was enjoying himself, how George was feeling about the party, what Irene in another whim of temper might take it upon herself to do. Was it such a good thing, she wondered bitterly, that there were people in the world like Carl to open windows if there were always Harrys to slam them shut?

7

ON HIS WAY home from the Dilworths' Carl stopped at
Lorna's. He was stirred up by the party and his own
reactions to it, and he wanted to talk. Finding her and
Henry at supper, he sat with them and told them about
it.

"The funny thing about people like Mr. Dilworth is
that they aren't simply bored with me. They're fundamentally hostile."

"Naturally. They hate writers. Essentially, they hate
all artists."

"But why, Lorna? Why should they?"

"Because you make them feel they might be missing
something in life. That's why they want you to conform, to be like them. Think how admiringly they
speak of a writer who's also an insurance salesman or a
doctor."

Henry looked up at her.

"You think I should become an insurance salesman,
dear?" he asked bleakly.

Lorna turned her big eyes on him in loving reproof.

"Don't be an idiot. You're a genius, and that's different." She turned back to Carl. "But seriously, Carl, you
have to watch your step. If you hang around with
people like that they'll make you do all the things they
can do better than you. Like the English and their
hunting. You end up either by becoming ridiculous or
by becoming one of them. Or both."

"You mean it's a conspiracy?"

"In a way. An unconscious conspiracy."

"But even if what you say is true," he protested, "it doesn't fit Eloise. Eloise is different."

Lorna laughed. It was not a nice laugh.

"My dear boy," she said mockingly, "do I have to be the one to tell you what it is that Eloise wants?"

Carl was upset by this remark and thought it over during the next two days. He knew, of course, that Lorna was possessive about the young writers whom she gathered around her, but still, she was nobody's fool, and women could sense these things about other women. The idea, however, was oddly unpleasant. Though he found Eloise attractive, older than himself, of course, but still attractive, he preferred to think of their relationship as—well, a platonic one. He flushed at the thought of what Lorna would say to that. She, of course, would say it was corny. But then who in hell cared what Lorna said? There were plenty of women for sex; he had never had trouble with that. And damn it all, he liked to think that a woman like Eloise, the wife of a successful man, a mother, all that, should value so highly, perhaps more highly than anything else, her own ability to feel with a young man the agony of other confused young men in the hot horror of the Pacific war. But now, if all it was was the other thing, if she was just another bored society woman out for a jag, excited at the prospect of an affair with a young writer whom people talked about, well, hell, sure she could have it, yes, but it was a letdown. And as for her friends, that smug, superior crowd, was that the way they thought of him, as Eloise's little boy, Eloise's pet? He worked himself up into such an angry mood that he decided to ask her to lunch with him in the Village to show her that he could still wear a blue shirt open at the neck and a coat with a belt in back.

When she came, of course, she never noticed his clothes. They met in a small Italian restaurant and sat in the back by a window that looked out on the yard and the soft glare of the autumn sunlight. Eloise did most of the talking, reaching down from time to time to pat the small grey poodle which sat obediently at her feet. She seemed to sense his constraint; she talked on, without waiting for his comments, about her childhood and the dreams she had once had for her life and how foolish they seemed now, how she had wished to be a singer, an actress, to run for Congress, to be watched and loved and praised. She laughed at herself and said that, of course, she had known all along she had been destined for just what she was. She was nervous, he could see, at their first meal alone, and there was a slight note of self-consciousness in her tone, but it was not too much, not really, and she was lovely to watch, dressed in grey like the poodle, lovely to listen to. His mouth and throat felt full, and he was giddy with the confusion of his own thoughts and the Chianti that he kept drinking. What did she want of him, he kept asking himself, as he listened to her voice now, not her words. The poodle that kept staring up at him with expectant black eyes made him think of what Lorna had said of people being made to conform. And suddenly the thought of taking Eloise to his apartment, of boxing her cared-for loveliness into that small atmosphere, obsessed him. He couldn't even answer her when she asked him a question.

"But, Carl, you haven't been listening!" she protested. "I might as well have been talking to George."

He looked at her fixedly for a moment.

"Will you go home with me?" he asked. "To my apartment?"

She didn't understand him for a moment, and when she did her eyes opened even wider than usual.

"Oh, no, Carl, I couldn't do that. Oh, you poor boy, did you feel you *had* to ask me?"

"I suppose I've shocked you," he said angrily, ignoring her question. "I suppose you'll tell me you're disappointed in me."

To his further confusion she smiled. It was a nervous smile, but still, she smiled.

"I don't blame you in the least," she explained hurriedly. "People can never believe that I mean what I say. But I do. You see, Carl, I'm a perfectly ordinary wife and mother. I live in a busy, routine little New York world. It's the way I am."

He stared down at the table, resting his forehead in his hands.

"I'm sorry, Eloise. I don't know where I'm at. Why don't you go on home now and let me just sit for a while? I'll call you again. And don't worry. I'll be good."

He didn't look up as she slipped away from the table, even when the poodle barked at him.

8

BOBBIE CHAPIN'S failure to live up to the dark picture of himself which Miss Ranick had drawn for Hilda in the washroom was quite deliberate. If women were important to him, his freedom was no less so, and he was not so unsubtle as to suppose that Hilda would take even the mildest advances lightly, particularly after her remark that choosing a husband was like choosing a career. That had certainly given him pause. It seemed a wanton risk in a city full of girls like Elaine, who enjoyed their liberty as much as he enjoyed his own, to play the reformable rake to an apparently humorless girl with auburn hair and serious eyes, just the kind of girl, as everyone said, that men like himself ended up by marrying. Oh, sure, he had heard it a million times, but what really worried him was a small, sneaking inclination on his own part to see this conventional tableau as a romantic one, an inclination, as he knew perfectly well, that was based on nothing but the sloppiest kind of sentimentality. When Hilda, therefore, came into his office one morning to tell him, with uncharacteristic timidity, that her father and stepmother wanted him to go out to dinner and the theatre with them the following week, he thought it best to decline.

"I'm not much at those family affairs, Hilda," he said with what he thought was his pleasantest smile. "Why don't I pick you up after the show and take you out for a drink? Wouldn't that be better?"

He could see immediately that it wouldn't be. Not a bit better. He was always surprised at how seriously his friends took their families. His own parents, who lived in Pittsburgh, were elderly now, and as his two brothers, both married, lived near them, very little was expected of him in the way of family duty. He called up his mother from time to time and sent them all expensive presents at Christmas. Occasionally in the summer he visited them for a week. But that was all.

"Oh, please, Bobbie," she urged. "I do want you to meet Daddy. I know you'd like him."

He saw that she was really in earnest, and relented.

"Okay, Hilda. Anything you say. I don't have to put on a monkey suit, do I?"

"I'm sorry. Daddy always wears a black tie to the theatre."

Holy smoke. He was really in for it.

"You're the boss," he said.

He regretted his decision more acutely on the night he was to meet the Dilworths as he stood before his mirror and tied and retied his black tie. In the next room, Larry Weavers, who shared the apartment, was giving a cocktail party that he wanted very much to join, a wish that seemed rather unreasonable in view of the somewhat superior attitude that he had been recently taking towards Larry's parties. Larry, who had been his classmate at Dartmouth and a fellow pilot in the Pacific, was his best friend, but he was beginning to wonder if Larry, at thirty-two, had not remained too resolutely faithful to what Elaine always referred to as the old razzle-dazzle. The noise of his party, however, as it came down the corridor, brought irritating reflections as to the sober, stuffy evening that undoubtedly awaited him with Hilda's parents. It even occurred to him to telephone her and suggest that she come over to his place instead. But no. As he again tied the wretched black piece of cloth around his neck he smiled rather unkindly at the thought of how such a proposal would shock her. She and her ideal husband. Oh, to hell with her, to hell with the whole thing, he thought disgustedly, as he buttoned the double-breasted coat of the closely fitted, midnight blue tuxedo that he almost never wore and went down the corridor to the living room.

"Why Bobbie!"

"Talk about being all dressed up and no place to go!"

"Have a drink with us, Bobbie?"

"Or are you too good for us now?"

He waved an arm at them and went out the front door. Larry followed him to the landing.

"Some of us may end up at Leo's," he said. "Why don't you bring Hilda after you've packed her folks off to bed?"

"I don't think so, Larry. I don't think it's that kind of an evening."

"Can you spare me thirty then?"

"Jesus, Larry, again?"

"Make it twenty-five."

He felt even more deflated as he went down the

91

stairs, having parted with five crisp bills from the check that he had only cashed at noon. Why, he fretted, did he always have to be the easy handout, the guy with clothes to borrow, a car, bighearted Bobbie? What was the result of it but to have Larry spend his money while Hilda dragged him to some boring show? Oh, Hilda was all right, sure, he liked being with Hilda, but alone with her, at a place like Leo's where he could at least have a drink, not tied up in a theatre with her family. Lord, couldn't he picture that family, in from the suburbs on a three-day fling with a highbrow play every night and meals at some dark little tearoom!

He had to admit, however, that the restaurant where he was to meet them was more than a tearoom. As he followed the headwaiter to Mr. Dilworth's table he took in the almost menacingly expensive atmosphere, the wide spaces between the tables, the green paneled walls, the big white menu cards crayoned in blue and red. Was this how a receptionist's family lived? Then he saw Hilda, looking tense, and in a moment he was being introduced to a blond, rather pale-faced lady about his own age and a forceful middle-aged man with thick black hair.

"I've taken the liberty of ordering for you, Chapin," Mr. Dilworth said to him without even a suggestion of apology. "We don't want to be late, you know. Hilda, what was that red wine we had here on your birthday, do you remember?"

While he and Hilda went into this, the blond lady turned to Bobbie.

"Tell me, Mr. Chapin," she asked brightly, "are you what George calls an 'uptown' lawyer?"

So that's who he was. George Dilworth. Hunt & Livermore. And he, Bobbie, had been telling Hilda who was who in the legal profession. The little minx.

"I suppose he thinks we're all ambulance chasers," he said, smiling a bit sullenly.

"But aren't you? It would be such fun to think of Hilda working for a firm of ambulance chasers."

"She'd reform us all pretty quick, don't you imagine?" he asked, glancing at Hilda who was obviously listening to them as she pretended to study the wine list.

"Which would be such a pity."

"You think?"

"Well, I'm a great one for leaving things as they are," Mrs. Dilworth explained. It was hard to tell from her alert, attentive manner when she was joking. "That's the basic difference between Hilda and myself."

He was almost deciding that he liked Mrs. Dilworth when her husband, finished with the waiter, took a firm hold of the conversation.

"I understand that you're a partner of Alvin Herbert's, Chapin. I don't happen to know him myself, but I remember he represented a mortgagee in a bankruptcy proceeding in which I was referee a few years back. It was really quite an interesting thing, you see—"

And he was off. It lasted during most of their rather hurried dinner while Hilda played disconsolately with her food and Mrs. Dilworth looked around the dining room, occasionally nodding, rather absently, to an acquaintance. The play, however, was worse. It was in modern blank verse, by an Englishman, and totally incomprehensible. Mr. Dilworth closed his eyes and slept without even a pretense of listening, while Hilda, determined to give every playwright his fair chance, sat still and concentrated, shaking her head deprecatingly each time Bobbie tried to whisper to her. Mrs. Dilworth was the only one who seemed to be enjoying herself; she laughed quite spontaneously at several points in the action. Mercifully, however, it was short, and when the lights went up at a quarter to eleven and people started reaching for their coats, he was overcome with the friendly feelings of relief.

"Now it's my turn," he said cheerfully. "I want to take this party on to Leo's."

Mr. Dilworth looked at his watch.

"I insist," Bobbie protested. "At least for a nightcap."

It was impossible to tell whether or not Hilda was pleased. She simply looked at her father to see what he would do. Mrs. Dilworth, somewhat to Bobbie's surprise, made the decision.

"Come along, George," she said, slipping her arm under her husband's. "We'll go for just one drink and then leave Hilda and Mr. Chapin. You haven't taken me to a night club in ages."

Leo's seemed very small and crowded when they got there, and their table was next to a larger one where Larry Weavers, Elaine and the remnants of the cocktail party were rather boisterously enjoying themselves. They all stared at the Dilworths, but they were too well coached by Larry to do more than nod to Bobbie. The latter's good humor, however, had been quite restored by the familiar atmosphere, and he was anxious now to show off his new girl friend and her family.

"Mrs. Dilworth," he said, leaning over to her. "I'd like to have you meet my roommate."

This was followed by a general introduction and, because of the proximity of the tables, a merging, only partly intentional, of the two parties. Larry Weavers politely asked Mrs. Dilworth to dance, and she accepted, with her same pleasant, rather surprised smile. Elaine found herself next to Mr. Dilworth and began to talk to him, after darting a mischievous glance at Bobbie, in a manner very different from what Hilda's father might have expected of a girl who was only a few years older than his daughter. Bobbie could see in Hilda's troubled face that the move had been a mistake, but it angered him that she could leave nothing to his judgment. He felt a sudden rough urge to make her listen to him entirely, to blot out with the force of his own personality any lingering attention that she could give to Elaine and her father.

"Let me ask you something, Hilda," he said abruptly. "Very frankly. Do you mind?"

"Oh, no, Bobbie. Why should I?"

"Why do you work for that funny little firm of ours?"

"But don't you think I ought?" she asked, taken aback. "Don't you think a girl ought to earn her own living?"

"Maybe. Sure. But when you've got—" He made a vague gesture in her father's direction. "I had no idea your folks were in that sort of league. I'd always thought of girls whose fathers were partners in Hunt & Livermore as being sophisticated and slinky and—well, as spending all their time in the Stork or places like that. Why do you want to pound that machine in our shop?"

"I suppose I should be sorry you don't find me slinky," she said in a small voice.

He laughed.

"Oh, you don't need to slink, Hilda. You're fine the way you are. For me, anyway." Her hand was resting on the table; she withdrew it quickly when he put his own on top of it. "Well, have it your way," he said, frowning as she glanced covertly towards her father's end of the table. "It takes all types to make a world. But do you really think your father's going to kill me if he sees me touching your hand?"

She turned around quickly.

"Oh, Bobbie, why do you say that?" she protested. "You *know* it isn't done to hold hands in public places!"

He glanced around the dimly lighted room and smiled.

"You mean to be honest, Hilda," he said, shaking his
95

head. "You really do. But you don't succeed. You don't even succeed in being honest with yourself."

"With myself?" she repeated in alarm. "What do you mean by that, Bobbie?"

"You and me, for example," he said, and then paused, wondering if he really wanted to get into it. "We've been going about together. We've been to parties together. Yet we couldn't be more different, could we?" He frowned again and shrugged his shoulders, suddenly irritated with himself as well as with her. "I guess we just like each other."

"But we're friends," she pointed out in dismay. "You said so yourself in the beginning."

"Yes, Hilda," he said after a moment, giving it up, "I guess you're right. I guess that's exactly what we are."

Just then they heard Elaine's voice, sharp and clear, coming down the table towards them.

"Are you a divorce lawyer, too, Mr. Dilworth? A member of what they call the keyhole bar?"

Hilda's lip trembled.

"Bobbie," she said, "would you mind terribly if—"

"I know," he finished dryly. "You have a headache."

"Daddy can take me home," she protested. "He's ready now, anyway."

"I'll take you home," he said firmly.

"No, please, Bobbie!" She was alarmed again. "I *want* to go home with Daddy. Really I do!"

Ten minutes later, when, defeated, he had seen Hilda and her family off in a taxi, he returned rather moodily to Larry's table and sat down by Elaine.

"If you want to talk about Hilda," she said sourly, "I'll give you five minutes. No more."

He thought of the dismay on Hilda's face, that childish, prudish dismay.

"I wish you'd got off one of your real cracks,

Elaine!" he exclaimed and sat for a few moments staring into his glass. Then he looked up and saw her surprise. "Oh, hell. Forget it. I was thinking of this whole evening. What a goddam stuffy affair. Not for me, no, sir. Not for this kid."

"Not even Hilda for this kid?"

"Not even Hilda. She's too good. She's too damn good."

"Oh, is she? And what about me? Am I too good?"

"But you don't have any pretensions about that sort of thing, do you, Elaine? Seriously, that's what I like about you."

Her expression showed how little she took this as a compliment.

"I see it all," she retorted. "You want me to persuade you you're in love with her."

"Now why in God's name should I want you to do that?"

"Because like all philanderers you're afraid you've never been in love," she said sharply. "You want to rumple that blond hair of yours the way you're doing now and kid yourself that youth and innocence have finally won their way into your rugged heart. Oh, I know you, Bobbie!"

"What brought this on?"

"But where you've made your mistake," she continued relentlessly, "is that this time there isn't any youth or innocence. That gal is hard as nails."

Well, maybe. He shrugged his shoulders. He certainly wasn't going to discuss it with Elaine. He had other plans for Elaine.

"And then there's her family," he said, as if he had been thinking aloud. "Why her father's a goddam Wall Street lawyer. She's been holding out on me."

"Oh, she has money." Elaine nodded her head now as if she saw all. "I thought she seemed awfully confident about something. My congratulations."

97

"All right, Elaine," he said shortly. "My five minutes are up."

In the taxi driving down Fifth Avenue to Fourth Street Eloise sat between Hilda and George. There had been a silence for several blocks, and she smiled in the dark at George's obvious irritation at having to go so far out of his way. Hilda, after all, was his daughter, not hers. The balance that it was her role to strike between the girl's filial adoration and his parental indifference made her feel useful but not responsible.

"It was a nice evening, Eloise," Hilda said finally, in a deliberate tone. "Thank you so much. And thank *you*, Daddy."

George grunted. This was followed by another silence.

"I liked your Mr. Chapin, dear," Eloise volunteered. "I was rather sorry we had to go to the theatre. I wanted to have more of a chance to talk to him. I think he's attractive."

"You do?"

"Yes. He's gay. Full of fun."

"Oh." Hilda sounded very dubious. "Did you like his friends, too?"

"Well, I really don't know. Nobody did anything wrong, did they?"

"Oh, nothing wrong, Eloise, of course not," Hilda retorted with an impatience that showed the strain of the preceding hours. "It's just rather humiliating to me that Bobbie can't face an evening with my family without surrounding himself with his old drinking crowd."

George looked up at this.

"It didn't seem to me that Chapin had much to drink," he observed. "It seemed to me—"

"Not tonight, no."

"Now wait a second, Hilda, until I've finished," he said testily. "You young people are always interrupting.

All I want to say is that he struck me as a perfectly agreeable young man. I don't think much of the kind of law he practises, but that's neither here nor there. And what's more, I understand from that girl he introduced me to that he has a damn good war record."

Hilda said, nothing. It must have been hard, Eloise reflected, glancing at her, for girls her age, who had had no emotional commitment in the war, to have it always flung in their faces. It must have seemed as if the veterans strutted about, flaunting indulgences that were no longer for sale.

"Aren't you being just a touch prudish, my dear?" she asked her, as gently as she could. "Is it necessary to condemn every young man who likes a drink?"

"*A* drink!" Hilda looked at her almost pityingly and then abruptly changed her tone. "Anyway, it doesn't matter," she said flatly. "I really don't care how much Bobbie drinks. Or who his friends are."

"Oh? You've had a quarrel?"

"That's so like you, Eloise," the girl retorted. "You always have to dramatize everything. I simply mean that Bobbie and I aren't really interested in each other. Not that there's any reason why we should be. But the fact remains we're not."

Eloise smiled.

"I don't know if *he* sounded so uninterested when he talked about you tonight," she said.

Hilda snorted.

"Bobbie gets around every woman he talks to," she declared. "He's always flirting. Even with you, Eloise."

"Even with me! Well, thanks. Anyway, I'm sure other girls find him attractive. I'm sure Elaine Whatever-her-name-is does."

"Oh, indeed!" Hilda agreed, raising her hands in the air.

"Well, you can't expect to have him to yourself right

99

away," her father cut in irritably. "What do you want? No competition at all?"

"Daddy," Hilda protested wearily, "Daddy, you don't get the point at all. Would it interest you to know what his relationship with Elaine *is?*"

Eloise and George exchanged glances.

"I'm sure I don't want to know anything about Bobbie's private life," he said sternly. "And I often wonder, Hilda, if the girls of your generation don't know more than is good for them."

"More than is good for us!" she exclaimed indignantly. "Is *that* what it boils down to, all the teaching you and Grandma Dilworth gave me? Is that the way I'm supposed to face the major issues of life! By turning my back on them?"

George threw his gloves roughly into the hat on his lap.

"What brought all this on, for God's sakes?" he demanded angrily. "Can't a man make a simple remark without causing a scene? I guess I'll never understand you, Hilda!"

Eloise put her arm around his stiffening daughter.

"Come dear, let's not go on with this," she said soothingly. "We're all tired."

They drew up before Hilda's apartment, and Eloise got out and walked to the front door to say good night to her. When she came back, a few minutes later, for she had been telling her not to mind George's sharpness, she found that he had switched on the light in the back of the cab and was already deep in a printed galley that he had taken from his pocket.

"What's gotten into her, anyway?" he muttered as she got in.

His irritation, she could see, had passed, but not because of any renascent sympathy for Hilda. He had given himself to a legal problem and to the pleasure of turning the wheels in his cerebrum and feeling their

100

easy integration as the whole smooth assembly line moved towards its solution. Such were his moments of satisfaction.

"She's crazy about that boy, obviously," she answered. "She thinks he doesn't care about her because he took us to a place where his old girl was. That's so like Hilda. She won't see it for the compliment it is."

He shrugged his shoulders.

"Well I can't worry about that," he said as the cab started off. "She ought to be able to do a lot better than Chapin, anyhow."

"But if she loves him, George?"

"Oh, posh. Girls get over that."

How would he know, she reflected as they drove silently uptown. How would he know if he had never cared himself? If he had never taken even two minutes to try to put himself in a woman's shoes, her own or Hilda's, even Irene's? For he was a man as other men, taking advantage of her weakness, not his strength; she had helped to make him that way herself, through the years, she and Hilda, giving in to him. She shrugged her shoulders, suddenly tired, and closed her eyes, hoping that it was not pleasure that she felt at seeing Hilda finally at grips with a problem that she could not solve by her principles. For Hilda's little principles, Dilworth principles, had rung out hollowly in their argument that night; they had for once seemed childish, not menacing, pathetic instead of high-minded, and she could lean her head back and think of Carl and what he had said to her at the restaurant with something very different from her usual fear.

9

SHE HAD MEANT IT when she had told Carl that she was not offended. She looked upon his proposition, on the contrary, as the greatest compliment that she had ever received. Indeed, the only reason that she had hurried away from the restaurant had been to be alone with the idea of it and hug it to herself. There was no disloyalty to George in this. It was not as if she had even contemplated infidelity. But from the beginning her inner life had been her own, her dreams and fantasies, and the outer code had no application to them, no relevance, for they had dreamlike and fantastical punishments of their own, harsh enough even for George. First, however, she could enjoy the exultation, she could sit by herself in her bedroom, her hands grasping the arms of her chair, and listen to her heart pound as she re-created that scene. And it was better to be alone, anyway, for she hadn't the least idea how to handle such scenes, how to reject without hurting feelings, how to show gratitude without encouragement, affection without commitment. Except was it even affection, she asked herself desperately, if there was no commitment? Maybe not, probably not, but whatever it was, the turmoil within, self-love or worse, it was her own.

Carl telephoned her early the very next morning.

"I've thought it all over," he told her, as she sat in bed frowning nervously at herself in the mirror across the room. "You told me the first time we met that you wished we could be friends. Do you still mean it?"

"Of course."

"Even after yesterday?"

"Certainly, after yesterday."

"Then we will be," he said in his most serious voice. "And I understand now the sort of friendship you mean."

"Oh?"

"I don't want you to think I'm so wedded to the philosophy of muscle that I can't understand anything else."

"But I don't," she said vaguely.

"Good then. We'll be friends."

There was a long pause, awkward as only telephone pauses can be.

"You make me feel as if we ought to sign something," she said, laughing rather tensely. "Or as George would say, that we need a notary public. Why don't you come in and see me this afternoon? I'm always home after five."

"I'll be there," he said, a little, she couldn't help thinking, as if it were his first assignment.

Peggy and Jo were with her when he arrived which she had planned, for although he was obviously not used to the domesticity of children at teatime, they lessened the constraint of the atmosphere. He told her about his rather lonely childhood in White Plains, about his high school years, about his career in New York University that had been interrupted by the war. She accepted his self-consciousness as she accepted her own and was encouraged, the next time he called, that he left with her the manuscript of a short story about a Central American revolution. It was not good, but when she ventured to criticize it, even mildly, he was peeved.

"You don't want me to write about anything except what I've actually experienced," he told her. "You want to limit me to my home town and Iwo Jima. It's a kind of snobbishness, like your crack the first day we met about the officers in my novel. No one can write about officers but officers. No one can understand Eloise Dilworth but a Dilworth."

"That's foolish, Carl. You understand me."

"I do, like hell. Could I write a book about you?"

"But that's only because nothing has ever happened to me." She sat back in her chair and gazed at the fire. "I believe there are lots of people like me, too. Exempt from crisis and catastrophe. It doesn't always last, of course. I may blow up some day and turn into a subject for a Carl Landik novel. I almost should, shouldn't I? You need a subject."

"There's a limit to what I exact of people," he said, mollified. "Besides, I'd never use you, Eloise. You're my friend."

"You will, dear, you will." She nodded her head. "That's the wonderful thing about artists. They use everything. And you're quite welcome to me, Carl. Can't I deed my character to you, the way one leaves one's body to a hospital?"

Sometimes they met in the park in the afternoon and walked for an hour in the brisk, autumnal air before going home to tea with bouncing, emotional Peggy and Jo who had promptly developed crushes on Carl and crawled all over him, chattering about their school and which teachers and girls they liked and which ones they really, really hated. When they went off at last to their homework, after much lingering and stamping of feet, many giggles and blown kisses, he would talk, more easily than if the girls had not come in, about his difficulties at high school and in college and in the war, mostly the war. She loved to hear him describe himself and his friends in the Marine Corps; she wanted to know everything about their reactions to friendship and discipline and battle. She could always identify the men in his novel from his descriptions of actual people. She knew it, indeed, almost by heart; she had read it over twice more since their first meeting, and he told her that she gave him the feeling, rare enough to writers, of a communication almost complete.

It would have been perfect but for her fear of boring him. She had never before had a real friend of her own whom she did not have to share with anyone else and for whom she had no uncomfortable sense of responsibility. The sick at Bellevue to whom she read aloud, the veterans at Halloran with whom she played checkers, Aunt Gladys and George's mother on whom she assiduously called and the wives of the Hunt & Livermore partners with whom she dutifully lunched, all these were part of the world of her obligation. But Carl was her private corner, her recess, her underground in a world of action and assumed good feeling; Carl was all that Irene had not been, and she could hardly believe in her own luck that this morose, tense young man, with his unhappy, hard eyes, should find her company worth his while. What could she possibly offer him? Surely, it was only a matter of time before he would discover his error, before, careful as she was, she would tip her hand and show him what poor cards she held, a fear that made her spoil her pleasure in the very moments when he was with her, seeking to engrave them in her memory against the day when she would no longer have him.

Yet she clung to him, despite her foreboding, as the one patch of green, of moisture, of shade, in the dry plateau that her life seemed to be becoming. Irene, it was true, who loved to gossip, telephoned her every morning and saved on her allowance by coming to lunch, but having regained her health and with it her independence of spirit, she had already assembled about herself a rather frayed and grimly sophisticated little group of ex-expatriates in whose gin-loving, blue-headed midst Eloise found little sympathy. She tried to be happy about her mother's new vigor and life, but she had brought her home, after all, to be taken care of rather than to be entertained, and she felt at those spirited little parties in the two cluttered rooms at the Stafford something of what an old-maid nurse must feel, spotless in her starched and unadmired uniform, when she stands outside the patient's room hearing the gay chatter of the first recuperative cocktail party, the same patient, now calling so loudly for ice, who a few days before had been content to lie flat and listen to her stories of a simpler life.

If she was disappointed, however, at the impersonality of her relations with Irene, she did not equally regret the new distance between herself and George. For ever since she had acknowledged to herself her error in giving in to him about Irene at Storey Beach, the shadow of his disapproval had seemed less threatening. She had made up her mind, nervously and tentatively, but still with as much resolution as she could muster, that in a future crisis she would behave quite differently. George himself seemed partly aware of this change of attitude; he could tell, she suspected, that the expression on her face as she listened to his evening summary of the day was more dispassionate, at times almost critical. He showed his bad conscience in his rather deliberate enthusiasm for any new interest that promised to divert her. Her friendship with Carl, for example, had not elicited the least expression of disapproval.

"Seems like a nice enough young fella, that," he said after running into Carl one evening as the latter was leaving. "What's he got, a crush on you or something?"

"Oh, no. Carl just wants someone to talk to."

"Well, if you have time for it, fine. Personally I should have thought you had too much to do being the good housewife you are, my dear, to have time for all the neurotic complaints of young writers. They *are* neurotic, aren't they? Or am I unfair?"

"You just said yourself you thought he was nice, George," she pointed out.

"Well, he can be nice and still neurotic, can't he?"

"Carl Landik happens to be a very distinguished young man," she said. "It's not a question of whether I have time for him. It's quite the other way round. It's a treat for me, George. Can't you see that?"

He shrugged his shoulders.

"Well, treat or no treat, my dear, it's certainly up to you. The only thing I can't see is how, with all that's going on in the world today, a young man can possibly be satisfied sitting at home writing novels. But I suppose it takes all kinds, as they say."

She said nothing to this. It annoyed her to think that he probably didn't even believe it himself, that it was something one said, one of those things that in his world went undisputed.

If Carl, however, had so much to offer Eloise, it was equally true, no matter how little she knew it, that she had a great deal to offer him. Since his mother's death when he was sixteen his relations with women had all been of a single kind. Now he had an older sister or a younger mother—it didn't matter, he assured himself defiantly, what nasty psychological term Lorna would have used—an approving, encouraging female friend whose sympathy seemed limitless. Sometimes he felt embarrassed at his own greediness for this sympathy, at the completeness of his surrender to her strange charm. At such moments his condition seemed unmasculine, almost ridiculous, as if he were ignoring fundamentals in favor of teacups and roses, as if he were exalting chatter and degrading love. He would feel this most keenly when he had stayed longer than he intended and George Dilworth, home from the office, would walk in on them. For George seemed to accept him with the same easy good manners that he might have shown to a tutor for the girls. When he found him in the living room, getting up hastily to make his departure, he would put his hand firmly on Carl's shoulder and force him back into his chair, telling him that he could not leave without a drink, that he, George, like Eloise, had too few opportunities of talking to famous authors. Once he read over Carl's contract with his publishers and pointed out a possible construction in Carl's favor that his agent found very valuable. His attitude, generous and hospitable, was obviously that of a husband, completely confident, who was glad that his wife has found so inexpensive and innocuous a pastime. Carl, on the defensive after such encounters, would tend to be surly at his next meeting with Eloise. This happened one afternoon in the park where they met to discuss the outline of a new novel that he had given her to read. It was to deal with the State Department and the curious revelations of an ex-Communist who had also become a Catholic. The hero, of course, was unjustly smeared by these revelations.

"You don't think it's too topical?" she suggested as they walked through the Mall between the double row of grey, weather-beaten statues.

"Topical? Of course it's topical," he retorted. "I'm not writing for posterity. I'm writing for nineteen-forty-nine."

"I see." She paused doubtfully. "But does it never occur to you that readers may consider you a writer and not a journalist?"

"That's specious, Eloise. We live in critical times. People have to take sides. They have to speak out."

"Individually. But as novelists?"

"Particularly as novelists."

"I don't see why," she protested. "People care about Carl Landik the writer. Nobody cares about Carl Landik the commentator. If they want advice on reform, it's not to you they'll come."

There was something rather devastating in her simplicity. It may have been in her instinctive ability to separate the vicariously from the immediately felt. It was as if she tapped his work with a small silver hammer, and he could hear for himself when it failed to ring true.

"I suppose that's what I should expect of you," he said irritably. "Lorna was right when she said you read for escape. You're a reactionary at heart, Eloise. You don't want anything to be written that might even joggle your precious status quo!"

"Did Lorna say that? That I read for escape?"

There was a faint flush on her cheeks, and he bit his tongue.

"Not really," he said quickly. "We were talking about readers in general. Hell, everyone reads for escape."

"Don't be afraid to say it, Carl. I don't mind. I was just startled for a minute, that's all. But you're wrong about the status quo, political or otherwise. I don't care about it. One way or the other. Those things don't really exist for me."

His irritation had disappeared in the embarrassment of his break.

"What does exist for you, Eloise?" he asked, almost politely.

"The things I have to do. Or feel I should do. Little things. Daily things."

"Don't you have a god? I should have thought a person like you would have a god."

"Not for myself," she said after a moment's reflection. "For other people, yes. I believe there's a god for George and Hilda and Peggy and Jo. But not for me."

"Because you don't deserve one?" he asked with a smile.

"Maybe. Maybe because I don't need one."

He stopped and stared at her.

"Because you don't need one? Eloise! You mean that timidity of yours is really self-assurance in disguise?"

"It isn't self-assurance, it isn't that at all," she said anxiously, shaking her head quickly and walking on as if she suddenly couldn't bear to be still. "It's nothing in the least praiseworthy, quite the contrary. It's a kind of preoccupation, or obsession if you will. You see, if you don't fit in, Carl, into your own world, that is, or think you don't, which is the same thing, fitting in can be everything to you. Everything. That's the secret of the maladjusted. You don't need faith of any kind, even faith in the world you're trying to fit into. It's like a picture puzzle, completely absorbing."

"But what is this, Eloise, about not fitting in? You seemed perfectly at home at that party the other day—"

"Don't you think that's enough about me?" she interrupted, with a slightly tense smile. "Aren't we getting rather far afield from your novel?"

Which was all he had been able to get out of her, but had anyone else got more? Lorna, for example, her closet friend, had never even suspected that she might be an interesting person.

"What you can't bear to admit, Lorna," he had told her once, "is that you might have had a pearl all these years and never known it. Oh, I know how we feel about childhood friends, that it's just a quirk in ourselves that makes us like them, that nobody else could. But most of us will admit it's prejudice when we really consider it. That's where you're so stubborn, Lorna. You'll never admit you're wrong."

Lorna had not known what to think. In fact, she had not known what to think of the whole relationship between Carl and Eloise. It seemed on the one hand almost incredible that they should actually be lovers, but on the other, and especially by the standards of her circle, it seemed equally incredible that they shouldn't. She became rather feverishly interested in the question and taxed Carl with it whenever she saw him. She hated to have people crawl out of the pigeonholes where she had placed them, and Eloise seemed unmistakably to be emerging from hers. Carl, however, much amused, took a lofty tone with her.

"I wouldn't expect you to understand a friendship like mine and Eloise's," he said, in the last of their conversations on this topic. "You and Henry would find sex in a stone. Something unphysical isn't simply unbelievable to you. It's indecent. You're actually shocked, Lorna, by my friendship with Eloise."

"What do you expect to get out of her, then? Material for a new novel?" She snorted. "Maybe you're smart at that. They say Edith Wharton is coming back."

"Now you're just being nasty!" he said with a maddening calm. "I told you you wouldn't understand it. You can't. You feel we have to be earthy every minute. It's really quite boring, Lorna."

"Well, if I were going to be a gigolo, Carl Landik," she retorted angrily, "I'd at least try to fulfill my side of the bargain!"

She was sorry that she had said this, but it was too late. He slammed out of the apartment, and her last source of information was closed.

10

IRENE WAS enjoying herself. It was her favorite time of the day, the cocktail hour, when she could drink with the comforting knowledge that the rest of the world was drinking too. On the coffee table before the sofa in her living room at the Stafford Hotel was a large glass shaker which she was gently stirring and beside it two glasses, one for herself and one for Arthur Irwin. The atmosphere was cozy, even intimate, for it was not the first time that the great banker had called. His card, in fact, had been left at the desk on the very day after she had met him at George and Eloise's cocktail party where they had been so obviously and absurdly worried that she might shock him. She liked to imagine what George's expression would be when he found out about these visits. The very prospect almost made up to her for the ridiculous rumpus he had made over her little toast at the dinner party at Storey Beach. It showed how little he knew of the smart world for all his nervous desire to get on in it. He could still come to Irene for lessons, poor battered Irene whom he had reduced to two little rooms at an apartment hotel without even a personal maid. Well, he would see. Even Eloise would see that her precious George didn't have all the answers.

"You certainly have fixed this room up nicely, Irene," her visitor was saying. His plain brown business suit sat on him without wrinkles. His thick wiry white hair seemed almost to blend with his forehead. He raised his glass slowly and deliberately to his lips and sipped with an unexpected smacking sound. Only a small tremble in the hand that held the glass showed his age. "It just goes to show how little I know the city I live in. I didn't even know they let you have your own furniture in hotels."

"There's always a way with a price or a smile," she said, rather sadly. "As I don't have the price, I usually have to depend on the smile."

"You're not going to get any sympathy out of me that way," he said stoutly. "With that smile you're better off than I am."

"Oh, Arthur." She poured him a cocktail and followed his eyes around the room. "Yes, it is rather sweet. I can't bear not to be surrounded by my own things."

It was hardly necessary to tell him that the only things of her own were her portrait by Speicher, bobbed and cigarette-smoking, a relic of the early twenties, and the cluster of bibelots that adorned the tops of the several small Chinese lacquer tables: ivory elephants and knives, gold coins and snuffboxes, tiny jade figurines and porcelain shepherds and shepherdesses. Everything else, besides the two hoop-skirted floppy dolls on the sofa, had come from Eloise. But what of it? It was her arrangement, not Eloise's that made the room. No one could have compared it with that overdecorated living room of Eloise's in New York, and as for the house in Storey Beach—

"It's so cozy here."

"It *is* cozy," she agreed, as if she had been waiting for someone to supply her with just that word. "One thing I pride myself on is being able to make a comfortable home. Heaven knows, I ought to be able to. I'm not exactly a novice."

She watched him as she made this flippant reference to her matrimonial past. There was a pause, a definite pause, but he finally smiled. Oh, she knew how far she could go with him; she knew her tycoons. He would resent everything she had been born with and grown up with, as he resented it in Gladys and Gerald, but she had the advantage of having thrown it away. Alone and poor, dependent on a self-made son-in-law, she was a perfect illustration of what he would consider the great moral of life: that acquisition was virtuous and disposition extravagant, except disposition by those who had acquired. She could look up, so to speak, from the mud into which she had tumbled and admire his passing show.

"Yes, I suppose you've had to do over a lot of those châteaux in Paris, or whatever you call them."

"Oh, come, Arthur. I was never that grand."

He sipped his cocktail contentedly.

"I guess that's where Eloise gets it from," he said. "I think she's made George pretty comfortable, don't you? He's a good boy, George. Not like some lawyers I could mention who spend their time sounding off with general statements and going to cocktail parties to meet new clients."

"Dear me, you are hard on Gerald," she said with a disloyal smile, but stopped when he frowned. Obviously, he did not like to have his points underlined by others. "Anyway, I agree about George. He has common sense. And so few have that." She knew she had to endorse his remarks about George. Arthur was almost paternal about George. "But dear Eloise, my angel, whom I adore, of course, I suppose she makes George comfortable enough, but the poor darling is simply devoid of taste. But *devoid!* Maybe it comes from having too good a soul. It helps a woman to live abroad a bit."

"I suppose it must," he agreed, looking at the lacquer tables as though they too had come from France.

She nodded. It didn't pay to be too humble. One

could show pluck. Pluck, in fact, like acqusition, could be a virtue.

"I saw Eloise this week," he said. "Last Saturday afternoon in the park. I always walk around the reservoir, you know, on Saturdays."

"Did she go around with you? She's so healthy."

"No. As a matter of fact I didn't see her to speak to. She was with a young man who wasn't wearing a hat. I think I saw him at that cocktail party where I met you. I noticed also that he had a yellow scarf on. Probably some sort of artist. Frankly, Irene, I was rather surprised."

She looked up.

"Carl Landik?"

"And who, pray, is Carl Landik?"

"Oh, I keep forgetting. You great men don't read, do you? At least you don't read war novels, the kind we have today. Full of big feeling and small words."

"Oh, he's one of those, is he? No, I certainly don't have any time for them. I like books with facts in them. What does Eloise see in a boy like that?"

She shrugged her shoulders, raising her eyebrows slightly at the same time. He looked shocked.

"You don't mean to imply you think there's anything between them?"

"Why, Arthur, what do you take me for?" she retorted immediately. "He's a beau, that's all."

He grunted.

"What does she need a beau for?"

"Oh, Arthur. What does she need a beau for? What would you need if you were a beautiful girl, married to a man who spends his days and nights working for Arthur Irwin?"

"George works hard, sure. We all work hard. It's the way we get things done over here, Irene."

She looked into his cold green reproving eyes, at those set, thin lips that barely touched. It was odd at such moments how, although not large, and although moderately round in figure, he could seem actually gaunt. The pink white flesh under the white hair dimmed almost to grey.

"But you're right, Arthur!" she exclaimed hastily. "Of course you're right! It's this terrible 'business' you men have all the time here. It drains the energy. How have you managed to escape its consequences? How have you held on to your looks and your hair and all those wonderful things?" She laughed at his blush. "Maybe it's getting to the top of the heap that saves a man. Is that it?"

They were back again on the safer topic of Arthur's philosophy and of his rise to riches which led them in due course to the malfeasances of his grown-up children, all of whom, in his opinion, had more money than was good for them. A widower, he watched, with a rather grim detachment, what he considered the inevitably corrupting process of money that had not been earned by its disbursers. This lasted them for two more cocktails and through most of dinner at the French restaurant where he took her later, but Irene, only half listening, hardly minded. She could nod sympathetically at the right intervals and glance discreetly about the room with its red velvet curtains and red-shaded table lamps, rubbing her thumb and forefinger up and down the stem of her champagne glass, enjoying the warm afterglow of her martinis. There was plenty of time for her own thoughts and for a fuller consideration of the meeting in Central Park, of which her interpretation had been immediate and direct. Eloise, obviously, was having an affair. It explained everything, the presence of that boy at the cocktail party, his strange, cocksure attitude and Eloise's subsequent evasiveness. Oh, it didn't seem like her, of course not, but that was just the point; women like her, the least likely, were the kind to go furthest. And was it so terribly mischievous of herself, she reflected, assuming a pained expression as Arthur moved on to the story of his first and favorite child's death, to exult a little that this should happen to George?

Driving home afterwards on the wide back seat of his town car, her legs warm and comfortable under the fur rug, she was surprised to hear him bring up again the one topic that was on her mind.

"You know, it worries me about George and Eloise," he said. "It's the way those things start. Couldn't you do something, Irene? Couldn't you persuade George to take Eloise off on a trip? She wouldn't need this boy, I'm sure, if George was around more."

Irene smiled grimly to herself at the thought of George's reaction to this.

"Why would he want to listen to an old thing like me?"

He leaned over and patted her hand which rested on the rug beside him.

"Because you know more about the heart than all of us put together, Irene. And George knows that. Deep down."

She smiled again. Arthur would respect knowledge of anything if it was extensive enough, even knowledge of the heart. But she turned his idea over in her head that night and the following morning. What intrigued her about it was that it offered such a valid excuse to get into a situation that she was dying to get into. She knew that she would never get anything about Landik out of Eloise who had become increasingly evasive with her, despite their daily telephone calls, but to be able to go to George with sensible, homespun, painful advice, advice, too, that *ought* to be given, even if the bearer did derive a subsidiary satisfaction from giving it, and to know, in addition to this, that she was giving it with the backing and at the instigation of his biggest client— well, if that wasn't made to order what was?

117

Her opportunity came when she called at the Dilworths' one evening that week, on her way out to dinner in their block, to find Eloise out and George in his dinner jacket reading the evening paper in the living room. He looked up in surprise when she came in. It was not a pleased surprise.

"Oh, hello, Irene. You're not expecting to dine here, are you? I'm due at a firm dinner in twenty minutes."

"No, I'm dining in the neighborhood. I thought I'd just stop in. You don't mind, I hope, George?"

"Mind. Of course, I don't mind. Can I get you—can I get you a drink?"

She smiled thinly.

"No thanks, George. I think I'll just sit here for a bit." She sat down, and for a moment they simply looked at each other. "Where's Eloise?"

"Gone to the theatre."

"By herself?"

"No, that young friend of hers, Landik, went with her."

"Oh." Irene paused significantly between her monosyllable and her next remark. "The young man at your cocktail party? I didn't know he was a beau."

George lit a cigarette. Then looking up suddenly, he apologized and offered her one. She shook her head.

"Landik's not a beau," he said in an unconcerned tone. "He's more like a kid brother. You know Eloise. She always has to have a lame duck to look after."

"She does, yes. But that's not going to keep the lame duck from thinking he's a beau, is it?"

"You don't get the picture, Irene." He exhaled heavily and fixed his gray eyes on her. "He's an artist. He's probably got a couple of boy friends in the Village whom he's much more interested in."

Irene laughed in sheer surprise. It was a nervous, mirthless laugh.

"I've only met the young man once. But he didn't

118

strike me as that type at all. Quite the reverse, I should say."

"Well, let's hope so," George conceded. "There are too many of the others around by a long shot."

Irene stared. She had not expected, even of him, a self-assurance so sweeping.

"Does it ever occur to you, George, that you may be taking Eloise a little too much for granted?"

He stiffened.

"What do you mean?"

"You assume so completely that there's no danger in leaving her to her own devices. Now, I'm not saying there is. Perish the thought. But the assumption is not flattering, George. It makes life so drab. When, for example, did you last do something to surprise Eloise?"

"You're the one who provides the surprises, Irene," he said coolly. "I'm a little too busy doing the providing. As you of all people should know."

She caught her breath at this. She was not accustomed to men who took the offensive so quickly.

"I don't mean in big things, George. I mean in little ones. Tonight, for example. Couldn't you have passed up your dinner, just for once, and taken her to the theatre?"

He folded his paper and placed it beside him, giving it a sharp pat.

"What is this?" he demanded, looking up at her. "Advice to the lovelorn? Are you trying out a first installment on me, Irene?"

"It mightn't do you any harm to listen," she retorted. "Marriages have been saved by clichés before."

He stood up, suddenly angry.

"Do you think, Irene, that your own matrimonial record entitles you to give advice?"

She got up herself, very pale now. His brutality had filled her with a sudden sense of a world in which women no longer retained even a formal advantage, a bleak, dead world.

"You certainly take a very high tone, George," she said with what dignity she could muster, "to a person who's only trying to help you. If I were your age with a beautiful wife admired by a much younger man, I might be many things, but I'd never be complacent."

He snorted.

"You think Eloise is tired of me. You'd like to think that, wouldn't you, Irene? You've never thought I was good enough for your Riviera set."

"You're being childish, George. I'm only saying a very obvious thing, which is that when couples are of different ages, it's only natural to expect that a time will come when they won't—well, how shall I put it? When they won't want the same things at the same time, when one is less—well, shall we say less passionate?"

It was the look in his eyes that stopped her, the unpleasant fixed emptiness. As she watched it she became uneasily aware that his color was changing too, that red and purple were seeping into the blue of his closely shaven cheeks. It was the high flush of real anger, a massive, crushing, un-sex-differentiating anger.

"So I'm no good, is that it?" he said in an ugly tone. "I'm too old for it, is that what you think, Irene?"

Instinctively she moved a step toward the door.

"I didn't say that, George."

"What did you mean then?"

"I simply meant that it's foolish to *assume* that everything is all right. Even when it is."

For another moment they stared at each other, and she could hear his heavy breathing.

"Tell me about Landik," he said, abruptly changing the subject. "What do you know about him?"

"Practically nothing."

"But enought to assume he's her lover, is that it?"

"George, I never assume things like that. I either

know or I don't. And I most certainly don't know that he and Eloise are lovers."

"What do other people think?"

"I doubt if people know anything about it. What is there to know?"

He got up and walked slowly over to the fireplace. He picked up the poker and began angrily rearranging the logs to break up the dying fire.

"It's time we both left, I guess," he said shortly. "Has Eloise spoken to you about this?"

"Not a word."

"I suppose you'd have to say that."

"I suppose I would. But she hasn't." She lingered there as he said nothing. "What are you going to do, George? I hope not anything foolish."

"Foolish?" He turned back to her from the fire. "I'm just going to see that she sends this young whipper-snapper packing, that's all."

"You can't be so stupid!"

"Stupid!" he retorted. "You've just been telling me that I take too much for granted. Well, I don't intend to go on taking too much for granted."

"But don't you know what that'll do to her? Don't you know anything about women?"

"Don't you know anything about decency?" he almost shouted back at her. "Don't you know anything about marriage vows and loyalty? Of course you don't! You wouldn't believe in them if you did. This is all your fault, Irene. Eloise and I had no trouble before you came back."

"You mean no trouble that you knew of."

"I do not. I mean no trouble at all."

Irene looked at him in dismay, slowly shaking her head.

"You're a fool, George," she said flatly, "and I suppose there's no point arguing with fools. They're always determined to be themselves."

121

11

WHEN GEORGE HAD CLOSED the front door behind his
mother-in-law, neither so much as nodding good night
to the other, he returned to the living room and lit his
pipe. He knew what anger did to him, and he wanted,
if possible, to get it under control before he went to his
dinner. As he sat before the fire he could feel it rising
within him, then ebbing for a few moments, then rising
again to the bursting point until his chest felt tight
against his starched shirt and he could feel the sweat in
his ears. He thought carefully about a piece of paper
getting bigger and bigger until his mind was almost a
blank, but at the last moment, as if someone had rudely
ripped a corner open, the whiteness was shattered by
the image of Eloise and her mother sitting on the porch
at Storey Beach gossiping about him with sly giggles,
comparing notes about husbands and how many times
and when and how and who could and who couldn't
and was it true that Count So-and-So could still at the
age of ninety? While he had been imagining that she
was simply "catching up" on her mother. Catching up
on that old slut! As if her past was anything but a series
of rumpled beds! Oh, yes, he knew how Irene and her
set talked. They made a lot of their culture and their
wit and their general sophistication, but when you got
right down to it, what was it but pornography, pure and
simple? Of course, he had never thought of Eloise as
having anything truly in common with her mother, but
they were both women, weren't they? And didn't most
women have the same attitude about sex, that they were

entitled to it whenever and however they wanted, that the male who wasn't always eager was always deficient, that all the remarkable things in the city, in the whole country, for that matter, with its industry and production and law, were as nothing when placed in the balance with a little act that monkeys could do as well as men? What did it matter to them that a man might break his health working for his family, that he might become one of the best corporate lawyers in the city? No, all they cared about was *that* and how much of it they got and when they got it. He had been a fool to think that Eloise was different, that because she was quiet she was undemanding. He had been an idiot to take it for granted that she appreciated that a busy man in his later forties, subject to the constant pressure of heavy responsibilities, was apt to be less enthusiastic than a boy about—not, of course, that he couldn't. Not that he hadn't performed competently in his day and still would when he wanted, sharply and quickly, he liked to think, and not lingering over it in dirty modern way. For what were people who made a fetish of it, who wrote poems about it, who called it the greatest thing in life but a bunch of decadents who were glad enough to shriek "impotent" at any man who put his life work ahead of the simple animalism of evoking those silly squeals? God! And to think when he *had* been in the mood, one night a week after he had packed her old bitch of a mother back to the city, she had said she had a headache. Well, she would see, she would be sorry, if she expected that she could make a fool of him, flaunting herself around town, wearing the clothes he had bought for her, the jewelry, in the company of some two-bit hack writer whom he wouldn't have employed as an office boy!

When he got to his club he found the other lawyers already seated about an oval table in a private dining room under a large dark portrait of General Grant. It was a dinner given for the litigation department of the office by Harry Hamilton, their senior trial lawyer, a semiannual forum where the different associates of the firm could learn about each other's cases. George was not himself a trial lawyer, but as a partner and as a good friend of Harry's he was always asked and always went. Enthroned at the end of the table as moderator of the evening, Harry enjoyed himself with a completeness that was rather terrible to behold. His personality entirely dominated his weight, making it seem firm instead of soft, imposing, even menacing, and the steady gaze of his large black eyes, the sweeping hook of his nose and the almost obscene baldness of his great round head were Roman in their dignity. Even the implied buffoonery of his red velvet evening jacket and scarlet bow tie could do little to mitigate the commanding impression. A bachelor, Harry's life turned emotionally around Hunt & Livermore in whose sober and mild environment he could play without rival his chosen role of enfant terrible, the bane of the new clerks whose breaking in was his particular specialty. He would insult them flagrantly; he would fling his hands in the air and thunder at their ignorance; he would even threaten to fire them, and they frequently had to be caught emerging crestfallen from his office, their hopes dashed, their futures in pieces, and reassured that this was only "Horrible Harry's" way. Once accepted by Harry, however, they were accepted altogether, and they could then join the little clique of admirers who aped his cynicism, his heavy humor, his extravagant passion for baseball, and who, every evening at six, were to be found ambling after him down the corridor on their way to dinner at the same waterfront restaurant. There Harry, released from the competition of his partners, of office routine, of home lives, would hold forth at his ease, over dry martinis and steak, about Lord Eldon and Joe DiMaggio, about perpetuities and shortstops,

124

until it was time for the little group to amble back to the Wall Street office where the squares of light along the fifteenth story testified until midnight of their nocturnal industry.

At the dinner it was his habit to call on people without warning to report on their cases, but even after they had risen to their feet it was Harry who held the center of the stage. Each speech had to be delivered against the running flow of his comment.

"I believe that decision was overruled last week," he would drawl, or, "Williston to the contrary, of course," or, simply and abusively, "Crap." When not interrupting he would look around the table with a rather bleary stare that seemed to protest, with a tired resignation, how hard it was that even paying what the firm paid and selecting only from the law-review boards of the country's leading law schools, it still wasn't possible to find young men who knew enough to state the facts, simply the *facts*, his upturned eyes would seem suddenly to agonize, on which a court's decision had been based.

George that night did not listen to the speeches. He sat in grim silence, answering the associates who spoke to him in monosyllables. They soon left him alone. After the last talk, when Harry had glanced at his gold pocket watch, pushed back his chair and pronounced the meeting adjourned, the group rose and filed slowly into the bar for a final drink. George remained in his seat at the empty table, glowering over the crumpled napkins and coffee cups, puffing at his cigar. Harry, waiting for him, raised his eyebrows when he saw him still sitting there and ambled slowly down the side of the table.

"Will you not repair with us to the adjoining chamber?" he asked. "Will you not partake of the customary concluding libation?"

"Let's have it in here, Harry. I want to talk to you."

125

"Bill." Harry had turned immediately to the last man in line who was filing out the door. "Bring Mr. Dilworth and myself double scotches, will you? That's a good boy."

Slowly, solidly, he settled himself in a chair beside his friend. George, however, gave him no time to make himself comfortable.

"Have you heard anything about Eloise and a young writer called Landik?" he asked bluntly.

Harry blinked at him solemnly for a moment and then took a long puff from his cigar. When he took it gingerly from his lips and deposited the ash in an empty coffee cup, the whole end was damp and black. He coughed.

"I was wondering about that," he said with a sigh. He pushed his glasses up over his eyes and rubbed his eyebrows with his thumb and forefinger. "I almost spoke to you about it after your cocktail party for Arthur."

George looked at him carefully. He knew that Harry could never bear to admit that he was hearing any piece of gossip for the first time.

"What were they doing at the cocktail party?" he demanded. "I didn't notice anything. Were they holding hands?" He snorted, angry now at Harry for confirming his suspicions. "Were they necking in a corner?"

"No." Harry shook his head solemnly. "Nothing of the sort. Don't get upset, George. I notice things that other people would never dream of noticing. Perhaps it's my own nasty mind. I simply noticed that Eloise seemed very cozy with a man considerably younger than herself who obviously knew no one else at the party. That's all." He shrugged his shoulders. "People have hanged for less. Innocent people, too."

George wondered resentfully if anyone but Harry would have made such a point of it.

"Well, if you thought it was odd, I suppose other

people did, too," he said heavily. "I just hadn't thought of it. I really don't know anything about Landik. He's been to the house several times, and Eloise has never made a secret of it. It never occurred to me that anything was wrong until—" His face darkened again as he thought of his mother-in-law. "What do you think I should do about it, Harry?"

Just then the young associate arrived with their drinks, which gave Harry time to prepare one of his speeches.

"Eloise may be as pure as snow," he said ponderously when they were alone again. "I've no doubt she is. But you know my attitude about women, George." He lowered his voice, even though there was nobody to overhear. "If they didn't have what we were looking for just where we need it—" here he pointed significantly— "we'd keep them tied up." He nodded several times, his expression grave, as though to confirm the solidarity of men. "And I don't admit to any exceptions. My wife, if I had one, or yours."

"Okay, Harry, okay." It exasperated him that Harry should pick such an occasion to sound off with his oldest saw. But Harry took any reaction to his stories as complimentary. He nodded, as though George had given him the proper response, and placed his hand on his shoulder.

"Will you leave it to me, George?"

"Leave what to you?"

"The whole thing." Harry tightened his grip on his shoulder. "Harry the Snoop. He'll find out for you. Leave it to the old litigator. And don't worry. Eloise will never suspect a thing. Unless."

"Unless what?"

Harry shrugged his shoulders.

"Unless she's up to something that she shouldn't be up to. Do I make myself clear?"

There was a rather weighty pause, and then George

127

nodded. He got up immediately afterwards and left the room without a word.

Harry followed his friend into the little bar a moment later, a weary half-smile on his large pale face. He stood with his drink in one hand, the other on his watch chain, in the center of the little group of associates that immediately formed around him. He answered their questions with unusual mildness and even admitted that there were some decisions of the present supreme court that might be considered sound. He actually complimented one of the younger men on part of a brief that he had written and told several stories of the practice of law in New York when he had first been admitted to the bar which period, although little more than two decades back, he managed to invest with an almost Dickensian flavor. All the while, however, as he talked, swaying slightly backwards and forwards in a rocking motion, he was filled with a tingle of pleasure that Eloise should at last be showing herself in what he was quick to deem her true colors. Poor George. Harry's big eyes became limpid with sympathy. For once, anyway, the male was going to stand up and assert himself. There would be no driveling this time about "being a gentleman," no graceful and cowardly giving in to the too often victorious female. It was still a man's world if men would only realize it. And he would show them. He and George.

12

ELOISE AND CARL had been to a play about the cure of a woman alcoholic which Eloise had rather enjoyed.

Carl had hated it, but his reactions, she reflected, were rarely moderate.

"Sentiment," he said disgustedly, in the taxicab afterwards, "gush. The 'hardboiled' Broadway audience. That's a laugh." He snorted. "I'll bet it's the most sentimental audience in the world. And they sneer at the movies. Jesus!" He slapped his hand on his forehead. "At least the movies don't always end on the note of life opening up again. Of rebloom."

"I like sentiment," she said stubbornly. "And fundamentally you like it too."

"Isn't that just like a woman?" he retorted. "Because you happen to like something, you assume anyone who says he doesn't is a hypocrite. You won't even admit the possibility of higher standards in others. Why, I could write a better play than that with—"

"Then why don't you?"

"Ah. The feminine challenge. Well, maybe I will. I'll bet it's all poppycock that it's so hard to write a play. It can't be more than a question of keeping people interested in what's going on on the stage. Hell. That's what every writer has to do. Fundamentally."

The taxi stopped before Eloise's apartment.

"Will you come up for a drink, Carl?"

"No thanks. I think I'll take a walk. I want to get some of that hot air out of my lungs."

Upstairs, in the living room, she found George. He was sitting on the sofa with a brief on his knees. He glanced quickly at his watch as she came in.

"Where have you been?"

"Where have I been?" She looked at him in surprise. "Why, to the theatre with Carl, of course. Where did you think I'd been?"

"I'm sure I can't guess every place that young man chooses to take you."

"But I told you, George. Don't you remember?" When he said nothing she shrugged her shoulders and

129

turned back towards the front hall. "I think I'll look in on the girls."

He stood up.

"I've just been in. They're sound asleep. Please sit down, Eloise. I want to talk to you."

"Is anything wrong?"

He stood in front of her now, his arms behind his back, his chin stuck forward. He was staring at the floor with a rather glassy concentration that struck her suddenly as pompous.

"I want to know about you and Landik."

So there it was, she thought. It was quite wonderful that she should never have consciously predicted it and yet never have doubted that it would occur. And here I am, she thought blankly, sitting here, having it happen.

"What is it that you want to know, George?"

"I want to know if I've been a fool to have taken him as casually as I have. I've trusted you, Eloise. I've taken the whole thing at face value."

"And is there any reason you shouldn't have?"

"That's what I want to know," he said immediately, looking down at her. "I've been told by two people tonight that they considered me a very modern husband. I assure you, they did not mean it as a compliment."

She thought of where he had been, of his firm dinner.

"Harry?"

"Never mind who," he retorted. "It only matters whether or not there's anything in what they said."

There was a long pause.

"What do *you* think?" she asked suddenly. The question startled her almost as it did him.

"What do *I* think?" he said angrily. "What do you think I'm asking *you* for? Do you think I do it to hear myself talk?"

She stood up quickly at this.

"George, if you think I've been having an affair with Carl, I think you'd better come right out and say so."

"Well, have you?"

She had not been prepared for such roughness. It threw her off balance and for a moment she could only stare at his angry, unfeeling eyes.

"Have you?" he repeated, raising his voice.

"No," she said finally, almost as though it was an afterthought, "I haven't." She turned and took a cigarette from a box on the table beside her.

"You're just good friends, is that it?" he pursued.

"That seems to be it."

"And he's never suggested that you should be more than that?"

She lit her cigarette carefully.

"I didn't say that, George."

He took a step towards her.

"Why, the little——!" he exclaimed and then stopped. "And you go on seeing him after that?"

"I do."

"To encourage him to keep trying, I suppose."

She looked down, embarrassed.

"You're being very crude, George," she said quietly. "You don't give me credit for being able to handle either myself or him. When Carl and I first became friends he was a bit confused, that's all. There was nothing more to it than that."

"Then it's hardly fair to perpetuate his confusion," he said sarcastically. "I'm sure you won't think me unreasonable if I ask you not to see him again."

She stared.

"You mean not at all?"

"I mean not at all."

"You mean I should just slam the door in his face?" she exclaimed.

"You needn't slam it. Only close it. He'll understand.

He must know there are people like me in the world, however much he may deplore us."

She took a deep breath.

"I don't think I can allow my life to be run so arbitrarily, George," she said with a firmness that surprised her. "I think I must be the best judge of what is and what is not wise in my friendships."

He closed his lips tightly and wiped them with his large silk handkerchief.

"You mean you're going to continue to see him?" he demanded ominously. "You're going to go on with this thing even after it has caused talk?"

"If I see fit."

"Even though I ask you not to?"

She nodded slowly.

"Even so, George."

In the pause that followed this she felt a return of something like her old timidity, but it was not this time any fear, however nebulous, of what he might do to her, but rather of the position, humiliating as it suddenly struck her, into which she had put him. George was so accustomed to prevail when he was angry, and now he hadn't. What could he do about it but glare at her?

"Very well," he said in a dry, hostile tone. "I realize that the observance of marriage vows is going out of fashion. But I warn you, Eloise. Be discreet. I don't relish the idea of being made a fool of."

Dumbly, she watched him go out of the room. Then she sat down to finish her cigarette. She wanted to savor for a moment the illusion of her triumph before she went to his room to plead with him.

"George," she said, when she had opened his door and found him standing in his shirt sleeves before his bureau, "let's not leave things like this. It's so grim."

"I feel grim," he said, without turning to her.

"But isn't it all really too silly?" she asked, looking helplessly about the room. It was neat and masculine, with two heavy mahogany bureaus with large brass handles on the drawers. It was hard and chaste and rejecting. Sometimes in the daytime, when he was downtown, she would stand in the middle of it, knowing that it bruised her, that it would never compromise. "Nothing's worse than this sort of fuss. I'll see less of Carl if you want. I'll be discreet. Oh, you can't imagine how discreet, George."

George turned and looked at her coldly.

"That's not what I want, Eloise," he said. "I don't want you to see Landik at all. I thought I made that quite clear."

She looked at him with a sudden mixture of awe and repulsion.

"I guess you did at that," she said. "I guess it was just that I couldn't quite believe it."

And closing his door quietly behind her she slipped down the narrow corridor to her room.

13

HARRY HAMILTON had done everything to make his office in Hunt & Livermore as different from the other partners' as he possibly could. Not for him was the paneled sobriety of George Dilworth's uncluttered room with its gleam of new furniture and huge crystal ash trays, the sanctuary of the corporate expert; not for him, either, was the fussy elegance of Gerald Hunt's great green chamber with its French armchairs and photographs of diplomats. Harry, indeed, had nothing but sneers for the whole redecorated office at 21 Wall Street, for the green oval reception room with its prints of old New York, for the wide white corridors hung with colored lampoons of English barristers, even for the neat still library with its glistening rows of reporters and Chinese rugs. He tried in his own office, the door of which was always closed to keep out the silvery sound of the endlessly repeated autocall, to strike the note of a less conforming era, to suggest an Ephraim Tutt without going so far as a roll-top desk, to act, in short, as an ineffective but vociferous protest against a uniformity that was devouring even the most individualistic of the professions. Harry had books and files everywhere, on his desk, on chairs, even on the floor, placed there and left there for months at a time, in a disorder that only he could understand and that was never allowed to be interfered with by the despairing file clerks or librarian. He had a giant leather swivel chair, specially constructed for his large figure, a glass cabinet with his collection of Spanish cutlasses and on the wall behind him a rather sentimentalized battle painting from the Civil War in which his grandfather had allegedly been a combatant.

His office geographically was just down the corridor from George's, a proximity which Harry had insisted on in the recent relocation of rooms after the new decorating. His habit of ambling down the hall to call on George every day after lunch had become an indispensable part of his routine and one that even George, who disliked any social interruption in office hours, had long accepted. For George, however undemonstrative, knew how to assess devotion, and Harry had always been devoted. They had met in the beginning of their first year at Harvard Law at the same party at which George had met Hilda, his first wife, then a nursing student in Boston. When George had taken Hilda on to dinner afterwards, Harry, quite drunk, had insisted on accompanying them, but he had somehow succeeded in amusing rather than irritating them, and this triple date had been subsequently repeated until it had bloomed into a solid and enduring friendship. It was a friendship, however, that had been based in large part on Harry's and Hilda's mutual dependence on George and their recognition of this dependence in each other. Such a recognition might well have resulted in jealousy but for the gentleness of Hilda's nature and her passionate fear of antagonizing. Sharing George with Harry, even after she had become Mrs. Dilworth, or perhaps, to put it more accurately, sharing with Harry the small part of George that she dared to call her own, had eased her feelings of guilt and enabled her to live out a continuing apology for her presumption in having accepted so superior a husband. Harry, for his part, had been almost servile in his respect for George's singlemindedness. Speculative, disorganized, self-dramatizing, he had been fascinated by the contrast of George's efficiency, his silences, his moods. Jointly and happily he and Hilda had ministered to this man who had taken them as completely for granted as they had fundamentally both wished to be taken, and his strongly knit and innocuous triangle had only been broken by Hilda's tuberculosis and death. It had been said by the shocked and sorrowing friends that Harry would miss her more than George, and it was true. He had erected a stained-glass window in her memory beside his pew in the church that they all had gone to together, and had prayed beneath it every Sunday morning afterwards, his eyelids tightly closed, his fat, white hands clasped in prayer, his head full of memories of a relationship that he knew too well could not be duplicated.

There had been compensations for Harry, however, in George's widowerhood. Even Harry had known himself well enough to admit that. George, for example, had asked him to move into his house, ostensibly to keep him and little Hilda company, but actually, as Harry well knew, though without in the least resenting it, to take over the bothers of housekeeping which George detested. Harry had almost enjoyed the shared melancholy of that first winter after Hilda's death. He had even allowed himself the desperate little hope that the arrangement might become permanent, that he and George might somehow continue their domestic as well as legal partnership, their joint lives dedicated to an elevating but not necessarily despondent vigil before poor Hilda's tomb. But he had reckoned, of course, without George. It had been obvious to everyone but Harry that George was planning to marry again at the earliest possible moment. He was not the kind of man who could remain single for long; there were too many things, despite all Harry's assistance, that could only be taken care of by a woman. He needed a mother for little Hilda, a hostess, a housekeeper, and after all he was a healthy man and only thirty-four years old. When George had been asked to bring his daughter down to spend his vacation with the Hunts at Storey Beach, Harry had thought it merely the kind of nice thing that Gerald would have done for any junior partner who had been so unfortunate as to lose his wife. Others, however, had thought of Gerald's niece, so like poor Hilda, so sweet and thoughtful and anxious to help her aunt, but somehow, perhaps because of her lack of confidence and poise, perhaps because of the very pathos of her eagerness to be good and do what was right, so definitely on the family's hands.

Oh, that summer! Everything went back to that summer, Harry reflected with bitterness the morning after the firm dinner and his talk with George. He had not even been aware of the threat until he had gone down to spend a weekend with the Hunts and found George monopolized by that tall, blond, lanky girl who had followed him about everywhere and gazed at him across the table at meals with such offensively adoring eyes. He quivered even now with distaste at the memory. It might have been true that George hadn't minded it, but it was equally true that he wouldn't have had a chance if he had. She had taken every advantage of his loneliness, thrusting herself into his path at each opportunity, rising early to have breakfast with him and in the end probably even climbing shamelessly into his bed. And what a catch for her, too, the penniless daughter of a woman too disreputable to bring her up, living on the charity of an uncle! He tingled again as he did each time he remembered that awful September day when George had told him, as casually as if he had been buying a new car or planning a fishing trip, that he and Eloise were to be married the following week. When he had spluttered about it being hasty, too ill-considered, George had simply smiled and told him with that disarming candor that characterized their relationship: "I'm not like you, Harry. I see no point in mourning. The dead are dead. If it's all right to marry Eloise in a year it's all right to marry her now." Harry's head had spun. It had been throat-filling, heart-compressing, excitingly horrible to think of Hilda dead only six months and Eloise already in her bed.

Looking up sharply now and shaking his head to dismiss the thought of it, he picked up his telephone and told his secretary to send in Tom Haighter. Tom was an affable young man with curly blond hair and expensive tweed suits, the nephew of one of Harry's partners and exuberantly anxious to show everyone that he expected no favors. He was not yet a member of the Hamilton inner circle, but Harry had an eye on him, still not sure that he wouldn't turn out to be too tweedy, too social for the discipline and dedication of the litigation group.

"Tom," he said in a hearty voice when the young man came in, "how would you like to be my lawyer?"

"Your lawyer, Mr. Hamilton?"

"I have a matter of some delicacy that calls for the

services of just such a man of the world as I take you to be."

Tom looked pleased, but suspicious. Oh, they knew him all right, these young men, Harry reflected comfortably. They knew how much faith to place in these compliments.

"What's it about, sir?"

"Well, it's not strictly speaking a legal problem," Harry continued, carefully inserting the tobacco in his pipe. "Not yet anyway. It involves getting in touch with that detective whom we use in personal matters— Fitzgerald. I want you to arrange to have a certain person watched."

"What person, Mr. Hamilton?"

Harry smiled at the eagerness of his tone. There was no necessity, he knew perfectly well, of bringing Haighter into this; he could have more easily talked to the detective himself. But to have had no one to whom he could denounce the iniquities of Eloise's conduct would have been to forego the greater part of his pleasure in knowing them. Now, moistening his lips, he prepared his stroke.

"Mrs. George Dilworth."

"Mrs. Dilworth!" Tom exclaimed. "What has *she* done?"

"You see why the matter is confidential," Harry continued briskly, underplaying the drama of his news. "It's a question of whether or not she is having an affair with a young writer called Carl Landik."

Tom seemed upset.

"Does Mr. Dilworth know this?" he demanded, almost accusingly. "What you're doing, I mean?"

Harry looked up in astonishment. It was distinctly not the tone of a Hunt & Livermore associate. He moved quickly to quash the impertinence.

"George know?" he demanded with an air of incredulity. "Why of course George doesn't know! I make it a habit," he continued sarcastically, "of taking it upon myself to check on the fidelity of my partners' wives. You might say it was my hobby."

Tom flushed and looked down at the floor.

"I'm sorry, Mr. Hamilton."

"George has done me the honor," Harry went on in a drier tone, ignoring the apology, "of confiding in me, as I am now confiding in you. He suspects that his wife shows every sign of being less exclusive in her devotions than he could wish."

"But do you agree with him, sir?"

Harry stared at this second impertinence.

"You'll learn in life, Haighter," he answered majestically, "that there are two kinds of rumor that are always true. One is that people are dead. The other is that they're committing adultery."

He had to admit, however, that Tom did not seem impressed. The boy had probably met Eloise at one of those annual firm cocktail parties while she was skulking around the edges in that way of hers, pretending to be shy and democratic and anxious to talk to the clerks when she was actually only interested in the proximity of young men. Oh, sure, like better men before him, Tom would have been taken in by the dishonest humility of those eyes.

"I don't think it's right to spy on a woman," Tom protested. "Particularly a woman like Mrs. Dilworth. I'll bet you anything Mr. Dilworth is wrong about her!" There followed a pause in which he perhaps reflected that he had gone too far. He smiled a rather tense smile to show that he was still on Harry's side. "Don't you think yourself, Mr. Hamilton," he continued in a halfhearted effort at banter, "that you may be letting your well-known misogynism affect your judgment?"

To have his moral anger taken as the expression of a personal animosity based on his own lack of something

139

which this healthy young animal seemed so struttingly to represent was to have his little scene devolve very differently from the way Harry had planned it.

"I am not letting anything affect my judgment!" he roared, sitting up straight and using the voice that he usually kept for recalcitrant witnesses. "I am simply endeavoring to help an unhappy friend who is in the grip of the most wretched suspicion that a man can suffer from! If Mrs. Dilworth is as innocent as you surmise and as I sincerely hope, my investigation will at least have borne the happy fruit of restoring his faith in her."

He paused here and glared at Tom.

"I guess that's so," the latter said, abashed. "I hadn't thought of it that way, sir."

Harry immediately pressed his advantage.

"Of course, if you find helping me in this matter distasteful," he continued, shifting to a softer, more menacing tone, "I have no wish to have you act against your conscience. I am reasonably sure there are others in the department who will listen to my cry of need."

Tom's ambition, which had been dozing, reawoke with a start.

"Oh, no, sir, I'll be glad to help."

"You're quite sure now?"

"Quite sure, sir."

Harry eyed him speculatively for a moment.

"Have Fitzgerald in my office this afternoon at three," he said abruptly. "Thank you, Haighter."

He glowered at the young man's tweeded back as he left the office. It was unfortunate that he had not picked one of the older associates. Haighter's spontaneous crudeness had almost spoiled his morning.

14

ELOISE WAS RELIEVED when she woke up the next morning to remember that George was leaving for Chicago for a week on business. He didn't say goodbye to her when he left, but she heard his voice in the passageway speaking to the girls, and she sat quietly in bed, holding the edge of the spread tightly in her fists until the voice and his heavy tread had passed by outside her room and she heard the front door slam. Then she breathed again, but her relief was a blank, empy relief.

"Hi, Mummy! Daddy's going to Chicago. Why does he have to go to Chicago?"

Peggy and Jo burst into her room, dressed in their green school uniforms.

"He has to go on business, dear. He has to make money."

"Is that what they do in Chicago?"

"I guess it must be."

"Will Carl come today, Mummy?"

"Yes, will he, Mummy?" Jo reiterated. "I have a pocket comb in a tortoise shell case to show him. I got it at a trade in school for the doll with the bust eyes."

"But, Jo, that doll was worthless! You were going to throw it away."

"That's why I traded it."

"Isn't she terrible, Mummy?" Peggy protested. "All the girls say she's a cheat!"

"They do not!"

"But would you like it if they did, Jo?" Eloise asked reprovingly. "That's the point."

"Will you read to us this afternoon, Mummy?" Jo demanded. "Will you read *The Scottish Chiefs?*"

"Yes, will you Mummy?"

"All right. I promise."

When they left she lay back in bed with a curious numbness. She felt as if something had given way within her, with a gentle but nonetheless distinguishable snap; she didn't know what it was, or just how vital, but she had a sense of floating precariously in a sort of undulating void, being slowly propelled in a direction in which she was not sure that she wanted to go. It was as if the thin wire that had held her all these years like a marionette in the exact performance of assumed and imagined tasks had parted.

The telephone rang; it was Irene.

"I was waiting for your morning call, darling," she began. "Is anything wrong?"

"What do you think might be?"

"Oh, nothing." Her mother's voice sounded surprised. "Is George all right?"

"He's gone to Chicago." She was suddenly quite certain that Irene was one of the two people who had spoken to George the night before.

"Then we'll be able to spend an evening together," Irene continued. "Shall we set a date? Tonight? Tomorrow?"

Eloise raised her eyebrows at her own reflection in the mirror across from her bed.

"I'll have to call you, Irene. I'll have to see what I've got on this week."

"Oh." Her mother sounded hurt. "Well, that's fine, child. You call me."

When she had dressed and gone into the living room she was surprised to find Hilda turning the pages of the morning paper in a desultory fashion. She looked up as Eloise came in.

"Oh, hello," she said. "I came to see Daddy before he went to the office. But I see he's gone."

"Yes. He's gone."

"Can I come around for supper tonight? I want to talk to him."

"You can come for supper, of course. But I'm afraid you won't find George. He's gone to Chicago."

"Oh." Hilda looked utterly discouraged. "I didn't know. He never told me."

Eloise sat down opposite her. "I don't suppose I could help, could I?"

Hilda looked at her doubtfully.

"I've quite my job."

"You have, really? I'm sorry. That is, if I should be sorry. There wasn't any trouble, was there?"

"Not trouble exactly. It was Bobbie. I didn't think I should go on seeing him."

Eloise sighed.

"And I thought he was so nice. Well, I suppose there's no help for it," she added, shrugging her shoulders. "Would you like to take a trip? I believe that's what people do under the circumstances. George is away, but I'd be glad to give you the money."

"Oh, no thanks." Hilda seemed flustered by the ease with which Eloise took it. "I'll get over it. It won't kill me, after all. And it must be better to go through this now than get involved with someone you can't really respect." She paused and then appealed to Eloise, suddenly, almost belligerently. "Don't you agree, Eloise? Really?"

"I don't know, dear. I really don't."

"Oh, Eloise, why do you always say things like that?" Hilda exclaimed, suddenly irritated. "When he gets drunk at parties and loose as—as I don't know what? I suppose you wouldn't know," she continued bitterly. "You fell in love with Daddy. A man who had everything. You probably can't conceive what it's like to find yourself caring for someone like Bobbie."

"I could imagine it, couldn't I?" Eloise speculated, watching her and smiling. "I should think I could imagine it just be seeing how down you look. If life is like this without Bobbie, I can't help wondering, dear, could it be so much worse with him?"

"I have to do what I think is right," Hilda said impatiently, turning away from her. "If you don't see it that way, I don't see how I can explain it to you."

Eloise studied her for another moment. She had the same detached feeling as when she had been talking to her mother.

"I know you've never really liked me, Hilda," she began, but stopped immediately when she saw the girl's expression of horror. "No, I shouldn't say that. It's childish to say that. Let me put it this way. I know you've never felt that I've been any help to you, and maybe I haven't. I don't apologize, because I don't think it was altogether my fault. It's not easy to be a stepmother, particularly when you had to start as young as I did. But I still think you're making a mistake to be as hard on Bobbie as you've been on me. And on yourself. Of course, it's your life and you must lead it, and nobody knows that better than you, dear. But I feel sorry for you, Hilda, and I don't say that with any sense of superiority."

Hilda was speechless for several moments, staring at her. Then her fortitude suddenly collapsed.

"Oh, Eloise," she cried, getting up and hurrying over to her, "don't say I don't like you! Please don't. It's not true." She leaned over and kissed her with tears in her eyes. "I've been jealous of you, I know, and there have been times that I've thought unkind things about you, but it isn't that I haven't liked you. It's just the oppo-

144

site, really." She sat down by her, suddenly quite humble. "Do you really think I'm being stiff and prudish?"

"Well perhaps just a bit, dear. Don't you think so yourself? Just a bit?"

"Maybe." Hilda nodded morosely in a mood of immediate self-condemnation. "Maybe I am a prude. Maybe that's what I deserve to be, a prudish, censorious old maid."

"Dear me."

"But it's true," the girl exclaimed excitedly. "You know it's true!"

"Hilda," Eloise said firmly, putting her hand on her arm, "why don't you ask Bobbie for dinner here one night while your father's away? Just the three of us?"

Hilda shook her head gloomily.

"He's in Florida. On one of those divorce cases of his."

"Then he doesn't know you've quit your job?"

"No."

"Well, that's good," Eloise said hopefully. "I was afraid you'd had a scene with him. Now he won't have to know why you quit."

But Hilda shook her head again.

"Yes he will."

"How?"

"Oh, he just will." Hilda sighed. "He'll ask me, and I'll have to tell him."

"Oh, Hilda." Eloise raised her eyes to the ceiling. "Stop being a Dilworth, for pity's sake. For once in your life."

When she finally sent Hilda back to her apartment, the girl seemed moderately cheered up. She had promised to write Bobbie a letter saying that she had quit the job to take a business course, and she was planning to absolve her conscience by actually enrolling in one. Eloise, alone at last, went out for a walk in the park.

She was surprised at her own serenity. She had

defied George, after all, even if nothing had happened. Well, what had she expected would happen? What had she thought he could do to her? Beat her? Strip her and expose her to a mob of jeering men as in her fantasies she saw herself, the agent of Irene's world punished by the stern people of his? No, after all, thank God, she was still rational; one could fear the anger of a man like George, fear it neurotically, but when it came it had to be an anticlimax. There was nothing else, by simple definition, that it could be. As she walked along she thought less guiltily of Carl and of how clear and young the skin on his cheeks was beneath the older look in his eyes, that expression of habitual impatience. thought of him working at his desk, staring out the window, concentrating, not thinking of her. She didn't really want him to be thinking of her. She wanted to think of herself as accessory, as only there to console and relax him when he was tired or couldn't write. And a sudden excitement took hold of her when she thought what other people might be saying about them, not only Irene and Harry Hamilton, but others, lots of others—a squirrel crossed the path in front of her in two quick bounds, and she stopped, her heart beating as if she had heard a sudden sound in the night.

When she got home she found that Carl had telephoned. She called him back, and he asked if he could come to tea.

"I'm afraid not," she lied with a glibness that surprised her. "George's mother has come down from New Hampshire, and I expect to be tied up for the next few days. You know how eager they are at that age. The Planetarium, top of the Empire State, Grant's Tomb. I'll call you when I'm free."

He grumbled, but he believed her. She could tell that, and she was proud of herself, as she had been proud when she had put Irene off.

She read an hour to the girls that night and sent

them to bed to talk about William Wallace while she went alone to the movies. The next day and the one after that she kept to herself, putting her mother off in the morning call, telephoning Hilda but not seeing her, canceling her luncheon engagements, even failing to turn up at the board meeting of her club for neighborhood children. She walked in the park and went to the movies and felt bored but clear-minded, restless but free. She was even beginning to wonder if she might not be readier to give up Carl than she thought, if she had not at this point given him all the sympathy he needed, indeed all that she could really give. And perhaps there was something in what George said; perhaps it *was* rather ridiculous for her to be seen about town accompanied by someone as young as Carl, someone who ought to be seeing girls his own age or even thinking of marriage. She wanted him to marry, of course. But she was quite sure of one thing. She was not going to give Carl up because George had snapped his fingers, even if George should think, when it happened, that this had been her reason. She would give him up perhaps, but not until she had signified in some way to herself that she knew what she was doing, that she was not being coerced, that it was the free act of a woman who realized that the whole relation was by its nature temporary, that there could be no real future for that kind of friendship between a woman like herself and a young man like him.

"You're so hard to get hold of these days," Irene told her the third morning on the telephone. "Anyone would think you were having an affair."

"Anyone can think what they please," she said rather grimly. "I'm sick of anyone."

"I hope you're being discreet," Irene continued, more sharply. "You don't think you could use the advice of your old mother? She knows her world, you know."

147

"Oh, Irene, you can have your world," she said wearily. "Are you so sure that you understand other people's?"

"All right, dear, all right. I was only trying to help."

This interchange, unpleasant as it was, had made her face up to the fact that it was exactly an affair that she was contemplating. It was small wonder that she had been avoiding people, that familiar faces had filled her with sudden panic, now that she realized that what had formerly been a guilty, secret thought might unbelievably become a fact, now that she could picture the stiffening of friends' cheeks, the narrowing of their lips at her playing publicly, as in a nightmare, the role that she had always reserved for her fantasies. While she kept away from people she could be alone in the privacy of her imagination; what she was thinking seemed more logical, less terrible. Didn't they do it, too, other people, even, perhaps, the people she feared, wasn't it recorded in all the novels and plays that she read? Wasn't it love which, everyone seemed to agree, gave life its enduring significance? If she could go to Carl once, just once, she reasoned desperately, she might be able to return in peace to her role of wife and mother for as long as need be, but to give him up and go back to her old life without ever knowing, as she was sure now that she had never known, the embrace of a man who really wanted her, particularly now, when she felt at the crossroads of life, with the possibility of courage actually and for the first time ahead of her, would be to achieve the bitter plight of Phèdre who never plucked the fruit of her disgracing passion. She thought of it as she lingered alone over her solitary teacup until the girls came bounding into the room, and she blushed and expiated by reading *The Scottish Chiefs* until her voice was tired, way past their bedtime.

"Carl," she heard herself say late one afternoon when she had called him, dialing the number with a

148

trembling hand, "I'm off duty. The dear old lady's gone home. How about a cocktail?"

"I was just thinking of a cocktail. I'll be up in a half-hour."

"No, Carl." She paused to swallow. "You know, I've never seen your apartment. Could I come down? It's so bleak up here. The girls have gone to a birthday party, and George is away."

"Come along. Would you like me to get Lorna and Henry over?"

"Oh, no." She paused, having said it too quickly. "Let's just be cozy."

"Sure thing."

My God, I've done it, she thought. I've really done it. But don't even think about it, Eloise, she whispered to herself, get in a taxi and go, just go, for God's sake! All the way down in the cab she kept repeating over and over the burning lines of Phèdre's declaration to Hippolyte.

She wondered if his smile was suggestive when he opened the door; she couldn't be sure. She stepped quickly past him into the small living room and sat on the stool before the fire which he had lit. She heard him mixing the cocktails behind her, but she didn't turn around until he came over and put one in her hand. Then she took in the room with its cracked ceiling and dark green walls, its battered furniture and the plain board bookcase stuffed with books, new books still in covers, old school textbooks, theatre programs. Several paintings by friends, unframed, nudes and landscapes, hung on the walls.

"But, Carl, you have no rug, you poor dear," she said looking down at the bare floor.

"I keep meaning to get one. But you know. I never get around to it."

"Let me give you one. Please."

He sat down in the armchair near her stool and poured himself a drink from the shaker.

"Sure. I'd like a rug."

"As a matter of fact," she said, looking around, "I could do a lot for this apartment."

"No, just the rug, thank you. Why is it that women always want to change things? I'm quite happy the way this is."

"Well, then this is the way it should be," she conceded. She drank her cocktail quickly.

"Did you give your mother-in-law a good time?"

"Oh, she didn't come," she said almost casually, turning again to look into the fire. "That was just a story. I wanted to be alone for a couple of days."

"Eloise!" he exclaimed, laughing. "You don't have to tell me stories. Just say you don't want to see me. I'll understand."

There was a silence.

"What did you want to be alone for?" he pursued.

"To think."

"About what?"

"Myself. What do we ever think about?"

"I'm learning more and more about you. I had always thought of you as practically without an ego."

He poured her another cocktail, and they discussed the ego in a desultory way, he doing most of the talking. It was like their first lunch together, she reflected, when she had done the talking because he had had something else on his mind. Now their roles were reversed. As she stared at the two flaming logs she had a dreary, dull feeling that the moment had passed and that she would never dare make her proposal now, that she would simply sit on, drinking her cocktail, listening to him talk and then go home alone in a taxi to the endless unfolding of her own life. It would happen that way because it had always happened that way, or rather had not happened. She was destined never to participate, never to do anything but lend a nervous cheerfulness to the lives of people who not only disliked cheerfulness but distrusted it. She could go back to *The Scottish Chiefs* and to children who were less interested in it than she was herself. She took a long swallow of her drink and turned to him desperately.

"Carl."

"Yes?"

His dark eyes looked worried; when he rubbed his cheek with his hand he seemed almost too boyish.

"Carl, do you remember what you suggested the day we had lunch together in that Italian restaurant?"

He flushed.

"Of course."

"I wish you'd suggest it again."

She saw how she had startled him and turned miserably back to the fire. He was repelled, of course, why wouldn't he be? She was repelled herself.

"I'm sorry," she said and closed her eyes. "I should know there's a time and place for everything. I had my chance and missed it. I should have let well enough alone." She shook her head. "You'll have to forgive me, Carl. I'm new at these things."

"Eloise. Poor Eloise."

She felt his hand on the back of her head; he was turning her around; he was kneeling down beside her stool, but still she wouldn't open her eyes. He kissed her on the lips, and it was the firm kiss of deliberation. He was being kind to her; he was probably shocked at what must have seemed to him an almost incestuous idea, but she no longer minded. His lips were as warm as the fire she had been staring into, and she clung to him greedily, not caring now what he thought of her or even what she herself thought of anything. When he released her he stood up and took his shirt off. He said nothing at all, and she watched him lean down and remove his shoes. He looked matter-of-fact, almost indifferent. Then he looked at her and smiled and, over-come with embarrassment, she got up and hurried into the next room, almost dark in the twilight, and cold. She took off her clothes quickly, almost frantically, and stood by the bed shivering, running her hands up and down her arms and her sides. In a moment he was beside her, and she lay down, suddenly oblivious of the cold, with a shudder at the feeling of the sheet against her back and shoulders.

This is it, this is everything and everybody, this is what I wanted; this is what I planned, this is *me*, she kept thinking desperately, until she almost ceased to think, until she seemed to become a blend of all her guilt and excitement, until she thought she heard a sound, and then again, and it was nearer, and then—

The light on the ceiling went on, and there was a blinding flash. The room seemed suddenly to be full of people, and a flat male voice was saying:

"Sorry, folks. Don't let us disturb you. Just getting a snapshot for the lady's husband."

When Carl got up she had a glimpse of his bloodshot eyes. He swung at one of the four men in the room, the one with the camera, but two others grabbed him and held him there, naked, while the camera man photographed him. She sat up and reached wildly for the blanket; she pulled it over her and threw herself back, turning over and burying her head in the pillow, deeper and deeper with a writhing motion. But there was to be no unconsciousness of this, deliberate or otherwise. Her nightmare had at last come true.

Part Two

1

THE HERBERTS' apartment was grey and modern and dominated by a single, large abstract painting hung over a fireless hearth concealed by a fire screen. Hilda Dilworth, knowing nobody at the party, stood at the edge of the group with an untouched cocktail in her hand and tried to look as if she were listening to the man who was telling her how sick he was of hearing about Albert Schweitzer. But Hilda was too preoccupied even to disapprove, as she normally and vociferously would have. She only wanted to be unnoticed or at least unspoken to; she felt as lifeless as the grey cushion on the L-shaped divan or the green ash tray with the cartoon stenciled on its surface. What was she doing there? she kept asking herself. But what, for that matter, would she have been doing anywhere else?

Mr. Herbert, fat and offensively merry, was wearing a paper cardinal's hat and mixing cocktails in an enormous shaker.

"You don't know how much we miss you at the office, Hilda," he said as he came by with the shaker. "Already. We're hoping you'll come back to us. Keep it in mind, will you?" He glanced disapprovingly at her untouched cocktail. "How are you doing? Anyone here you'd like to meet?"

"Oh, I'm doing fine, thank you, Mr. Herbert."

"You're the mousy type, aren't you?" he continued with a wink. "Do you know that all the time you were with us I never knew you were George Dilworth's daughter? Not until last week when you quit and Miss Ranick told me. I don't happen to have the pleasure of knowing your father personally, but I know several of his partners. Harry Hamilton, for example. And, of course, we all know Gerald Hunt by reputation. Mr. Hunt is your uncle, isn't he?"

Hilda stiffened.

"No."

"Really? I thought he and your father were related."

"He's my stepmother's uncle. That's what you may have been thinking of."

"I see, I see." He nodded, confused at her coldness. "Well, anyone you want to meet, don't be shy. Come right over and tell me. Bobbie Chapin's quite a pal of yours, isn't he? He'll be along in a minute. Just back from Florida and brown as a berry. Tried to tell me he'd been working down there, but the old boss knows better. Still, he's a good boy, don't you agree?"

"I'm sure he must be."

He glanced at her uncertainly.

"Well, as I say, he'll be along any minute," he said, obviously anxious to carry his shaker to more cheerful parts of the room. "I didn't tell him you were coming. It'll be my little surprise."

He moved on, and Hilda turned back to the man who was still talking about Schweitzer, trying to forget how intensely she had looked forward to this party and how little she was enjoying it now. When Mrs. Herbert had telephoned her only three days before she had accepted without even hesitating, though she had known perfectly well that they were only asking her because they had found out who her father was. But she hadn't cared; that was the point. For the first time in her life she hadn't cared what motive anyone had for anything. The mere possibility of seeing Bobbie had made her shiver as if an impudent hand had slipped

156

suddenly around her waist. Eloise had almost convinced her that such shivering did not have to be a crime.

That, however, was *then*, before her life had been splintered by her father's call. Come home, Hilda. Please come home right away. Peremptory, demanding, even pitiful. And she had gone to find him in a terrifying, a desperate rage, Eloise evicted, the little girls awed but curious. This is you, Hilda, she had told herself, this is your moment, your chance to take the powder to the fort in your apron, to tell cheering stories to the faint of heart in the lifeboat. Once to every man and nation. She had gone to her old room, now hers again, after that first talk with her father and had stood alone in the middle of the rug and clenched her fists to make herself realize that it had actually happened. Oh, yes, it was her world, after all. Not Eloise's, not Eloise's kind of world. She had not prepared herself in vain.

"Let me get you another drink, Miss Dilworth. Is there anyone else here you'd like to meet?"

It was Mrs. Herbert this time, too blond and too thin, with tired eyes and shiny dark circles under them.

"No thanks. I'm fine. Really."

"Then come and talk to me a minute, my dear. I've always wanted to know what goes on in Al's office. I'll bet he spends all his time making passes at the girls. That's what men call work, isn't it?"

Hilda sat down with her, but not to discuss Mr. Herbert's office habits. Instead, she had to listen, or seem to listen, to the discomforts of Mrs. Herbert's weekend in her new country place. To such a state as this, she reflected grimly as she looked around the room at the discontented faces, the nervously chatting mouths, come those who worship false gods. And suddenly she thought with a sick disillusionment of her last talk with Eloise and how she had been almost persuaded that if happiness beckoned, happiness should

157

be pursued. That was why she was here, in this room, amid these terrible people, Bobbie's friends. Maybe it was good for her; maybe it was salutary to see them at their worst, just as it might be salutary that life was obliging her to face Eloise's betrayal in all its enormity. For what was it, after all, but the final proof of her old theory about Eloise, that behind the charm there was a void, behind the airy kindness a moral emptiness? And she thought with a shudder of Pearl Harbor Day, listening to the radio and watching her father's face darken as he almost whispered: "Why, the little yellow bastards!" But Eloise's face, that was the thing. Hadn't she suspected her even then? When Eloise had simply shaken her head sadly, as if to agree with him, to deplore everything? No, Eloise believed in nothing, and she had been found out. They could all go back to living now.

"Take it from me, my dear, and don't go near the country," Mrs. Herbert was saying. "Do you live with your family?"

"I live with my father."

"You know, dearie, I don't think you should do that. I think every girl should be on her own."

Hilda kept glancing at the door, not even caring now how obvious she made her disapproval. She had almost made up her mind to leave without waiting for Bobbie when she heard his voice in the hall loudly greeting Mr. Herbert. As he came in it was very obvious that he had been drinking. He glanced rather blearily around the room and saw her. Immediately he raised his arm and whistled in surprise. The girl with him, Elaine, of course, seemed to be in even worse shape than he, and Mrs. Herbert hurried across the room to cope with her. Bobbie, however, seemed quite unconcerned; he came over and sat heavily down in Mrs. Herbert's place on the sofa.

"Little Hilda," he said, rather thickly, "who'd have

158

thought it? Whatcha doin' here? I thought you were running away from me. Isn't that why you threw up your little job?"

"You're quite wrong," she said with dignity. "It was just that I'd learned as much about being a receptionist as I thought I needed. You told me yourself there was nothing to it."

"Look, Hilda, don't try to kid me. You were running away, and you know it."

She glanced around nervously to see if anyone was watching. "I would have told you about it, but you were away, Bobbie. You were off on that trip."

"That's for the birds," he said rudely. "You were running away from me. It's written all over you."

"It seems to be settled, then," she said sharply, "that I was running away."

He nodded his head, accepting her concession as though it were sincere.

"And all because I took your family to that night club," he said. "All because I tried to give them some sort of fun after that goddam boring show. Hell, I know I like parties. I like drinking, too. But only at parties. You and I have to face up to something, Hilda. Let's not keep on avoiding facts." Here he held out his glass to Mr. Herbert who was passing by with the shaker. "I'm just straightening this little girl out, Herb," he said. "Why didn't you tell me she was going to be here? I might have left that lynx at home." He laughed loudly as he looked across the room to where Elaine and Mrs. Herbert seemed to be having an argument. "But to be serious, Hilda," he continued, turning back to her as Mr. Herbert moved on, "to be absolutely serious—and dammit, why shouldn't we be?—I think you're a wonnerful girl. Not like the rest of this crew." He took in the room with a careless gesture that upset a glass on the table beside him. "And you like me, too.

You may not approve of me, but you like me, and you know it."

As he paused to pick up the pieces of glass on the rug and place them with slow carefulness on the table, she was able to realize that the moment was actually coming and that it had not caught her unprepared. She noticed each aspect of his condition, the way he slurred his words, the way he kept pushing his blond hair, now messy, back over his head, his clumsiness in picking up the pieces of broken glass and the deliberation with which he ranged them side by side on the table. She shivered with the sudden coldness of her detachment, and it was almost with pride that she moved her shoulders, as if to feel the new freedom in the air around her, and looked him straight in the eye.

"And what comes of facing these facts, as you call them, Bobbie?" she asked.

He shrugged his shoulders.

"We may have to get married," he said, closing one eye and squinting at the row of glass pieces on the table. "You may have to learn to put up with my friends. And I may have to learn to behave myself with your family." He paused and swallowed in a final effort at articulation. "You may have to be nicer about my parties. And I may have to learn to put up with your abstem—abstemiousness."

The severity of her stare at last penetrated even the thick coating of his good will.

"You don't like it?" He shrugged his shoulders again and picked up his drink. "Okay, Bobbie, you're a jerk."

"I assume I'm not meant to be taking this any more seriously than anything else that is being said in this room," she said in an even, grating tone. "I assume that I'm not really expected to give you an answer. Or at least not until I've had as many cocktails as you've had."

He turned on her.

"You know it's serious!" he exclaimed roughly. "You know damn well how serious it is! And don't try to kid yourself."

Their eyes met, and this time it was she who looked away.

"It's always been serious between us," he went on, moving nearer to her. "And in case you don't realize it, you're the only girl I've come this close to proposing to. Which is a compliment, the way I look at it, whether you like it or not. Why do you have to be so damn prissy? Why don't you catch on to yourself? Why not, kid?" And he suddenly put his arm around her shoulders.

She jumped up in a passion of alarm.

"Never!" she exclaimed. "Never!"

She managed to control herself enough to say good-bye to Mrs. Herbert. She was even able, after a hurried dash for her coat, to stand with moderate dignity in the lobby as she waited for the elevator, though the front door was open and the eyes of the cocktail party, attracted by her sudden exit, were on her. She heard someone say something and mention Bobbie's name; it was followed by a general muffled laugh, mercifully cut short by the rumble of the opening elevator doors. Then there was the ride down as she stared at her shoes and at last the escape through the dark lobby to the fresh air of the street. It was free and cool and reassuring; it was her element, unlike the smoky air which she had just left, with all the laughter and the rattling of ice. As she hurried down the sidewalk she made a final, desperate effort to enjoy the knowledge that she had met her test as George Dilworth's daughter should have met it.

2

Eloise had taken a room adjoining her mother's small suite at the Stafford. She had gone there because she hadn't known where else to go and because it had seemed cruel not to let Irene, who professed to be almost distracted with guilt, have an opportunity, at least in her own eyes, to make up in some fashion for the sorry, gossiping role that she had played.

"I'll never forgive myself," she moaned to Eloise. "I had no idea he'd be so violent. Oh, but he's a horror, that George! A brutal, vicious horror!"

"George is only being himself, Irene," Eloise answered calmly. "I would not have expected him to behave otherwise."

"What must you think of me, my child?" Irene raised her thin white hands to her temples. "What have I brought you but trouble and tragedy? It sometimes seems to me that you've spent your life just turning the other cheek."

"And here I am. Right back where I started from."

She could afford to be generous with Irene, for she had never been less involved with her. Irene's remorse was probably sincere, as sincere, that is, as any feeling that Irene ever had, but Eloise had no need of it. She could not connect her mother's meanness with the magnitude of what had happened; it seemed almost presumptuous of Irene to cast herself in a casual role when she had been only the unwitting agent of the strange gods who had struck her daughter down. Ever since the departure of the detective and his men, when Eloise had raised her head from the pillow to face a Carl shaking with sobs of humiliation and anger, a Carl who had turned to her for sympathy like a small boy, ever since she had gone home to find her bags packed and waiting for her in the lobby of the apartment house, she had been certain of one thing. It was her own nemesis, to be handled her own way. She would share it with none, not even with Carl. The gods had been holding off their thunderbolt all her life. Now they had hurled it. It was doubtful if there was anything more under the sun for her to be afraid of.

Not indeed that her path in the future was going to be plain sailing. Far from it. She had not been allowed even to see Peggy and Jo, although the nurse telephoned every day to tell her how they were. She had no idea what arrangements George would make about them or how she and Irene were going to live. The future was a white page. But at least she knew now the things which worried her. They were all in the open. She would do nothing, not even hire a lawyer, despite all of Irene's protestations, until George made his next move.

"We'll wait to see what he offers," she kept putting Irene off with. "He knows where I am. And don't worry. George is not a man who can bear to have things unsettled for long."

It turned out that George indeed was not, for the day after she said this Harry Hamilton called upon her. She received him alone in Irene's little sitting room. He kept looking out the window as if the interview was boring and purely routine and pinching the bridge of his nose with his thumb and forefinger. His big, protruding eyes tumbled in their sockets.

"I've come on George's behalf," he began, shielding a sudden, unsettling yawn behind his fat palm, "to offer what I'm sure you'll agree are equitable terms under the circumstances."

She nodded and said nothing.

"In the first place," he continued with a little cough, "George has decided to bring an action of divorce against you. He has decided to bring it here, in New York."

"I see."

"Of course, as you may know, there's only one ground for divorce in New York." Harry sighed and pinched the bridge of his nose again. "It happens, however, to be precisely the ground that George is relying on."

"Thanks to your carefulness, Harry."

His whole countenance, however, was bathed in a bland indifference to anything that she might have to say.

"There's no reason, I believe, that the proceedings should receive publicity," he went on. "When both sides are agreed on that, such things can be arranged. Judges are normally averse to scandal. I assume there will be no difficulty about this with what I might describe as the more vulnerable of the two parties to the action?"

He looked up at the ceiling, touching and retouching his fingertips together, and she was suddenly sure that he had rehearsed this scene to the last gesture. She had been wrong about many people, she reflected quickly, but not about Harry. He had always hated her.

"You needn't assume anything," she retorted. "Publicity might be valuable to me. I can't tell yet."

Harry continued to gaze at the ceiling.

"I should have thought you might have considered the welfare of your children in this respect."

"You can be sure I shall consider it, Harry Hamilton!" she exclaimed, giving in suddenly to a sharp stab of temper. "That's exactly why I don't intend to throw away any potential weapon I may have. What does George propose to do about the girls?"

164

He paused.

"Do you have a lawyer?"

"No."

"But you will have?"

"Obviously, I'll have to."

"It would be wise." He nodded. "But that needn't stop us now. All I want is to tell you what George's offer is. It's very simple. He will give you five thousand a year, for life or until your remarriage. This, considering that a court would probably award you nothing, is, in my opinion, handsome. He will, of course, retain sole custody of the two girls, but he is willing to give you his informal assurance that when you have established to his satisfaction that you are leading a life the example of which is beneficial to the children, he will allow them to visit you at such times and in such places as he may designate."

She grasped the side of her chair.

"You can't mean it!"

"On the contrary I most certainly mean it."

"And if I refuse this ridiculous offer?"

Harry's shrug was monumental.

"The financial offer would then, of course, lapse. And we would have no alternative but to go to court and try the question of your fitness as a parent."

"Why mine and not his?"

"Isn't that fairly obvious?"

She gave a shudder of distaste.

"As if a man who did what George has done to me could possibly be a fit parent," she answered. "Would Peggy and Jo have to go to court?"

"The judge would probably talk to them in his chambers."

She thought of Jo excitedly telling a dark robed figure about the murder of William Wallace's wife and Peggy trying to stop her, trying, as Peggy always did, to identify herself with the adult side. She raised her hands instinctively as though to shield them, dropping them a second later and staring with a certain awe at this man who could say such things to her.

"You must be enjoying this, Harry," she said. "I suppose it's the only way you get your pleasure."

He simply stared at her with a blankness that was meant, she assumed, to be annihilating.

"I wonder if our courts will go along with you," she continued. "I wonder if it's possible for people like you to do such things to people like me. I think it may be important for me to find that out. More important, perhaps, than anything else."

He rose to his feet, nodded and picked up his hat and cane. Watching his slow movements she reflected how useful it was for censorious people to be fat. They needed surface for the full expression of their venom.

"Tell me one thing, Harry," she asked him. "I'm beginning to see, now that I face true antagonism, that I used to imagine it in situations where it didn't actually exist. But I didn't imagine yours, did I? You've always hated me. And I have no conception of why. What did I ever do to you that you should hate me so?"

He turned toward the door.

"Get a lawyer, Eloise," he said, ignoring her question. "Get a lawyer and tell him what I've told you. He'll tell you that it makes sense. If he's any good, he will."

No sooner had he left than Irene emerged explosively from her bedroom.

"Eloise, who do you think is downstairs waiting to see you? Carl Landik! Oh, I told him to go away, of course, but he won't. My God, do you suppose Mr. Hamilton will see him as he goes out the lobby!"

"I neither know nor care what Mr. Hamilton sees," Eloise said sharply, getting up and going to the telephone. "And you had no business, Irene, to tell Carl to

166

go away. I shall make my own decisions about my own visitors."

"Eloise, what are you going to do!"

"I'm going to ask him to come right up."

"My child, don't be crazy!" Irene was across the room in a moment, both her hands on the telephone. "You've got to consider how things look. You're not your own boss any more, dear girl."

"On the contrary, it's just exactly what I am. And for the first time, too. What difference can it possibly make whether or not I see Carl? Harry Hamilton has all the dirt he needs."

Irene shook her head violently.

"He has one incident," she said, holding up her forefinger solemnly. "One single miserable little incident. That may get him his divorce, yes, but what about the children? What will a judge think if you continue brazenly to see this boy in your room?"

"Irene, you were listening at the door!"

Her mother brushed this aside.

"Of course, I was listening. How else am I to protect you against yourself? We're going to prove to that court that you're a better mother than George if it's the last thing we do! And we're not going to do it by entertaining Carl Landik up here!"

Eloise hesitated. The vision of Jo talking to the blackrobed figure flashed again across her mind. But it was degrading, soul destroying, this sudden reduction of her life to a chattering monologue played out before the respectability of suspicion.

"You mean I can't see him at all?" she protested.

"That would be best."

"But that's so mean, Irene. The poor boy is sick over this whole thing. I owe it to him."

Irene sat in the chair by the telephone, guarding the instrument with one hand and picking at her scarlet lower lip with a long fingernail. The picture of Carl brooding in the lobby had evidently touched her readily available sympathies.

"We might go down, I suppose," she said at last. "Both of us, I mean. We could see him in the lounge."

"Or the bar."

"No, the lounge. We'll have tea."

"Tea, Irene? That sounds so odd, coming from you."

"Well, you'll see." Irene nodded, quite happy with her own ingenuity. "No one could think that tea was wicked. And, after a bit, I might even stroll up and down the lounge and let you and Carl talk. But not for long. It mustn't be for long."

"All right, Irene," she said, after a pause. "We'll try it your way. This time."

They were a strange threesome, she refleced, when they were seated in a corner of the lounge, she and her mother on a dark couch and Carl in a tall Italian chair placed at right angles to them with a potted palm between. Carl looked utterly miserable and could hardly say a word. Irene's spirits, however, were high. She loved conspiracy, ordering tea in a brisk, cheerful voice which she dropped to a whisper the moment the waiter had gone, warning Carl, with a good deal of head-nodding, about the necessity of precaution. Eloise watched him listening reluctantly, humbly. And suddenly it was not just strange any more. It was horrible.

"Irene," she said suddenly, "isn't it perhaps time for that little stroll of yours?"

Her mother started at her tone.

"All right, dear. But, remember, I won't be long. And I don't think I really ought to be out of sight."

"Sometimes I think Irene really cares," Eloise said to him as her mother moved away across the lobby. "But more often I wonder if she's ever had a better time in her life."

"Eloise," Carl said quickly, moving over to the sofa, "there must be something I can do?"

168

She shook her head.

"For God's sake, Eloise!"

"But there isn't, Carl, dear. That's the thing about lovers. There isn't a thing they can do."

"Don't talk that way."

She simply shrugged her shoulders.

"How do you want me to talk? This is one thing that I have to face alone. It's so obvious, Carl. But don't look glum. I *want* to face it alone."

Carl was at his most restless. One arm ran along the back of the couch; the other was raised to his head as he scratched his hair.

"You talk as if you were a sophomore and I was nothing but a punk freshman," he said sullenly. "I want to do something in this mess. I've *got* to do something. Even if it's only punching that rotten husband of yours in the eye."

"That would be so helpful."

"Well, it would show him how I feel, anyway. I lie awake at night worrying if that bastard could possibly be thinking that I'm ashamed of myself. Hell, I wasn't taking any part of you that he cared about, and you know that's true, Eloise. And how he can sit there, that stuffed shirt of a dog in the manger—"

"Please, Carl. This doesn't help."

"But it's the truth, Eloise!"

"What does it matter? If you only knew how little I worry about George! The only thing that matters is that I don't want the girls handed over to him. But we don't get anywhere by abusing him."

"That's not the only thing that matters," he objected, his lower jaw forward. "There's another thing that matters. One hell of a lot, too. To me, anyway. I want to marry you, Eloise. Just as soon as Dilworth gets his divorce."

She sat there, absolutely still, feeling a constriction about her heart that was at once exhilarating and

169

threatening. In her sudden excitement she lost her confidence and wondered if she could rise to this, even conversationally, if she wouldn't antagonize him by saying something fatuous and flat.

"Oh, Carl," she murmured, "you are sweet."

"I'm not sweet at all," he said indignantly. "I mean it. I love you, Eloise. This isn't just a gallant gesture. You know what I think of gallant gestures. Don't you believe me, Eloise?"

"I believe you." She nodded nervously. "Of course, I believe you. But I wouldn't dream of holding you to it."

He grabbed her hand.

"Do you love me, Eloise?" he demanded. "You must or you wouldn't have come the other night."

She stared at him for a moment and then nodded soberly.

"I suppose I must," she agreed. The words sounded incredible in the big dark lobby with the passing people. She saw a fat man, as fat as Harry Hamilton, walking towards the elevator followed by a porter carrying an enormous bag. She wondered indifferently what he would think if he could hear her. "But it's very hard for me to tell. You see I don't think I've ever loved anyone before. I'm not even sure I've ever even liked anyone before."

He looked confused.

"But you will marry me?"

"Oh, that doesn't follow at all," she said, leaning her head back and closing her eyes for a moment. She wondered, without really thinking it would, if this would hurt him, but somehow it seemed irrelevant. "I'm older and more married, and I have two children, and the circumstances are awful, and, oh, Carl, there are so many things."

"Not if we love each other," he said stubbornly.

"Darling, I couldn't possibly discuss it now," she

said, sitting up suddenly. "Maybe after the case, but not now. Nothing seems quite real to me now. I wonder if it does to you, either, you poor boy. We'll both be more sensible later. Now don't say anything," she continued as he was about to speak, putting a finger to his lips. "Listen to me. I want you to keep away from this whole wretched trial. If they call you, that's one thing, but I don't see why they should. I'm not fighting the facts. But for my sake, Carl, stay away until I send for you."

"No, Eloise," he protested, "if you think I'm going to run out on you. . . ."

"Darling, it isn't running out on me, it's helping me."

"I don't care. I don't like it."

"Carl!" Her voice was sharp, peremptory. "You must do as I say. *Someone* must do as I say."

"Am I too soon?" came a voice from above them, and there was Irene, actually simpering, with a waiter pushing a wheeled tea tray.

"No, dear, you're just right," Eloise said quickly, "Carl has been very sweet. He wants to help, but of course there's nothing he can do. I've told him to write me. You'll do that, Carl, won't you? And one day soon we'll be seeing each other again. When all this is over."

Irene sat down, and Eloise turned her attention to the tea things. Carl said nothing and stared at the floor. It wasn't until Irene tried to catch his attention by handing him his cup that he spoke, and then it was only to mutter an excuse and hurry away. Irene gazed after him, her mouth open.

"Your young man, I must say, has charming manners."

Eloise looked after his retreating figure and then turned back to the teapot.

"I wonder if I really believe in good manners," she said.

3

GERALD HUNT'S office, as might have been expected, was the largest and certainly the most impressive of the partners' offices of Hunt & Livermore. He sat in one corner with his back to a large window that commanded a view of the Hudson, protected from his visitors not by a desk but by a long, rectangular eighteenth-century French table. The green walls were hung with charcoal drawings of eminent contemporaries, signed by the subjects. In an alcove over the bookstand rested a large bronze bust of the late Justice Hunt, Gerald's and Irene's father, with the aquiline nose that was almost essential to sculpture of the heroic school. Gerald, like his partners, usually left the door of his office open, but today it was closed, and his elderly secretary, Miss Chotsworth, had received instructions that he would see no visitors and take no calls while Messrs. Dilworth and Hamilton were with him. He was leaning back in his chair, his hands folded in his lap, his eyes fixed on George who was seated in the chair opposite. Harry was strolling slowly back and forth across the room, his hands behind his back, his eyes rolling listlessly from picture to picture.

"I want to make one thing entirely clear," Gerald was saying, "and that is that I've tried to keep this whole tragic business out of the office. My first reaction, aside from my obvious personal distress, was that it must not be allowed to affect our relationships downtown. I pride myself that it has not. George and I were friends before his marriage, and we will be friends after his divorce. Isn't that so, George?"

"Certainly that's so, Gerald."

Gerald glanced at him and turned slightly away in his chair, one finger raised to his mustache. He did not like the brooding expression on George's face or his quick, rather belligerent assumption that everyone was on his side. Gerald had never been much of a side taker. He rarely cared enough, one way or the other. It mattered very little to him as a man or as a moralist whether Eloise was unfaithful to George or George to Eloise, but as the latter's uncle and as head of the Hunt family he could not be entirely indifferent to what was now being done to her. George's assumption of his partisanship seemed to take for granted that friendship, especially friendship for George, should transcend blood loyalties. Gerald was quite sure that this was a decision that George was not going to make for him.

"Good. Very good," he said, stroking his mustache and nodding. "We've got that out of the way, then. Which brings me to the only part of the whole sad business that I want to discuss here. The part of it, in other words, that affects the firm. Harry tells me, George, that he has instituted divorce proceedings on your behalf in New York County. He says that you have named Mr. Landik as correspondent."

"I have. Is there anything wrong with that?"

Gerald did not look at him this time.

"I think you might have consulted me before doing that, George," he said in a milder, drier tone.

"I saw no reason for it."

"You didn't? I'm sorry." Gerald picked up a silver paper cutter and examined its edge. "It didn't occur to you that such a case might involve considerable publicity? Not only for yourself and your family but for your partners and possibly even your clients?"

"If there's any publicity it will be because of your

173

niece," George retorted. "If you wish to avoid it, you might try to persuade her to be reasonable."

Gerald turned, his eyebrows slightly raised, and saw that he had read correctly the truculence in George's tone.

"I have no intention of trying to persuade Eloise of anything, George," he said sharply and decisively. "I have no intention of getting mixed up in your affairs any more than I already am. What I want to know is why, when all other civilized people go quietly to Reno or the Virgin Islands to get their divorces, you and Eloise must stay here and wash your dirty linen in public." He turned abruptly to Harry. "Can you answer that one, Harry? You're handling the case. You presumably advised bringing the suit here."

"I think I can answer that one, Gerald." Harry's equanimity was almost insulting in view of the senior partner's expressed concern. He stopped his roving and stood before Gerald's desk, his hands clasped behind his back, his eyes blinking. "It's very simple. George is really an unusual sort of man. He doesn't choose to let the state of Nevada or any other state or territory, for that matter, hand over half his income and the custody of his children to a woman who under the laws of New York might be entitled to neither. As I say, it's unusual." Harry's face became even blanker to point up his sarcasm. "It has become traditional for the husband, wronged or otherwise, to submit himself to the tender mercies of any state whose divorce laws are drafted by its chamber of commerce and whose climate is agreeable to his wife."

Gerald closed his lips tightly and turned his chair away. He had always detested Harry and his airs of superiority. It did not help, either, that he knew that Harry looked down on him as a lawyer which to Harry was identical with looking down on him as a man.

"You're off the point, Harry," he said gruffly. "I

haven't heard that Eloise is asking for any half of George's income. From what I've heard all she wants is to have her children with her half the year. Surely that's fair enough."

"Does it not occur to you, Gerald," Harry asked with a slight lift of the eyebrows, "that George may not wish his daughters to spend *any* part of the year with a mother who finds adultery to be within the scope of her marriage vows?"

Gerald considered for a moment asking Harry to leave the room. Rarely, however, did he act on impulse.

"Surely you don't think, George," he said, turning to the latter and ignoring Harry altogether, "that this mistake of Eloise's, reprehensible and regrettable as it is, means that she's no longer fit to bring up her own children?"

"I most certainly do. Until she's proved to me that she's ashamed of herself, anyway."

"I doubt very much if most people would agree with you," Gerald continued severely. "Those little girls seem to me to have been excellently brought up. Eloise isn't going to become the devil's advocate overnight."

"How do I know she hasn't always been?" George demanded in sudden anger, clenching his fists. "How do I know she hasn't been undermining them for years? I never knew she had this rottenness in her till three weeks ago. Oh, I know, most people smooth these things over, cover them up—anything to avoid publicity or to keep the children from finding out when they get older. Maybe children *should* find out. Adultery to me is a serious business, Gerald. I happen to believe in keeping the vows I take. There's too much moral flabbiness in the world today, and I don't want any part of it. For myself *or* my children."

Gerald looked down at the blotter before him and fingered again his silver paper cutter. It always embarrassed him when people claimed to be guided specifically by the general principles to which society professed adherence. Gerald was too much a man of the world to find in the application of broad moral rules to individual problems anything but the crudest possible taste. He professed many principles himself; few people, indeed, professed more; that was the way one lived, it was the secret, perhaps, of civilization. But to premise one's conduct on their absolute relation to reality, well, that was being childish, and being childish was something that the son of a famous judge had little or no time for.

"You're going too far, George," he warned him, shaking his head. "People aren't going to like this. You'll find them going over to Eloise's side."

"I don't give a damn whose side they're on," George retorted. "I intend to dissolve my marriage according to the laws of my state and to bring up my children according to the principles in which I believe. And I don't consider that anyone's business but my own."

"You don't care, in other words, about the reputation of the firm," Gerald said in a quiet, grating tone that rose as he spoke to a higher pitch of indignation. "You don't care how I'm made to look, the uncle who stands by while his niece is disgraced in public by his own partner! You don't care that by the time Harry has got through with his circus, this firm and the scandal will be on the lips of every purchaser of an evening paper!"

George's expression did not change. He never took his eyes from Gerald's face.

"If you're implying, Gerald, that you think I should disassociate myself from the firm before the case comes to trial, I can only say that I'm quite willing to do so. Harry and I have already discussed the possibility that you might feel this way. He has been kind enough to say that his actions will be governed by mine."

Gerald was too cautious at first to glance up from his desk. He continued for a moment simply to play with his paper cutter. Finally he looked up and briefly smiled.

"I think perhaps we're all getting a little hot under the collar," he said, standing up. "And that's never apt to be a good thing, is it? I didn't realize, George, how strongly you felt about this. Obviously if you feel that way, you must act accordingly. I don't deny I'm sorry about it, for everyone's sake. I simply wanted to be sure how things stood. Let's not say any more about it for the time being, shall we? Thank you, gentlemen."

When they had gone Gerald turned his chair around and gazed out over the harbor. It had not been a time to be dictatorial; he had been right to check himself when he had. He didn't even know, for example, how Arthur Irwin would stand if George left the firm, and Arthur's company paid an annual retainer three times the size of their next largest. Arthur, of course, was his contemporary and nominally his client, but George was closer to him and did most of his work, and Gerald knew better than to underrate such things. No, decidedly it was not the time to take a high hand. If he could be sure of Arthur—well, that would be different. Then George could be chastened. And George needed chastening; he was getting dogmatic and arbitrary. The future senior partner—if indeed he *was* to be that— should not be as rigid as George had just shown himself. He was good, yes, but nobody was indispensable. And as for Harry—Gerald bit into his pipe and smiled rather wryly to himself. Harry had certainly gone as far in Hunt & Livermore as Harry was ever going.

George and Harry in the meanwhile walked down the passageway to George's office without exchanging a word. When George went in he paused near the door, hoping that Harry would go back to his own room, but the latter followed him in and closed the door behind him.

"Do you think you should have gone as far as that, George?" he asked. "Do you think you should have said what you did about our resigning?"

"Don't worry, Harry. He won't do a thing. He wouldn't dare. I doubt if he could even run the firm without you and me."

"Maybe so. But does *he* know that?"

"I said don't worry, Harry."

He went over to his desk and sat down, spinning his chair so that he faced towards the window. He knew that he shouldn't let Harry see his irritation, considering all that Harry was doing for him, but he knew that otherwise Harry would go on and on with the subject, twisting his way deviously into its most painful corners, sucking his private peculiar satisfaction out of anticipating the very thing that he most dreaded, his own and George's separation from the firm that was fundamentally Harry's life. It was all very well for Harry to be impertinent to Gerald when George was present, but George knew only too well what qualms would soon send shudders up and down Harry's big frame. And the last thing he could face now was to spend the afternoon consoling Harry; the only thing he wanted and needed was to get back to work. He had made up his mind, and he had no intention of changing it, for Gerald or anyone else, but if they kept talking about it, if he and Harry had to waste all their time speculating on the possible consequences to themselves and everyone else, even he, George, might lose his nerve.

"Do you think Eloise really means to fight?" Harry continued. "Or do you think she's bluffing?"

"How should I know?" George said impatiently. "You were the one who talked to her."

"Yes, but I'd never seen that side of her before. I'd never seen her so cocky, George."

"Maybe she's learned it from Mr. Landik," George said bitterly, turning back to his desk. "Will you excuse me, Harry? I've wasted too damn much time on this mess as it is."

"Certainly. I was just going." And he left, trying too hard not to look offended.

Alone, George stared across the room at the mahogany breakfront which held the large black volumes of his bound registration statements. On its top, in place of the silver-framed photograph of Eloise, stood a round gold clock with discs where the numbers should have been. It was solid and heavy as he liked such things to be, and fixing his eyes on it he tried to calm himself by emulating its stillness. The terrible anger that had swept over him when Harry had telephoned him in Chicago, that had churned him up until he had been physically ill, had cooled by now to a grim but still seething determination to make Eloise pay for what she had done. Yet as he continued to stare at the clock its very expressionlessness seemed to take on some of the expressionlessness of Eloise's face, a quality which now, in the light of all the horror of his smashed home, his stolen property, as it were, he equated with self-assurance, an air almost of defiance, an attitude of "But did you *really* think, poor man, after all these years—?" Christ! There it was coming back again, that destroying temper, that waste of energy and feeling, and what in the name of heaven was the point of it now, with Harry irrevocably delegated to carry out the whole wretched plan? He took the draft of the prospectus for Arthur Irwin's new bond issue and held it fixedly before him while he forced his eyes to read and his mind to concentrate. Very slowly the words began to take on sense and his brain to turn over; he sighed, hardly daring to recognize his own relief, and suddenly he caught a point, the burying of a factory alteration in a mass of verbiage, the very thing against which he had warned the younger partner who had prepared the draft. Eloise left his mind immediately. Picking up the telephone to tell his secretary to call Mr. Irwin, he even managed a chuckle of satisfaction at the thought of Arthur browbeating a junior partner into doing the prospectus his way. They would pay anything, these tycoons, to retain George Dilworth and yet do anything to get around him.

"No, Arthur, it won't do," he began immediately when he had him on the telephone. "I've said so before, and I'm sticking to it. It's like describing a man by saying he has two eyes, a nose and a mouth. Not a misrepresentation, perhaps, but if the boys on the commission pick it up, they'll jump to the conclusion that you've got something to hide. And the point is you haven't. That's what I never seem to be able to drive through the heads of some of you tycoons, that you haven't really got anything to hide—"

Harry Hamilton, in the meanwhile, had returned to his own office and sent for Tom Haighter, his selected assistant in Dilworth *versus* Dilworth. The young man closed the door carefully behind him as he had been instructed always to do when this particular litigation was discussed.

"I've just been in with Mr. Hunt," Harry couldn't resist telling him confidentially as he sat down before his desk. "The old man is fussed up over this suit. No doubt about it. But he'll live. He'll live. Have you finished that memo on custody?"

He reached out his hand as he asked this and received the expected memorandum. It was the custom in Hunt & Livermore for all partners, even Harry, to be politely reasonable in estimating the time required for a piece of work. To hear them discussing this with their associates one might have assumed that a leisurely, almost a Southern atmosphere prevailed in the office. There were none so benighted, however, as to be unaware of the brief future that would await a clerk who availed himself of every deadline. Harry skimmed the pages of the memorandum while its author looked nervously on. It failed, however, to catch his interest as he was already familiar with the legal principles which it explored. It was frequently this way with memoranda that Harry ordered. He believed in the discipline of them.

"Well," he said impatiently, tossing the memo aside, "what do you really think? Do we get the children or don't we?"

"I think it's close, sir."

"Why?"

"I don't know if she deserves to lose her children. Just for that." Here Tom looked suddenly abashed. "Just for one time, I mean."

Harry held up his forefinger.

"One time *proved*, you mean," he corrected.

"One time proved. Yes, sir."

"How many times would you give her? And with how many men?"

Tom looked uncomfortable.

"Well, I don't know if I could name a number, sir—"

Harry held up both hands to interrupt him.

"Enough, enough," he said quickly. "I agree, of course. One proven act of adultery might not be enough to deprive her of custody. Conceded. But suppose she's proud of it? Suppose she glories in it?"

Tom looked astonished. His round, healthy face was blank.

"But will she?"

"Oh, youth, youth," Harry murmured, "where is the fight in youth?"

"But even if she thought that, she wouldn't say so, would she? Not in court anyway."

Harry slammed his hand down on his desk.

181

"You mean that Mrs. Dilworth is a liar as well as an adulteress?"

"Oh, I don't say that, sir."

"What *do* you say, then?" Harry exclaimed abruptly, and then as suddenly he was silent again, apparently lost in his own thoughts. "No, Eloise is truthful," he continued in a more reflective tone. "That's the thing about Eloise. And it's on her truthfulness that we must hang her."

"On her truthfulness? But would that be right, sir?"

Harry looked up quickly.

"Right?" he roared. "Of course, it would be right. What do you know of right and wrong, you babe in swaddling tweeds? It's *right* that she should tell the truth, and it's *right* that the court should hear the truth, and it's *right* that the court should award the children to George!"

Tom looked sullen. Awed as he was by Harry, there were still things that he could resent.

"Well, if that's all there is to it, why is there any case for us to prepare?" he grumbled. "Why don't we just sit back and let her talk?"

"Because she will have a lawyer," Harry replied with a smile of sarcastic sweetness, folding his hands before him on the desk. "We must assume that he knows what we know. We must assume that he, too, knows of her tendency to tell the truth. And he, therefore, will tell her what?"

"Not to tell the truth?"

"Oh, Tom." Harry shook his hands reproachfully in the air. "Tom, please. You must not be so crude. Let us assume that Eloise will not retain a complete ass. No, dear boy, he will simply coach her to be humble, to play the repentant wife, to assure the court with wide, shining eyes"—here Harry rolled his own lugubriously— "that never again will such a dreadful thing take place, that she was bewitched, that she cannot understand what could have happened to her—"

"And she'll say all that?"

"She will be so coached."

"And you'll make her deny it, sir? How?"

Harry settled back in his chair with an almost dreamlike expression in his eyes.

"You see, Tom," he replied, tapping a ruler slowly against the palm of his left hand, "I know Eloise. I know her type. She is a romantic or, as I prefer to put it, a sentimentalist. She has a highly confused sense of honor. Incapable of facing the badness in herself, the badness which we inherit from Adam and which only the realist is willing to face, she will try to dress up her act of adultery in moral colors. It was sweet, therefore it must be good. Isn't that the romantic fallacy? The more I yearn and yearn, the more I feel, the more I smell spring in the air, the more my heart pounds, the better a person I am." Here Harry clasped his own shoulders with each hand, closed his eyes and rocked his big body back and forth, pursing his lips. "And they'll go to the stake for their idea of themselves," he said sharply, opening his eyes suddenly and sitting up. "I've seen them do it!"

Tom, who had been staring at him, looked bewildered.

"They will?"

"Of course, they will!" exclaimed Harry, once more the judge. He then proceeded to destroy with heavy pounds his little caricature of the romantic with which he was disgusted to see that Tom had even temporarily identified him. But it was that way with all these blocky young men. Their minds—minds, did he call them?— were hopelessly literal. "The martyr, however, must be held to a certain pitch of excitement if he is to proclaim his faith to those who find it heresy. That is where we come in. I propose to define Eloise's adultery before her

183

in such a way as to make her angry. I propose to fling it in her face until she loses her temper. I propose to make her swallow it until she gags. And when I finally demand of her, in ringing tones, if she is not ashamed of her dark deed, I think we can count on her denial."

"And then?"

"And then, of course, we'll have her," Harry answered with only a shrug of his shoulders, his dramatic role played out. "She won't be able to wriggle out of it. Justice will be served, and morality. And truth. Don't forget that, Tom. Truth! For I, with all my fulminating, will be saying what I truly believe about adulterers, and she, with all her indignation, will be stating her own faith in herself. The truth will be before the court, and the court, as is quite proper, will apply the law of the land."

"Unless she sways the judge."

"In which case we will be victorious on appeal."

There was a pause, and Tom nodded doubtfully.

"I guess it sounds all right, sir."

Harry smiled more affably.

"I'll look over your memo later, Tom. There may be some points in it I can use."

He shrugged his shoulders again as the young man left the room. He knew that Tom still had doubts as to the morality of his procedure, but he knew that these doubts would soon be merged in Tom's admiration of the tactical advantages of his approach. For that was the way with these young men. They had really no moral values at all. No matter what was said against Harry Hamilton in the office, he knew that they could be counted on to pucker their brows, shake their heads and murmur, almost with surprise that any other value counted to anyone else: "But he's a damn good lawyer. You've got to admit that. Yes sir, that baby's smart." It was an adulation that he had always expected from them and that he had always received; he had loved it

184

and depended on it, but it was not enough, at least not enough to a man like himself who wanted everything from them, who would never really believe they didn't secretly despise him unless they accorded him enthusiasm on every level, not simply the intellectual. Yet they wouldn't, of course, any more than Gerald would; they wouldn't even give him the credit of conceding that he really believed in the things that he did believe in, in George's rightness and Eloise's wrongness and in the importance, the vital importance, that George be upheld in all his contentions. For they, all the young men, the world, were the real cynics; fundamentally nothing surprised or shocked them; they fornicated and took fornicating for granted; *they* were the cruel ones, not he, for they were willing to apply punishment to crimes which they didn't subjectively regard as crimes. Yet he, unlike them, believed in these crimes; he *believed* in the law of the land, and he was alone in his belief. Except for George. He thought with feeling of the first evening that he had spent in George's apartment after the terrible discovery. Poor George had been like a madman, and he had sat with him, hour after hour, or so it had seemed, refilling his scotch and soda and quietly listening as his poor friend paced the floor of his study and cursed his wife. Never had they been closer, yet even then—yes, even then—had it not struck him that there was a rejecting quality in the hard ego of George's temper? It was as if George took him a little too much for granted, as if he assumed too readily that Harry was immediately available as the instrument of his wrath. And then, too, when the wrath had simmered down to be succeeded by the more enduring mood of cold and determined anger which Harry now faced, had he not begun a little to wonder if the new George would even be as intimate a friend as the old? It was all so unfair, and it was all the fault of that woman! It was still the fruit of her adultery.

4

WHEN HILDA WALKED out of the Herberts' cocktail party, leaving Bobbie to be laughed at by those in the room who had observed their altercation, he was determined that he was through with her.

"I'm *glad* she made a fool of me," he kept telling Elaine sullenly as he continued to drink. "It's time this damn thing was over. No girl's ever treated me the way she has."

"And do you love it!" Elaine said scornfully. "You've always wanted to be made a fool of. You're bored with little girls who fall for your big blue eyes."

"Oh, dry up," he retorted. "I'm getting pretty sick of that theory of yours."

The image of Hilda that stuck in his mind was of a prim, exasperating creature who had no business to have any hold over him at all. He found himself constructing elaborate and rather vindictive fantasies in one of which, the most frequently recurring, he courted her under an assumed guise of meekness and sobriety only to fling it off, once she was his, and take her, a pale, quivering Christian slave, to scenes of Roman debauchery. He pictured the pain in her eyes with a grim satisfaction.

The direction of his thoughts, however, was drastically altered by a piece of gossip that Al Herbert told him at lunch a few days later.

"Have you heard about your friend Hilda's father?"

"What? Is he dead or something?"

"Maybe he wishes he was." Al laughed easily. "He's

just brought a divorce action against his wife. Named some young writer correspondent. I heard about it in court this morning."

Bobbie was too stunned to say anything.

"That's something to have happen to that bunch of stuffs down at Hunt & Livermore, isn't it?" Al continued. "Boy, I'll bet Gerald Hunt is having kittens."

"Who's Mrs. Dilworth's lawyer?"

"No idea. But he's got a job on his hands. They say Dilworth really has the goods on her. Pictures and all."

"The swine!"

"What's that?"

"I said, the swine."

Al laughed.

"I bet your friend Hilda doesn't take that attitude."

"No," Bobbie nodded bitterly. "I bet she doesn't."

He was unable to do any work that afternoon. He kept thinking of Mrs. Dilworth and her large, smiling, scared eyes. It was as if he and she had a sudden bond, having each suffered a deep injustice from the Dilworth tribe, as if it was Hilda's puritanism, so stubborn and so archaic, that had risen to strike them down together. No wonder, he reflected grimly, that Hilda had been so excited at the Herberts'. She must have known then that her little world had been knocked to pieces. He finally went downtown, canceling his appointments for the rest of the day, to the Supreme Court at Foley Square where a clerk, who was a friend of his, got out the record of Dilworth *vs.* Dilworth. There he found George's complaint, setting forth its brutal facts in the turgid legal phrases that were so well adapted to the promulgation of hate. He also found an affidavit showing that it had been served on Eloise Dilworth at the Stafford Hotel.

He discussed it that night with his roommate, Larry Weavers. They sat up late and drank lots of beer, but Larry always came back to the same point.

"What can you do about it, Bobbie? After all, it's Dilworth's marriage, not yours. We don't even know what provocation the guy had. She may have been cheating on him for years."

Bobbie looked at him peevishly. Larry, the playboy, the libertine, Larry, tomorrow's stuffed shirt.

"I don't think anyone ought to spy on anyone else. Husbands included."

"Okay." Larry finished his can of beer. "And when you do the world over, that's the way it'll be."

"And it'll be a damn sight better world, too."

"Maybe. Now go to bed." And when Bobbie made no move, he went on: "After all, it's Hilda's headache, not yours. And I'll bet Hilda isn't losing any sleep over the sad plight of her errant stepmother."

"Hell, no." Bobbie shook his head morosely. "She's behind the old man. All the way. That's one thing you can bet on. But I want her to know what *I* think of her, Larry. I want her to know that I think that she and her old man are *wrong*. Rotten wrong!"

"Oh, what the hell, Bobbie."

"You don't see it. Of course not. You haven't been around with her." Bobbie began to get excited. "The point is, Larry, she's right about a lot of things. I do drink a lot, and I like fast women. Granted. But she thinks because of that I have no standards at all. And God damn it, I *do* have standards! Higher ones than her old man's, too, even if she is always raving about him. Why, I wouldn't file a smutty petition like that in court for anything in the world!"

"Go see Mrs. Dilworth then." Larry yawned and shrugged his shoulders. "Maybe she'll let you be her lawyer. That'll show them. If she doesn't throw you out as a goddam ambulance chaser."

Bobbie got up. He had been trying all night to get Larry to say this.

"It's just exactly what I will do!" he exclaimed. "Just exactly what I'll do!"

"But not tonight, Bobbie," Larry protested wearily. "Let's not go tonight."

The next day Bobbie left his office at five and walked across town to the Stafford. When he sent up his name word came back that Mrs. Dilworth was out, but that she was expected back shortly. Mrs. Bleecker would see him, however, if he cared to go up. He got the impression from the clerk that Mrs. Bleecker would see anybody.

"Who's she?" he asked.

"Mrs. Dilworth's mother."

"Oh. Well, okay."

He had expected a grey-haired, motherly soul imported from the country to stand by a daughter in time of crisis, and he was startled when he saw Irene's thin, gaunt figure in the doorway and heard her deep voice.

"Mr. Chapin? Won't you come in, please. Eloise should be back any minute."

He came in and sat down rather awkwardly on the sofa, leaning forward so as not to crush the floppy doll behind him.

"Let me take Berthe away," she said, leaning over to remove the doll. "There." She sat down in the deep armchair and looked up at him, her dark eyes curious. "Could you be the Mr. Chapin whom Eloise has told me about? The one who's a friend of Hilda's?"

"I guess so. More or less."

"How do you mean, more or less?"

"Well, I'm not exactly in Hilda's good books at the moment. Sort of a lovers' quarrel, you might say." And if that one got back to Hilda, he reflected sullenly, he didn't give a damn.

"I see." She nodded. "Then you and Hilda, I take it, are lovers."

He looked up sharply and saw that she was laughing

189

at him. He took out his case and offered her a cigarette.

"You're quite a sporty old dame, aren't you?"

"And you, Mr. Chapin," she said, accepting his cigarette, "are quite a fresh young man."

"So we're even."

"Exactly. And perhaps now that we're even you'll tell me what it is that I can do for you?"

"You forget, Mrs. Bleecker," he said, wagging his finger at her. "I came to see your daughter."

She looked at him suspiciously.

"You're sure you haven't come from George Dilworth?"

"That stuffed shirt? Do I look it?"

At this Irene got up and went to the sideboard.

"Mr. Chapin, I think perhaps you and I are going to be friends, after all. George *is* a stuffed shirt. I've thought so from the beginning. Let me give you a drink."

He noticed that she poured the martinis into the shaker from a gin bottle that had a label "mixed" pasted to its side. When he tasted his, he found that it was very dry indeed.

"What I've really come for is to find out if your daughter needs any help," he said in a friendlier tone, settling back on the sofa. "I'm not looking for a job or a fee or anything like that. But it's a field I know something about, and if she'd like to know who are the good lawyers and who aren't—"

"But it's what I keep telling her!" Irene interrupted. "She must have a lawyer!"

"Then she hasn't got one?"

"No! she's been sitting around, completely *distraite*." Irene raised her hands in a gesture of hopelessness.

"The efficiency, I take it, has been all on the other side."

"Oh, yes. There's been no end of it there."

"Tell me, Mrs. Bleecker," he said, leaning forward, "what about Dilworth? If we were as efficient as he is, could we catch *him* at anything?"

He watched her as she looked down at her long scarlet fingernails. Obviously he would get things out of her that he would never get out of Eloise.

"I'm afraid not," she said, looking up at him. "I'm afraid you don't understand George. He's not interested in women. It's funny. You know, there's no country in the world with more sexual curiosity than ours. Everyone thinks there's always something terrific going on in his neighbor's house. And very often there is. But not always. That's what I'm smart enough to have learned about America, Mr. Chapin. Not always."

"You mean nothing goes on with George?" he amplified. "Wasn't he even interested in his beautiful wife?"

"He hasn't been for some time," she said, shaking her head firmly. "No, when I said nothing, I meant nothing. George is one of those who sublimates his sexual energy in his profession. He and Eloise haven't lived together, in the real sense of the word, for years."

He looked up suddenly.

"Are you sure of that?"

"Of course, I'm sure. Eloise told me so herself. But do you think she'd ever use that? Oh, no. She'd let him walk all over her first."

They hadn't heard the door in the lobby open, and they both started when they heard Eloise's voice.

"Would I, Irene? Let who walk over me?" She came in as she said this, taking off her gloves, a dry little smile on her face. "And who is this you're explaining me to?" She stopped as she took in Bobbie's face and then her smile broadened and the dryness disappeared. "Why, it's Mr. Chapin. Hilda's friend."

He got up to shake her hand, struck by the fact that

she was even lovelier than he remembered. Her large blue eyes seemed to have lost some of their timidity.

"He wants to be your lawyer, Eloise," Irene explained rapidly to cover her indiscretion. "I was just telling him how you needed one."

Eloise looked at him quizzically.

"Do lawyers come around now and knock on doors?"

He flushed.

"I'm sorry, Mrs. Dilworth," he said, "it's not what you think. I'm not looking for business or anything like that. Truly. It's just that I got sore when I heard what they'd done to you, and—well—I wanted to tell you that I'm on your side."

She continued to look at him gravely for a moment.

"Thank you, Mr. Chapin," she said finally. "I'm glad you're on my side."

"Eloise, you must *listen* to this young man."

She turned to her mother.

"Very well, Irene. I will. But I think it might be as well if I did so alone, don't you?"

Irene went to the sideboard, grumbling, and refilled her cocktail.

"I'm going," she said, "don't worry. All I want is to be sure you listen to him."

"I said I would," Eloise assured her. "But don't you," she added with a smile. "Please!"

When she had closed the door behind Irene, she came back and sat in the chair where her mother had been sitting.

"How is Hilda?" she asked.

"I haven't really been seeing her lately. She was pretty sore at me that time I took you all to Leo's."

"Oh, yes. She was upset about that girl. But I thought she'd forgiven you. Hilda can be very magnanimous."

He was afraid for a moment that she was being serious, and then she smiled. He laughed.

"Well, the next time she saw me I was loaded," he confessed. "Tough luck. It was at Al Herbert's. I had no idea she'd be there."

"I see. Well, that makes two of us she's down on. There's nothing, however, that I can do about my case. Yours, perhaps, is more hopeful."

"Hilda's a pretty good girl," he said awkwardly. "Fundamentally."

"I think she is. Fundamentally."

"She's awfully critical though."

"Very critical," she agreed.

He nodded.

"Is that why you want to be my lawyer, Mr. Chapin?" she asked mildly. "Do you think it would make Hilda less critical of you? I'm afraid it would have just the opposite effect."

"I agree with you. But that's the point. I want to take issue with Hilda. I want her to see where I stand."

"And where is that?"

"Against people who behave the way your husband has behaved."

There was another rather heavy pause.

"Do you really want to be my lawyer?" she asked, getting up and going to the sideboard to refill his drink. "I have no case, you know. I hate to ask anyone to represent me."

He shook his head to refuse the drink, and quite suddenly, without further discussion, there was a professional relationship between them.

"I've read the complaint," he said. "I assume he can prove it?"

"Completely."

"You don't want to oppose the divorce, then?"

"No. It's just the children."

"Tell me about it."

"The children?"

"Your marriage. George. The whole thing."

She sat down again and told him the story of her marriage. She was careful, he observed, to emphasize her own deficiencies as a wife and her husband's good qualities. She assured him that George had never given her the least cause for jealousy, that he had been liberal with money and that he had been uniformly agreeable to all the people whom she cared about. There had been the exception, she admitted, of her mother, but Irene, she explained, had always been something of a problem. When she came to Carl she pointed out that few husbands would have tolerated such a friendship as long as he had.

"I'm sure your husband's a wonderful man, Mrs. Dilworth," he said at last. "But he has a lawyer already. I presume he doesn't need another."

"Well, I want to be fair."

"If you really want to be fair," he said slowly, keeping his eyes carefully on hers, for he knew what a chance he was taking, "why don't you tell me what sort of husband he's *really* been? Basically speaking?"

She looked puzzled for a moment and then suddenly flushed.

"Irene!" she exclaimed. "Has Irene been talking to you?"

"She says you told her."

"I never told her!" she said indignantly. "Never! She's been snooping into things like that ever since she arrived."

"But it's true?"

"What does it matter whether it's true or not?" she said impatiently. "Does it justify what *I* did?"

"It makes it more understandable," he explained. "Judges are not always understanding, you know."

She appeared to think this over for a moment and then shuddered.

"I couldn't do a thing like that to George, Mr. Chapin. I really couldn't."

"Why not? Has he been so gentle with you?"

"But George is different," she protested. "George is like a child when his pride is hurt. I can't hurt him any more than he has been."

"Even at the cost of losing your children?"

She jumped up and walked up and down the room, puffing nervously at her cigarette. He watched her in silence until she turned back to him, flinging the butt in the fireplace.

"I see now that I've been living in a dream, Mr. Chapin," she said bitterly. "I was thinking that I'd been liberated by my own misconduct. That I'd been thrown out of a world I never really wanted to be in. I thought that once I'd heard all the sneers and felt all the brickbats, it would have no more terrors for me. If I'd paid the penalty, I could go my own way." She shook her head. "But it's not that way at all, is it? Even the person who's being thrown out never really gets out. The ones who belong and the ones who don't still have to play the same game according to the same degrading rules. As long as the world has any hold on you, and I guess it always does. Certainly as long as you're a mother, anyway."

"The world isn't a very nice place, Mrs. Dilworth," he agreed. "It's proved that to you recently. But if I'd been treated the way you've been treated I'd have no scruples. I'd kick back and kick back hard."

She shook her head again, several times, almost impatiently.

"But I don't *want* revenge, Mr. Chapin. I don't even feel the faintest desire for it. You don't understand."

He looked at the unhappiness in her eyes and smiled in spite of himself.

"If you'll only look at the judge that way, Mrs. Dilworth," he exclaimed, "our case is as good as won!"

5

IRENE WAS ALMOST satisfied with herself and with the world as she dressed that evening for dinner. If one believed in omens, and Irene rather did, it was certainly auspicious that at the very nadir of her and Eloise's fortunes Hilda Dilworth's young man should detach himself from the enemy camp and come over to command their forces. Who could tell what wholesale desertions might not follow so striking an example? She smiled at herself more cheerfully in the mirror as she rubbed rouge carefully into her pale cheeks. It was still going to be a fight, of course, but it was going to be a fight that they now had a chance of winning. Eloise might be surprised at her "they," for Eloise still didn't trust her, but that was all right. Eloise could hardly be expected to appreciate that under the brisk give and take of her gossip lay a maternal devotion all the stronger for not having been spent. Oh, true, she had given little evidence of it in the immediate past, but now things were different, as shown for example by her handling of Arthur Irwin. Arthur had been noticeably put off by the arrival of Eloise, the reprehensible Eloise as he regarded her, at her apartment, and for a time his little visits had been discontinued. And had she once reproached him? She had not. She had simply waited until, lonely, he had sought to renew his visits, and she had then been careful to ignore his past defection. Mere visits, however, were not going to be enough. She had little use for Arthur Irwin, neutral, in a battle where she had made her plans for Arthur Irwin, ally. She knew how much their little dinners had come to mean to him and the dependence that he was beginning to place on her sympathetic ear. She knew how little he trusted his own children and how much he liked to complain to her about them. And she knew, most importantly of all, how hard it was for him to make new friends and how difficult it would be to find another like her. Of course, she had to face the fact, at the same time, that there was more than a chance of failure and that failure could mean the extinction of any hope that she had of marrying him, but she had never been one to be afraid of a gamble. It was the element of chance, as a matter of fact, that gave the whole thing its excitement.

When she heard the buzz of her doorbell and let him in, she thought he looked embarrassed. Even after they were seated and she had mixed him a cocktail, she noticed that he glanced occasionally towards the half-open door of her bedroom.

"Arthur Irwin, will you kindly tell me who you expect to see coming out of my bedroom?"

He blushed.

"I thought Eloise might be there."

"Eloise has the room across the corridor. Besides, she's out for dinner."

"Oh. That's just as well then."

"What do you mean, Arthur? Why is it 'just as well'?"

"I think that should be fairly obvious, Irene."

"You do? I don't."

"I mean considering my friendship with George."

"Does being a friend of George's," she asked, looking him squarely in the eye, "involve standing behind him while he crucifies my child?"

"Oh, come now, Irene," he protested, shaking his head at her, "I can understand that you feel that way.

But George, after all, is my friend. Can't we drop it at that?"

"I'm afraid we can't, Arthur," she said in her gravest tone. "I want to know if you're my friend, too. That's something that happens to be very important to me."

He leaned forward a little in his chair and smiled at her.

"I'm glad it's important to you, Irene. It's important to me, too. Of course I'm your friend. You ought to know that by now."

But she shook her head stubbornly.

"I'm not sure you can be a friend of George's and mine, too, Arthur. At least not while this terrible thing is going on. I feel too strongly about it. I'm sorry, but I do. There's that poor child who's done nothing all her life but try to please people. She has pampered George and the children and that smug Hilda and George's fatuous old mother, to say nothing of my own brother and sister-in-law." Irene was warmly authoritative now; her eyes had a flash in them. "And what have they done for her in return? Have any of them appreciated one jot or one tittle of it? Not on your life. They've sat there like a bunch of harpies, waiting for my poor angel to make a mistake, one single mistake, so they could all jump on her. They call that justice, but I know what I call it, Arthur! I call it downright sadism!"

"But this mistake, as you describe it, Irene, was a pretty serious one." Arthur was scratching his head. "It seems to me fundamental that a man should be able to put aside a wife who's unfaithful to him."

"Put aside!" she exclaimed. "Arthur Irwin, this is nineteen-forty-nine! In a few months the twentieth century will be half over! And this whole episode has been out of a play by Dumas Fils."

By raising her voice she was able to dodge any serious discussion of the moral issues involved. As a

198

philosopher she knew that she would only alarm him. As an indignant mother she held his sympathy.

"I know it's been hard on you, Irene," he said consolingly. "I know you've suffered—"

"But do *you* agree with George?" she demanded, following up her advantage. "Do *you*, Arthur Irwin, think those little girls should be taken away from a mother who adores them? Who has looked after them day and night all their lives?"

"Well, that does seem extreme, I admit."

"But that's what your George is up to!" she exclaimed triumphantly. "And to accomplish what he wants he doesn't hesitate to stigmatize her publicly as an adulteress. Did I say Dumas Fils? It's pure Hawthorne. And did I say that he doesn't *hesitate* to do it? Why he goes at it with joy!"

"I don't think that's quite fair, Irene. I've seen George, and he looks miserable."

"And so he ought! And he's going to be more miserable still when he sees how this thing boomerangs! Mark my words, Arthur. You and George are going to find out that people won't put up with this sort of thing any more!"

"*I* and George!"

"Certainly you and George! Didn't you tell me you were on his side?"

It turned out that Irene had gambled wisely indeed. Arthur Irwin had a set of rigid moral principles, and he had applied them strictly to his own children, barely speaking even now to a daughter who had been involved in an equally scandalous but successfully hushed-up divorce. To his friends, however, when he saw fit, he reserved the privilege of applying different standards. Arthur had worked hard for his fortune; he felt that he had earned the right to friends and tolerances to which his idler offspring were not entitled. He was also coming slowly to the conclusion that Irene, while not exactly indispensable to him—no one was really indispensable to Arthur—was perhaps irreplaceable. She had just the right feminine combination of familiarity and respect; she made him feel important without letting him feel that he was pompous. She was interested in his money, of course, but wouldn't there have been something wrong with a woman of her age and situation who wasn't? Besides, Arthur, who tended to equate his money with himself, was perfectly willing to be loved for it. For any woman to ignore entirely the shining golden circle that he had drawn around himself might have seemed a kind of impertinence. Then it was also true that she had been married too much, but this had happened mostly in Europe, and he had a comfortable, isolationist feeling deep within him that things which had happened outside the country had somehow not really happened at all. But over and above all these considerations was the clear fact that his relationship with Irene, whatever he might ultimately decide to make of it, was certainly too valuable to be allowed to founder on an issue as remote as the custody of her grandchildren. Having once decided this, it was easy enough for him to take the next step and to speculate that, after all, she was probably right. A case like this one perhaps *had* better be settled. George, come to think of it, was going pretty far. It might be for the best all round if he dropped a hint to this effect to Gerald Hunt. It might even end the whole matter, and Irene would be pleasantly grateful.

His opportunity to do this came the following week at a wedding reception given in the ballroom of a ladies' club for the daughter of one of the Hunt & Livermore partners. He sat at a round table with Irene and watched the young people dancing after the breaking up of the receiving line. Irene was looking very well in a black dress with a white, wide-brimmed hat. She seemed almost smug as she drank her champagne.

"You see, Arthur, our side, Eloise's side, I mean, is really beginning to get somewhere. Obviously the Athertons had to ask Gerald and Gladys, and that meant it would be awkward to have George. But what about me? They certainly didn't have to have me, except they're terrible old snoopers, and they know I'm a friend of yours. So there you are. I'm here, and George isn't." She raised her glass in a mock toast. "Even Harry Hamilton wouldn't dare show his fat face. I tell you, Arthur, it'll split the firm yet."

He laughed. It was a short, dry laugh.

"If you have anything to do with it, it will, Irene."

"Well, a little splitting mightn't hurt it," she continued, looking around her critically. "Do they have to ask *all* the clients every time one of their children gets married? I never saw such dowdy women. Do you suppose they take courses in school to learn how to look that dowdy?"

"Well, don't worry. You'll never look like that, Irene."

"I suppose they can't help it, poor things," she continued, mollified, shaking her head. "That's the trouble with American business. From a wife's point of view, I mean. It takes twenty years to get anywhere, and then what good does it do them?"

"Money can be spent on other things besides personal adornment," he reproved her. "And what about your sister-in-law? She didn't have to wait twenty years."

They both looked over to where Gladys Hunt, serene under a pancake green hat, oddly floating over her billowing pompadour of grey hair, was standing, smiling inattentively at a little chattering group of younger women.

"No, you're right," Irene agreed. "There's no excuse for Gladys. No explanation for her, either. A big frog, I suppose. But oh, Arthur, what a puddle!"

201

"Why don't you go and talk to Gladys a minute? I've something I want to discuss with Gerald."

"Business? Even at weddings?"

"What's wrong with weddings?"

Irene shrugged her shoulders and went over to Gladys. Arthur smiled as he saw them peck at each other's cheek. Yet he was almost proud of Irene as he watched her; she was easily, despite her age, the most striking woman in the room. He would have been perfectly pleased to point her out as his wife and a man as distinguished-looking as Gerald as his brother-in-law. Of course, he was much too successful now and too old to have anything further to gain by a family connection with Gerald Hunt, but there had been a time when he would have cared a good deal about it. It was rather gratifying now, after all the hard years, to think that he might be about to acquire a group of Hunt relations for no reason more snobbish than his enjoyment of the martinis and conversation of a battered old girl who had no money to bring him and less reputation. And how they would jump to make up to her then! Oh, of course, it would be only another reminder of how far he had come in life, but multitudinous as such reminders now were, they still had their pleasant side. Then he remembered his mission and turned to look for Gerald. He found him holding forth to a group of young lawyers who were grouped respectfully around him. He raised one arm as Arthur approached.

"Aha, the distinguished Mr. Irwin. Boys, you know Mr. Irwin."

Arthur nodded to the circle of heads. He knew perfectly well that Gerald had no more idea of their names than he did, probably less, for he, at least, was apt to remember the boys in Gerald's office who had worked for him.

"Could I have a word with you, Gerald?"

"My dear fellow, of course."

The circle of young men promptly broke up, and they were left alone.

"I know it's a painful subject, and I mention it as a friend of Irene's rather than as a client of yours. It's this suit George is bringing."

Gerald put his hands behind his back and assumed his most serious aspect. He formed his lips into a circle and breathed in through his mouth.

"Bad business, Arthur. Very bad business. Nobody feels worse about it than I do. Terrible." He shook his head. "Terrible."

"I wondered if you couldn't call George off. Settle the thing out of court."

Gerald looked at him with a rather exaggerated expression of surprise.

"My dear Arthur, you don't think for a minute I haven't done everything I could, do you? But George is a madman about this thing. He won't listen to me. He and Hamilton have got the bit in their teeth, and there's no stopping them."

Arthur looked grave. He saw suddenly from the expression in Gerald's eyes what was expected of him, and it was a good deal more than he had been prepared to give.

"Nothing doing, eh?"

"Nothing."

For several moments he looked blankly at Gerald without speaking. Anger was growing inside him, accelerating, shifting rapidly in its search for a victim, from Irene for getting him into this, to Gerald for wanting what he wanted, to Eloise for being such a tramp and finally to George for having started the damn suit in the first place. But Arthur made up his mind quickly, and George was the last on his list. George was going to have to give up the lawsuit; it was as simple as that. And it was nobody's fault but George's own. He should have anticipated that Gerald would request the reassurance that he was requesting and that he, Arthur, would give it to him. George might be his idea of all a lawyer should be, but Gerald Hunt was not the kind of general counsel with whom one parted company over an issue like this.

"I would have thought you might have been in a position to exercise some pressure, Gerald," he said more sharply. "After all, Eloise *is* your niece."

Gerald shrugged his shoulders. He managed to express in this gesture the understanding hopelessness of a man of the world who still has a heart.

"What pressure, Arthur? I intend to watch the case, of course. It still may be possible to keep it out of the papers."

"You know the kind of pressure I mean."

"My dear Arthur," Gerald said again blandly, "I can do a lot of things. You and I both know that. But I have to know where I stand. The case is about to go to trial. Nothing under the sun will keep George from bringing it on now. If it's handled tactfully we may do well to leave it. But if it isn't, if it starts to become a public scandal, I should like to use very strong measures indeed and to use them speedily. I am delighted you agree, but let me ask you just one question. You mentioned just now that you were my client. Does that mean mine and no one else's?"

Gerald's tone became very dry indeed as he put his question, and he stared with none of his usual suaveness at Arthur as he finished. It was business, and he meant business; he was enough of a diplomat to know that although there was a place for smoothness, vital issues still had to be underscored. Arthur breathed heavily for a moment and then drew a cigar from his vest pocket.

"It means just that," he said, chewing off the tip. "You can count on it, Gerald."

"Thank you," said Gerald, nodding his head immediately and resuming his old manner. "That's all I wanted to know. Well, my dear Judge," he said, turning to a white-haired man who was bearing down on them, "I'm delighted to see you. You remember Mr. Irwin, don't you? With your customary wisdom, if I recall correctly, you ruled in his favor in that special dividend case last year. Let me see, how was it called? Irwin against the People's National Bank—?"

6

THERE WERE NOT many people in the courtroom early on the damp winter Friday morning when Dilworth *vs.* Dilworth was called, but as Hilda, sitting in a back row, reflected bitterly, there were a good many more than a routine divorce case would have called out. The group of men in the first row to the left were obviously reporters, and if there was even one of these, might there not as well be a dozen? Hilda felt cold and wretched, though she had kept her coat on and the room was warm; she looked up over the clean white wall to the big window and the dark grey sky beyond, as if searching for some symbol of the redeemability of herself and the little people in the far end of the room who sat behind the bar, of Judge Cory, so old and blinking and testy behind his pince-nez, even of her father, stiff and expressionless at his table. She had come because she had to learn these things. They happened. It was life. There was a man on the witness stand; she couldn't hear what he was saying, but she saw that he had a photograph in his hand. It was handed up to the judge who simply glanced at it and grunted. Then she saw Bobbie get up and heard him say something very fast that apparently was an objection. Nobody seemed to pay much attention to him, nor did he seem to mind; their voices were distant and unconcerned, like those of actors engaged in a line rehearsal where gesture and expression are superfluous.

Her father had briefed her on what was going to happen. There was to be no jury, as neither side had requested one. The plaintiff's case was now opening with proof of what had happened in Landik's apartment. Soon, perhaps in a half-hour, Mr. Hamilton would examine Eloise on the question of parental fitness. She made herself turn and look at Eloise and saw that, just as she had pictured her beforehand, Eloise was pale and beautiful. She was looking directly at Hilda now, but she turned her head immediately without even a nod of recognition. Of course, Eloise would never presume that they could still be friends. She would not take it for granted that people could forgive. And Hilda, watching Bobbie as he sat beside her stepmother, whispering to her, wondered sadly what was left for herself but a preoccupied father and the atmosphere of rather tired justice that filled the room like solid cubic blocks, justice that was one's own for the asking and that no one but Dilworths seemed to want. She had not seen people or done things, she had not even felt capable of attending her business-school courses since the terrible evening when her father had come home and asked her suddenly, with an unpleasant mixture of alarm and suspicion, if she knew that Bobbie Chapin was representing Eloise. It had been the first time she had heard of it, and her appalled expression had reassured him as to any part in the strange affair that she might have played. There had been nothing, however, to reassure herself. At first she had been simply, if violently, jealous, but little by little her jealousy had given way to a sensation that she could only describe as envy, a strange envy of the unexpected congeniality that she assumed now to exist between Eloise and Bobbie, of the undoubted harmony of their points of view, of the pleasant, joking time, even in Eloise's trouble, that they might be having together. And with the birth of this envy came a sudden, shocking impulse to surrender to them, to fling everything she believed in to the winds and rush pell-mell across the field of contest that divided her from them, in front of gaping crowds, and tumble down, a heap of quivering, senseless apology, before the grandstand of their basic good will. For Eloise alone she could fight, or even Bobbie, but this alliance, so odd, so utterly inexplicable, seemed to threaten the whole jerry-built structure of her sense of honor, filling its dusty emptiness with noise and wind. She found herself perversely anxious to exult in her own defeat, in her own agonizing exclusion from the shared warmth of their friendship. She closed her eyes and shook her head in the courtroom as she actually caught herself praying that Eloise would lose her case so that she might still befriend her with magnanimity.

George Dilworth had his arms folded across his chest, and he stared straight ahead at the railing of the empty jury box as he listened to the testimony of the detective. Just once he glanced out of the corner of his eye at where Eloise was sitting. She did not look at him, for she was looking at the witness, her features set with contempt. It was the first time that he had seen her since the night when he had asked her to give up Landik, but her expression was just as he had imagined it, one of bold, even defiant independence. If she had only come to him after her interview with Harry and asked his forgiveness, if she had even once, just once, tried to see him, things might have been different. But no. His first suspicions had been correct; she hated him for not giving her what she no longer wanted of him. She had ceased, in a word, to be his. And when he thought of what the little girls had said to Judge Cory in his chambers, how they had held out stubbornly to be with their mother, his anger seemed to freeze into something more like fear. For it was not only that she would carry on an affair under his very nose, she would take his children, she would happily, in fact, rip to pieces the very way of life that it had taken him so many years to build up. She might even, with those wide eyes and that dishonest smile, turn his downtown world against him, and for what? For defending his honor, his home? He put his hand over his eyes and thought of the beating of his heart. Surely it was too fast. Surely it would never do to go on with this excitement. Then some of the words of the testimony came to him, and he felt a quiver of even sharper alarm. Wasn't Harry going too far? He had a vision of Gerald and the other partners gathering against him; on all sides he began to see puckered brows and shaking heads—oh, hurry up, Harry, he groaned inwardly, hurry up and put that bitch where she belongs, make it irrevocable, get it over with, but *hurry*—

The law, however, was not to be hurried, nor was Harry Hamilton. He enjoyed litigation, and this case he was enjoying particularly. He strutted back and forth before the witness stand, the large photographs in his hand, held slightly away from him as if to avoid their contaminating effect.

"I think, Mr. Hamilton, if the defense has no objection," Judge Cory intervened, "we have enough evidence of this unsavory episode."

"Very well, your Honor." He nodded to Bobbie with a slight shrug of his shoulders. "Your witness."

"No questions."

Bobbie sat down again, impassive.

"Remember what I told you," he whispered to

Eloise. "You can make a fool of Fatty if you want. He's wide open. But don't let him get you mad."

She nodded.

"I mean it," he repeated. "It's vital." Then he suddenly smiled. "Have you seen Hilda? She looks like a stuffed prune. Poor kid. She didn't bargain for anything like this. How about you? Holding up?"

"I don't know. It's like a dream. I can't believe those men can be sitting there saying what they're saying. Right in public."

"Routine. Simply routine."

She glanced furtively again in Hilda's direction. He was right. She did look terrible. And why not? To have deified a father and to have one's god behave this way—well, would it cure her? She looked at George and shook her head sadly at the sight of his dark countenance. It was true, and for the first time she could really see it, that what they were doing to themselves was worse than what they were doing to her.

She felt Bobbie's hand on her arm.

"Here you go."

She walked, feeling numb, to the witness chair, raised her hand and took the oath. Then she turned to face Harry Hamilton. He was at his most seemingly indifferent, his stomach forward, his thumb and forefinger in his usual gesture of rubbing his eyeballs.

"Mrs. Dilworth," he began in a rather weary voice, "you do not deny, I take it, that you committed adultery with one Carl Landik on the date and under the circumstances just proved to this court?"

Bobbie was on his feet.

"Objection, your Honor. There's no reason why Mrs. Dilworth should be asked to incriminate herself!"

"Overruled," Judge Cory answered immediately. "The question is proper. But is there any need for it, Mr. Hamilton?" he continued, turning to Harry.

"Hasn't there been sufficient proof already of what you allege?"

Harry nodded several times, in a quick, offhand manner.

"I had thought the facts virtually conceded," he said airily. "But no matter. If Mr. Chapin wishes my questions to be hypothetical, I can certainly accommodate him. Let me start, then, if I may, by reading aloud to Mrs. Dilworth and to the court an excerpt from the opinion of Judge Vane in the case of Mason against Mason, Appellate Division, First Department, decided in nineteen-twenty-four." He cleared his throat and reached behind him, without even glancing around, for the volume which Tom Haighter promptly placed in his hand, open at the page in question. " 'Parenthood,' Judge Vane states, 'is the highest avocation to which a man or a woman can be called. The rearing and education of our youth are the foundation stones upon which our republic is built. Nor is anything more vital to the educational process than the teaching of proper moral standards where relations between the sexes are involved. Any parent who is unable or unwilling to undertake such indoctrination must be unfit to have charge of the education of minors.' " He turned abruptly to Eloise. "Would you agree with Judge Vane's point of view, Mrs. Dilworth?"

Bobbie was again on his feet.

"I object, your Honor. The question calls for the witness' opinion on matters that are not only vague but beyond the scope of this action."

"Your Honor!" Harry protested in a now thundering tone. "It is essential that the court know a parent's point of view on moral issues!"

"Objection overruled."

Harry turned again to Eloise.

"Do you agree with Judge Vane, Mrs. Dilworth?"

"It's a very general statement," she answered, looking at the judge as if he could not help but agree with her, "but I suppose I could say that I agree with it in principle. Yes."

She nodded her head as she said "yes," feeling sick as she did so. She looked for reassurance at Bobbie. He winked, and she was grateful to him, but she couldn't help reflecting that he did not really feel as she did. To him it was part of the game.

"Let me impose upon the court's time," Harry continued with a nod to the bench, "with a further quotation from the same learned justice, this time in nineteen-twenty-seven in the case of Pines against Pines. He speaks here of the evils of fornication and adultery. Fornication, as perhaps I should explain," he continued, turning to Eloise with crinkled nostrils, "is sexual intercourse between two persons not married to each other. If one of the fornicators be married—to a person, that is, not fornicating with him or her at the time—such married fornicator is also guilty of the crime of adultery. I trust I make myself clear."

"Your Honor," Bobbie protested furiously, jumping to his feet, "Mr. Hamilton is insulting the witness! I request that he be directed to moderate his language!"

Judge Cory nodded his head briefly.

"I wish, Mr. Hamilton, that you would use as few offensive words as possible."

Harry bowed to the bench.

"I shall do my best, your Honor. I assure you they are as distasteful to me as they are to you. The subject is not of my choosing." He turned back to his book and cleared his throat again. " 'No act threatens the home, the basic rock of our society, more dangerously than the act of adultery. That an adulteress could be a fit person in whose hands to place the rearing of young and innocent persons is almost unthinkable. Only if the crime is confessed and the adulteress truly repentant, only if the court has reason to believe that she has seen

211

the error of her ways and will not continue her adulteries in the future, should she be considered a fit guardian for her children.' " Harry closed the book impressively. "May I ask you, Mrs. Dilworth, whether you agree with Judge Vane's opinion in the passage that I have just finished reading?"

Eloise stared with a cold dismay into those large, watery eyes. She tried to keep her mind on Peggy and Jo and what this would mean to them, but it was no use. Harry was still in front of her, superior and sneering, trying, of course, to be as superior and sneering as he could, to exasperate her. Yet the only thing in the world that seemed to matter at all was that she should repudiate him, refute him, even if her repudiation and refutation were exactly what he was seeking. Do you want to be a martyr, she whispered warningly to herself. A martyr for what? But it wasn't only that, not really that at all—

"Shall I reread the quotation to you, Mrs. Dilworth?"

She shook her head.

"You needn't. I understand it. Judge Vane thinks that adultery is wrong. And so it may be. But I don't think it need necessarily be as wrong as that."

She caught a glimpse of Bobbie's warning eyes and turned her face away.

"Really, Mrs. Dilworth?" Harry queried, assuming again his bored tone, yet scarcely able to conceal a little quiver of excitement. "Perhaps you would tell us just how wrong you think it is?"

"I think it depends," she answered slowly. "If it's committed all the time, indiscriminately, promiscuously, then I suppose it's wrong."

"I see," came back the voice, now on a rising note of triumph. "But if it's committed from time to time, discriminately, unpromiscuously. . . ." Here Harry

212

rolled his eyes meaningfully at the judge. "Then, presumably, it's all right?"

"No, I don't mean that. It all depends."

"What does it depend on, Mrs. Dilworth?" he demanded in a strong, stern voice, but she didn't answer because she could think of nothing to say. "Perhaps I can help you," he continued more quietly. He placed his hands behind his back and gazed reflectively up at the ceiling. "Shall we break it down? Let us take your phrase 'from time to time.' Would you say once a month was all right? Once a fortnight? Once a week perhaps? Provided, of course, one was discriminating and unpromiscuous?"

"Well, of course, it can't be reduced to numbers," she said impatiently. "I'm only trying to draw a distinction between the woman whose attitude is serious and the woman whose attitude is not. I can imagine a woman whose husband has neglected her, for example, and who eventually falls in love with another man, and who, if they're discreet—"

"But suppose the husband has *not* neglected her?" Harry interrupted, almost with a roar. "Suppose he has worked hard and long to support her and the children? Suppose he has never so much as looked at another woman? Could adultery be justified under *those* circumstances, Mrs. Dilworth?"

"I don't know," she said, suddenly weary of it. "I suppose each case must be judged according to its own merits."

"Then there are no absolute standards?"

"How can I tell?" she protested. "Anyone can be made to look foolish in a discussion like this. You know that as well as I, Mr. Hamilton."

She looked up at him as he drew himself formidably up to his full height to retort. She felt a curious exhilaration, not unlike what she had felt after the first shock of the scene at Carl's apartment, a sense, again, that the

213

worst had happened. All the words that he had been using so violently, like adultery and fornication, words that she had never heard used this way by people to each other, certainly never in public, had suddenly lost their terror. They seemed like so many Easter bunnies and teddy bears scattered around the courtroom for other children to pick up and fondle. It was a nursery, and full of horrid children, but she at least was an adult.

"I'm not trying to make you look foolish, Mrs. Dilworth," Harry was saying now with the utmost gravity. "I'm merely trying to determine if you have a moral code and, if so, what it amounts to. It is unfortunately necessary to determine this where the custody of children is involved. If you believe that adultery is only occasionally wrong, will you not bring up your daughters to think as you do?"

"Oh, no!"

"Adultery, then, will be wrong for them but right for you?"

"Objection, your Honor." Bobbie was on his feet, looking desperate now. "Mrs. Dilworth never said adultery was right for her."

"I amend the question," Harry said blandly, rolling his eyes again to the judge as though in mutual recognition of the delays that had to be conceded to this impatient young man. "Does it not follow, Mrs. Dilworth, from what you have just said, that you would have one moral code for your children and another for yourself?"

"Not exactly," she replied, flustered between her effort to concentrate and her sense of the absurdity of the discussion. "But there are things that an adult—and I mean by an adult a person who is mature in every way—can do without injury to herself that a younger person can't do."

"Such things as adultery?"

214

"Yes. Perhaps even adultery."

"At what age, in your opinion," he sneered, "does a person become free to commit adultery?"

"Free? I never said free."

"At what age, then, to use your exact expression, can a woman commit adultery without harm to herself?"

She sighed.

"There's no set age, Mr. Hamilton," she protested. "That's ridiculous. It depends on her maturity and the circumstances."

"You would, then, teach your daughters that marriage vows are only binding until maturity has been attained?"

"Oh, no. I would want my daughter to be married happily. Very happily."

"But if they were not," he pursued rapidly, "you would tell them that adultery can be a morally justifiable remedy? Under certain circumstances, of course?"

"Those things they would have to find out for themselves, Mr. Hamilton. I didn't invent adultery."

"None of us invented evil or temptation, Mrs. Dilworth," Harry thundered. "What we invent, or should invent, is the moral armament to use against them. I fail to see how your children can be expected to develop such armament in a home where the most flagrant abuse of our moral code is treated as a mere matter of circumstance. Can you explain how they will, Mrs. Dilworth?"

"I don't think I would discuss such a thing as adultery with children, Mr. Hamilton."

"But children ask questions. They hear things at school, and it's only natural that they should turn to a parent as an authority. Your children may hear of this case, Mrs. Dilworth. What will you tell them?"

Eloise paused, breathless for a moment at the violence of this attack. She felt an impulse of sympathy

215

towards her in the air of the courtroom, but when she looked at the judge, he only looked away.

"I think I would tell them that they'd understand when they were older," she said quietly.

"Meaning that by that time they would have learned which adulteries were right and which were wrong?"

"No," she said firmly. "Meaning that at that time they would be able to make up their own minds. About their own parents."

"And does that not boil down to saying that you would refuse them moral guidance?"

"As to problems that may come up in the future which cannot now be visualized, yes."

Harry turned abruptly to Bobbie.

"Your witness," he said.

She hardly dared to face Bobbie as he got up and walked over slowly to the witness chair. He did not, however, look reproachful. He looked tired, but she thought again that he gave her the suggestion of a wink.

"Mrs. Dilworth," he began in a quiet, sympathetic tone, "you have told me that the incident which has been demonstrated earlier today was the first time that you had ever been unfaithful to your husband. Is that true?"

"It is."

"How long have you been married, Mrs. Dilworth?"

"Thirteen years."

"Thirteen years." He nodded gravely. "I see. Now my next question, I'm afraid, is going to be a rather personal one. Would you mind describing to the court just what your relations with Mr. Dilworth have been during the past five years?"

She stared very hard into his light blue eyes until the courtroom seemed to recede into dullness. Then her vision blurred and when it cleared she saw surprise in his eyes and then concern.

"Yes, Bobbie. I do mind," she said distinctly. "I mind very much."

He turned immediately to Judge Cory.

"Your Honor, I would like to ask for a recess. I'm sorry to do this, but I think my client is upset. I'm sure you will understand when you consider what she has been through today. Mrs. Dilworth is not a lady who's accustomed to hearing the kind of language that Mr. Hamilton has exposed her to."

"We'll adjourn till Monday at ten, if you like," the judge conceded. "Unless Mr. Hamilton has any objection."

"No objection, your Honor. But I would like to emphasize again for the record that the language to which Mr. Chapin takes such exception was the fruit of the defendant's own conduct and not of my invention."

Eloise rejoined Bobbie at counsel's table and then rose with the others as the judge left the courtroom. She saw Hilda slip out the door ahead of the onlookers, and from the corner of one eye she saw George talking to Harry who was putting papers in his briefcase and nodding his head.

"Come," Bobbie said to her. "I'll buy you a drink and some lunch."

"Oh, Bobbie, you don't have to. Poor Bobbie."

"Come."

He took her to a bar across the square from the court house and said nothing until they each had a drink before them.

"Drink," he said.

Obediently, she raised the glass to her lips.

"You know," he said, "I had a sort of suspicion that you'd do that. I never really believed that you'd let me handle this case as it ought to be handled."

"Are you furious with me, Bobbie?"

"I'd like to be. I'll tell you that." He took a long sip of his cocktail and then managed a smile. "You certainly made an ass of me today, Eloise. But I kept reminding myself that I was the one who had asked for it. You never came to me. I pushed myself on you. And why the hell did I? Can *you* tell me?"

"You wanted to make Hilda angry."

"Did I? That was part of it, I guess." His smile became rather sour. "She'll probably marry me now. Now that your case is all mucked up. I've probably won my way into her dark little heart at last."

"Oh, Bobbie, I'm sorry. Can't I tell people I went against your advice? Or do something to exonerate you? I seem to make such a mess of things."

"You do, Eloise," he agreed, nodding his head emphatically. "You sure do. You're too honest for this world. That's your trouble. Look. You're going to lose custody of those kids. Sure as shooting. You won't get a nickel out of George. You'll be all over the papers in the morning. But it'll be worth it to you. And why, in the name of God? Because you want to be the champion of adultery? Is that such a great thing?"

She knew how it was going to hurt later on, what he said and the truth of it, she knew how grim it would be when she got back to the Stafford and thought of Peggy and Jo with no one to read to them but old Mrs. Dilworth or George himself, in his literal, uncomprehending way. But now she could still feel and cling to the remnants of exhilaration.

"It's not that, Bobbie," she protested. "You're talking like Harry. It's just that I can't mouth their formulas. Even for my own children. Their meaningless, last-century formulas, conceived in hate and designed to inflict pain. I won't do it, Bobbie! And I won't tell them either, about George's—"

"Impotence."

"Call it what you will. Let George wash his dirty linen in public. I shan't wash mine."

He snorted.

"Too much of a lady."

"All right, too much of a lady!" she agreed excitedly. "I don't care what you call it. I know how George has sunk, and I won't sink to his level. I've talked their formulas all my life. Isn't that enough? Now I've washed my mouth out. And I intend to keep it clean!"

"Eloise." He shook his head sadly as he said her name. "Eloise, you're beyond me. You've brought back the past, don't you see? Anyone who heard Harry Hamilton this morning would have thought we were living a hundred years ago. Because they all fundamentally agree with you. They *do*. They're on your side. But you *force* them to go against you. Judge Cory wants to rule in your favor, I know. He talked to those kids. Anyone can see they're crazy about their mother—"

"Oh, Bobbie, please—"

"No, Eloise, I've got to say it. All you have to do is behave yourself in court to have things the way they ought to be and the way everybody but George and that son-of-a-bitch, Hamilton, really wants them. But no. You won't have it that way. You want to use the trial as a sounding board for a lot of ideas that you don't even believe in. For God's sake, be practical! Win your case and then do anything you want. Write a book if you must. But not here. Not in court."

She shook her head several times. In the silence of their booth, without the hateful booming of Harry's voice, it seemed clear enough to her, but she wondered if she could ever articulate it.

"Maybe it is foolish," she conceded. "But when Harry started asking me those questions I *knew* that I had to tell the truth. No matter what happened. It was as if I'd been living in a moral void ever since what happened with Carl. All my life before then I'd been living by what I thought was a code, and maybe it was one—I don't know—but it wasn't mine, that's the point. It was other people's. When I stopped being quite so afraid of other people, it seemed foolish to go on being quite so afraid of their code. Oh, Bobbie, don't you see it? I *had* to be on my own. And, of course, I make mistakes. But that doesn't mean I have to go home again with my tail between my legs. I have to find out the things *I* think are right and wrong. And I know all through me, all through myself, that what Harry and George are doing to me is wrong. We don't all have the luck, Bobbie, of finding great moral issues. Some of us have to make asses of ourselves over little ones."

"Here, here!"

"But we have to start *somewhere*, Bobbie. That's the point. And I've made my start."

"You've started all right. Right at the bottom."

"I'm sorry, Bobbie," she said disconsolately. "I'm sorry for what I've done to you. I hope we can still be friends."

"Oh, we'll be friends," he said, signaling the waiter for two more cocktails. "We'll even drink to that. Because I like you, Eloise. But you're an exasperating client. You're almost as exasperating as that stepdaughter of yours."

"Ex-stepdaughter."

He laughed.

"Not yet. Not for a few days anyhow. I wish the judge would put Hilda in your custody, Eloise. She's the one who needs a few new ideas." He scratched his head and then asked for the second time: "Why did I ever have to get mixed up with your family, anyway? Will you tell me that?"

7

THE FIRST DAY of the case of Dilworth against Dilworth
fell on a Friday, and on Saturday morning the publicity
which the newspapers accorded it exceeded even Gerald Hunt's worst fears. There were pictures of Eloise, of
George and of Carl; there was even one headline that
ran: "Wife of prominent attorney defends own adultery," and the testimony was reported in salacious
extracts. The public reaction was various, particularly
in that part of the city where the name of Hunt &
Livermore was a familiar one. There were a certain
number of fierce old maids, living on their memories of
other people's memories, and of conservative elderly
bachelors with repressed homosexual inclinations who
were elated to see a beautiful woman publicly exposed
and humiliated. Then there was the large and miscel-
laneous bracket of those who knew nothing of the case
but the quoted excerpts of testimony and who assumed,
with more curiosity than condemnation, and with some
surprise on the part of those who actually knew Eloise,
that this quiet and gentle woman had burst the bonds
of her repression to become the flaming advocate of
unfettered love. But there was also, and particularly
among the better informed of the downtown bar, a
group of prominent citizens who were deeply shocked
that George Dilworth should seek so public and scandalous a redress even for what they conceded was a
serious wrong. It was the attitude of this group that
even if the legal standards of parental morality operated
harshly in individual cases, it would be difficult to

broaden them without danger of destroying altogether such rules of conduct as were still believed in. There were rights and wrongs, in other words, in a general sense, and for somebody, particularly somebody in the position of George Dilworth, to allow his personal pique to induce him so to tamper with the precarious setup as to make justice seem tyrannical and morality antiquated was little short of outrageous. What, indeed, was Reno for but to keep the delinquencies of the respectable from prying eyes? In Reno, that innocuous source of a million newspaper stories, adultery became incompatibility; desertion, hurt feelings, and impotence the persistent failure to support one's partner's suit at the bridge table. It was to this enchanted city with its fairy-tale interpretation of facts that everyone recognized but that nobody wished to face that George should have taken his wounded pride.

Carl Landik spent Friday and Saturday in sullen solitude. He had not been called as a witness in the case as Harry Hamilton had not needed him, but he had refused to go out of town which might have had the look of running away. He had felt it his duty to be on hand and ready to help Eloise whenever she should need him, and he had called on Bobbie Chapin at his office to tell him this. Bobbie had been very nice about it, and Carl had felt for him the immediate liking which the intellectual often feels for the man of affairs who is frankly without interest in, but also without hostility to the world of the imagination. But Bobbie had had the same answer for him that Eloise had had.

"I can imagine what you're going through, fella," he had said, putting his hand on Carl's shoulder as he conducted him to the lobby. "But you're just a fifth wheel in this case. If I were you, I'd duck out of town. Leave me your address. I'll get hold of you if I need you."

"Thanks, Chapin. You're okay. But I'll be at my same address. The one I gave you."

On Saturday morning he read the papers and felt too sick to do anything but sit in his apartment and mope. After two anonymous and abusive calls and several others from reporters, he had his telephone disconnected. He could only indulge in the rather grim satisfaction of repeating over and over to himself that his chance to help her was not now but later, that he would make it all up to her in marriage, but it was a prospect that he faced without cheerfulness and sometimes, when he thought of the impetuosity of his proposal, with active resentment. For he had never really wanted to marry Eloise. He didn't really want to marry anyone, not for years anyway. He reflected with the gloomiest feelings how difficult if not impossible it would be to fit her into his life and among his friends, how patient but long suffering she would be at their drinking partes, what a struggle it might be to support her. He pictured already the patently brave, falsely cheerful resignation with which she would face his discovered infidelities, a resignation that he would never be able to criticize because he would know that it came from gratitude. Christ, what would she say if she knew that all during the period of their strange friendship and on the very day before her visit to his apartment, he had been living with that neurotic girl painter on the floor above? Oh, she would say nothing, she would never complain, she had been a true friend, there was no question about it, but if only they could go back to their original basis, to the mild grey uncommitting coolness of their autumn walks! This rest was madness. By evening he was so miserable that he had to see someone, and he called on Lorna, though he well knew she would be enjoying the newspapers to the hilt. She was, however, the only friend he had who knew both him and Eloise, and she was gratifyingly glad to see him, pouring him several stiff drinks, one after the other. It was only after the third double scotch that he would say anything at all about Eloise.

"If I could only think she'd let me make this up to her," he said moodily, to plumb her reaction. "If I could only think she'd marry me, I'd feel better about it. But there she is, all alone, with her life ruined. And whose fault is it but mine?"

"Carl, really. I know it's tough, but you don't have to be completely Victorian."

"Everyone else seems to be."

"Have you asked her to marry you?"

"Of course I have!"

"Well, don't jump at me." She sat back in her chair with her hands raised as if in self-defense. "Let me ask a simple question. Are you in love?"

"Certainly."

"And she refused you?"

He looked at her gloomily. "She implied that what's happened is no reason for getting married."

Lorna, for once in her life, looked impressed.

"Did she really? Well, she's right, of course. Even you, Carl, will come to see that. In time."

He turned away from her and finished his drink in a gulp. He hated himself for having sought the reassurance that Eloise would refuse him.

"Your trouble, Carl," Lorna said in a kinder tone, "is that you want to pay. And anyway you look at this, you can't help but come out of it unscathed. That's what you have to face, my friend. In a way, it's harder on you than anyone."

Irene had been in a state of nerves on Friday night. Eloise had gone out to dinner with Bobbie; they had asked her to go with them, but she had refused, saying that she would stay in her room and nurse a sick headache. She saw all in ruins because of Eloise's perversity, but for once in her life she felt too low even to

224

remonstrate. It was thus that Arthur Irwin found her when he called, stretched out on the sofa with an ice pack on her head and a whiskey and soda in her hand.

"I'm sorry, Arthur," she said wearily, "I'm too done in to dress up. You'll just have to take me as I am."

She could not have said anything that would have appealed to him more. To be accepted entirely as a friend, and at the same time to be recognized and revered as a potentate, was what he most desired. They talked about the case and Eloise's testimony, which had horrified him, but Irene, even in her state of emotional upheaval, never allowed herself to be caught in the pros and cons of the point of view which her daughter had expressed in court. She confined herself to what her "poor girl" was going through and reiterated, again and again, that Eloise had been too upset and hounded by "that fiend," Harry Hamilton, to have known what she was saying. Towards the end of the evening, when she threw up her hands and asked rhetorically what was going to happen to them now, he gravely made his long expected proposal.

"I think, Irene, that the time has come when I might be allowed to take a hand in your affairs. If I say so myself you would probably find several of your problems solved by the simple expedient of becoming Mrs. Irwin. At any rate, I think you should seriously consider it."

She stared at him for several moments with her eyes wide open. Then the ice pack fell from her head, the drink from her hand, and she sat up and flung her arms around his neck with an almost perfect simulation of surprise and spontaneity.

"Arthur! You mean you feel that way, *too!*"

And after he had gone to the telephone to order a bottle of champagne she straightened her hair and reflected elatedly that she was still adhering to her resolution of trying once again to be a good mother.

Was she not, after all, placing a fortune at her child's disposal?

Gerald Hunt had the most direct reaction to the turn which the case had taken. He received reports on Friday afternoon which made him realize that George had in fact crossed the Rubicon, and a glance at the papers the next morning assured him that swift action was necessary. Gerald, for all his diplomacy, could be very swift when he felt the future of the firm to be at stake. There were hurried telephone calls to the other senior partners and to certain old and trusted clients, including Arthur Irwin. The latter gave him an astounding piece of family news that strengthened his hand immeasurably and made the contemplated action now almost imperative. His last calls were to George and Harry to request them to be at his house at noon.

They met, the three of them, at the appointed hour in Gerald's dark Italian renaissance den at the back of the ground floor of his city house.

"I am sorry to bring you here on a weekend, gentlemen," Gerald began in his gravest tone, the one he reserved for his rare appearances in the federal appellate courts. "But I consider it a matter of the utmost importance to us all. You knew my concern about your case, George, with particular regard to the reputation of the firm. My concern, you will admit, has been justified. I find myself in an intolerable position. All New York is accusing me of standing by while two of my partners destroy my niece."

"I might point out, Gerald," George said sullenly, "that it's your niece who's causing the scandal. Not I."

"I don't wish to go into that, George," Gerald retorted, slightly raising his voice. "Any more than I care to go into the ridiculous issues that Harry has raised in court. The point is that a scandal has started and that as your wife's uncle as well as your partner my position is untenable. You will remember that when I first dis-

226

cussed this unhappy matter with you, you offered to resign from the firm if I thought it proper."

"I did."

"I had no idea then, of course, of taking you up on it. You're one of our ablest partners, and the matter, after all, was personal. But now the situation has changed. The matter has become regrettably public. Clients have been shocked by Harry's aggressiveness. There is only one thing I can do." Gerald paused deliberately and arranged his blotter folder neatly in line with a large ivory paper cutter. "I do not like to be in the position of giving ultimatums, but if I must, I must. I tell you, frankly, George, that unless you withdraw or settle this suit on Monday morning and proceed with your divorce in a less sensational fashion, I shall feel obliged to accept your offer of resignation. I might add that I have not come to this painful decision without the backing of a proper number of our senior partners."

George, breathing heavily, sat for several moments in silence, staring at the bland features of this older man who had for twenty years preserved a position of dominance in his life. It seemed indeed odd that after so long and arduous a struggle on his own part to gain the peak, he should now be releasing his grip from the very topmost boulder to slide back down the slope before Gerald's mildly curious eyes. And the oddness of it, he saw now with a dazed clarity, was the extent to which he had been caught in a process from which there was no longer escape, because the act of articulating submission to Gerald's terms had become impossible, not for reasons of pride or even, any more, of revenge, but simply and arbitrarily because it was impossible, because he knew, with a gloomy prognostication, that he was *not* going to submit.

"All right, Gerald," he said slowly, "I resign. We can work out the details next week."

"You're sure, George? You don't want the weekend to think it over?"

"I'm sure, Gerald."

There was a painful pause.

"I suppose you think I'm being unfair."

"You suppose correctly. I see no reason to discuss it."

Harry Hamilton rolled his anxious eyes from one to the other of these stubborn men. He no longer felt stubborn himself. He had been shaken by his duel with Eloise and by the bright, glittering hostility in her eyes as she had proceeded with the defiance of one who sees a trap and walks proudly into it, to walk into his. He had been shaken by the attitude of the other lawyers in the firm who felt that he had been rough, even brutal with a helpless woman. Harry had not been prepared for antagonism; under his burly and bristling exterior he craved, even more than most, the affection and approval of those around him. He could have borne it, however; he could have weathered the rising tide had he only felt that George was with him. But George, strangely and terribly, seemed to have lost his heart in the fight without his determination; he would no longer discuss it except glumly and sullenly. It might almost have been his attitude that the whole thing was Harry's fault and that he was backing him up, not because he wanted the divorce, or, at least, not under those terms, but only because Harry was his friend and he had told Harry he would stick by him. And was that the reason, the crazy reason, that with such bitter consistency he was now throwing away the future, breaking up the firm? Harry suddenly felt beads of sweat on his broad forehead as the realization dawned that Gerald would never be taking this attitude if he were not sure of Arthur Irwin. And if Arthur was loyal, the clients would stand firm. God! Did George know? But looking around at that brooding face he saw in a second that nothing would dissuade George, and the thought flashed through his mind, for the first time in their friendship, that maybe it was only common sense to leave him now, to go back to the normalcy and camaraderie and homeyness of his old firm, his club—

"And I assume, Harry, that you will stand by George," Gerald continued with a little smile. "As you said you would. I could hardly ask you to drop a case that you have started. Well, we shall miss you. But I am sure that the firm of Dilworth and Hamilton will enjoy a great success. I mean that, gentlemen. I'm sure it will."

Harry stared at him blankly, recognizing for the first time the hostility in those twinkling eyes. This, of course, was what Gerald had always wanted. Gerald had never wanted him to stay; Gerald had always hated him! His lips began to droop like a little boy's; he was afraid that his eyes would brim with tears. Or did he care? Did he really care what happened now?

He felt George's hand on his arm.

"Come, Harry. Shall we go now? We have a lot to talk over, you and I. Shall we go, friend?"

And Harry, grateful at least for the term of address, got up heavily and followed him out.

8

HEARINGS in Dilworth vs. Dilworth were resumed the following Monday, but they only lasted for a few hours. There was little more testimony to take. Two weeks later, Judge Cory handed down his decision awarding custody of Peggy and Jo Dilworth to their father. He wrote a lengthy opinion which was much discussed in legal circles and noted in several of the country's leading law reviews. It was obvious from the amount of precedent which he cited that he had found the decision a difficult one to arrive at, but he fell back in the end on the one proposition that he could not seem to elude.

"In reaching this conclusion I am entirely aware," he wrote, "that the defendant did not state that she believed that adultery was never a wrongful act. In fact, the implication is clear from the record that she believes that most adulteries *are* wrong. This, however, cannot alter the vital consideration that the defendant believes that the test of whether or not adultery is wrong is a circumstantial one—there is nothing to her *inherently immoral* in the unfaithfulness of one spouse to another. Such an attitude, viewed in the light of her own proven adultery, must under our law disqualify her as a guardian of infants."

Bobbie called up Eloise and read her the judge's opinion on the telephone.

"Well, that's that," she said dryly. "We expected it, of course."

"We still ought to appeal it."

"Do you think there's a chance?"

"Just that. A chance."

When she had hung up she sat on her bed and stared blankly at her reflection in the big glass mirror on the door. In the next room she could hear Irene on the telephone, ordering some part of her trousseau. It was an odd world. For here she was worrying about the costs of appeal, while Irene and Arthur were planning their fabulous trip around the world, a trip, it was true, on which they had invited her but which she had already declined. She called Carl Landik now, having promised to do so when the trial was over, and made an appointment to lunch with him. Then she left the Stafford and walked down to the building where Lorna's magazine had its offices.

Lorna treated her as if she were a patient and Lorna the doctor when she arrived. She jumped up and practically assisted her into a chair, carefully closing the glass door to her little office.

"You poor darling," she said solicitously, leaning forward, her elbows on the desk. "What can I do?"

Eloise told her briefly about the court's decision.

"What do they use for laws, anyway?" Lorna snorted contemptuously. "The Mosaic tablets? Poor child, what you must be going through. How about a snifter? I've got a bottle right here in the bottom drawer."

"No thank you, Lorna," she said, with just a touch of coolness. "I don't need a drink. I don't even need sympathy, as a matter of fact. But I do want advice. Or perhaps rather confirmation."

Lorna, visibly rebuffed, settled her features in an expression of less emotional concern.

"Shoot."

"What do you think I mean to Carl?"

Lorna started.

"What you mean to him?"

"Oh, come, Lorna, you know exactly what I mean. You and he have discussed me for months."

"Well, he's enormously fond of you, dear," Lorna said nervously, "and interested in you, if that's what you mean. And naturally, since this terrible case he hasn't been able to think of anything else, and he couldn't discuss it with anyone *but* me—"

"Carl came to me before the trial even started," Eloise cut in, in the definite tone of one who had been over the ground a dozen times before. "He asked me to marry him. Now I think he'd like to get out of it. Isn't that about the way it stands?"

Lorna turned very red and looked down at the pile

of typed manuscripts on her desk. She hesitated for several moments.

"Yes," she said finally, without looking up. "That's the way it stands, Eloise. I suppose I'm a bitch to tell you."

Eloise looked at her curiously, wondering what the new expression on her face meant, until she suddenly realized it was sincerity. There were even tears now in Lorna's eyes, but they failed to move her. She had had enough of the emotions of others. What help were people to one, really? First they had been sharp with her; now they were gushing. Like Irene.

"Thank you, Lorna, that's what I thought." She stood up.

"Oh, Eloise, dear. I *am* sorry."

"Don't be. I'm quite all right. And, incidentally, I shall be needing your advice. I'm taking a job. In the new Irwin publishing company. I'm only a reader, but anyway it's a start."

Lorna looked impressed.

"*Definitely* a start. I didn't know you knew anyone there."

Eloise smiled at the sudden revival of the old Lorna.

"What makes you think I couldn't get it on my own?" she asked as she turned to the door.

When she was walking down the street afterwards, in the brief mild winter sunlight, to her lunch appointment with Carl, she reflected in her still rather stunned state that she had known all along what Lorna had told her. And she really *had* known, too; it was not only hindsight. Now she could only close her lips tightly and pray silently to be delivered from the sooty cloud of self-pity that she felt roaring up behind her, knowing that if it overtook her she would never be able to fight herself free, that she would gasp and choke in it until her new being, the new being that she had cared so about, was utterly lost in the image of an Eloise bereft

232

and abandoned and of Lorna and Henry Sterne and Carl meeting for cocktails and telling each other how sorry they felt for her.

She met him in the same Italian restaurant where they had first had lunch. He had been waiting for her, obviously for some time, for he simply glanced at his watch, without getting up, when she appeared. He was really in one of his moods. During the meal he said almost nothing, watching her with preoccupied eyes, crumbling his roll into smaller and smaller pieces as she told him about Judge Cory's decision, about her new job, about Irene's impending marriage. The atmosphere that he created was constrained, even surly; it was like their other lunch there when she had done all the talking about her own life, but she became used to it as the meal progressed, hardened to it, playing a part.

"Of course, I don't want to be dependent on Arthur Irwin," she was explaining as she finished her ravioli. "That's one reason I took this job."

"Which you got from him, of course," he pointed out.

"Yes, but that's different from having him support me. Of course, I'm not going to be a fool. If I find myself really in a jam, I'll let Irene help. And if I ever get my children—George, I assume, won't be able to keep them forever—they're not babies, after all—I would let her help there, too. But in the meantime—"

"In the meantime what about me?" he demanded sullenly. "Do I play any part in this new life of yours?"

"But that's why I'm telling you, Carl," she protested. "To show you that I'm not as pathetic as you might think. I'm all right, don't you see? I really *am*."

"What is this? A renunciation scene?"

Yet she was even grateful for his rudeness. It eased the constraint.

"As a matter of fact, it is."

233

"And you're going off to the ball with the count?" he sneered. "Like Violetta?"

"If he'll ask me."

"Well, don't cough yourself to death. I might not be there for the final duet."

"What I do afterwards, Carl Landik," she said cooly, "is still my own affair."

He was looking at her now with resentment, a resentment, she reflected, that couldn't quite hide his shame.

"Is your count by any chance Mr. Chapin?"

"Mr. Chapin happens to be in love with George's daughter," she said in a sharper tone. It was too much that he had to cheapen her final gesture, that he was afraid even to owe her that. "As a matter of fact he's more in love with Hilda than he knows. Bobbie has a lot to learn about himself."

He blushed deeply at this and leaned forward suddenly, his elbows on the table, his forehead buried in his hands.

"I'm a heel, Eloise," he said in an abrupt change of mood. "You know that, don't you? I know all about what you're doing, and you know I know. You're giving me an easy out, and I'm taking it." He looked up suddenly, defying her to contradict. "And I think you're fine. I think you're wonderful!"

She stared at him for a moment, her eyes wide. If he was unwilling, then, to cheapen her least gesture, she at least owed it to him to put matters in their true perspective. There was an impulse to accept his tribute, to run out of the restaurant and lose herself in the sooty cloud that had threatened her. But it was only an impulse.

"This isn't really a renunciation scene, Carl," she said, looking down at the table again. "I haven't really anything to renounce. Oh, I'd like to think that you were crazy about me, of course. But not quite so much, I confess, as I'd like to think that I was crazy about you. It would be rather pleasantly melancholy, on top of all that's happened, to think of myself as loving and bereft." She shrugged her shoulders and smiled, looking up at him. "But that isn't quite the way things are, is it? I can't really kid myself, can I, Carl? What I know about love I may have learned from you, but it's still more of a teenager's crush than anything else. It isn't real because *I'm* not quite real. Do you see that, Carl?"

"You're a hell of a lot realer than you were, Eloise," he said gravely. "You've come a long, long way since that day in Mogue."

"Oh, do you think so?" she asked. "Do you really think so?"

He nodded.

"It's going to be all right," he said, looking away. "And what's more I'll tell you something. When you *do* fall in love, Eloise, I'm going to be awfully sorry it's not me."

She reached suddenly for her purse and gloves.

"I seem to be always walking out on you in this restaurant," she said, getting up. "Here I am doing it again." She found a handkerchief and raised it quickly to her eyebrows, just touching them. "Carl, dear," she said, in a nervous, almost social voice, "call me up in about two months' time, will you? By then I should be straightened out. And we can talk again like two civilized beings. Or we can try to, anyway."

She turned away abruptly, just as his hand touched hers, and hurried out of the restaurant.

9

TWO MONTHS LATER Eloise's appeal was heard by five justices of the Appellate Division. It was argued by Bobbie who made as much as he could of the point that a mother's fitness could not be determined by what she said in an abstract discussion of principle in a court of law. When he had finished, a rather subdued Harry Hamilton simply repeated the argument that he had used in the lower court. The court, though again troubled by the harshness of the result, could find no way to get around the point that had bothered Judge Cory, and his decision was consequently affirmed. As a matter of law, it was now decided, Eloise was unfit to bring up her own children.

When George read the opinion of the Appellate Division and realized that the fight was over at last, he felt little enough elation. Life without Eloise and without Hunt & Livermore had become a very different and a rather disheartening affair. Hilda had proved a poor substitute for her stepmother. In fact, she had become so gloomy that he really no longer wanted her in the apartment. She refused to confide in him and only murmured "Oh, nothing" in an irritable tone when he questioned her about her moodiness. He assumed, of course, that she was moping over that faithless young shyster who had taken Eloise's case, but he could only thank his stars that Chapin had shown himself in his true colors before things had gone too far between him and Hilda. He shuddered at the thought of a son-in-law who had been his ex-wife's lawyer and one, too, who had tried to put evidence—well, it was better not to think of it. At least there had been *that* decency left in Eloise. He had finally packed Hilda off to Mexico with a girl friend, overcoming her objections with the only argument that always worked on Hilda, an appeal to her duty of self-improvement.

"You can take a trip to Yucatan," he had pointed out, "and see the Mayan monuments. Here you've spent your whole life in America and never seen the remains of its earliest culture."

With Hilda gone his household was run by his mother who had come down from New Hampshire to help him. Mrs. Dilworth was a tall, straight, cheerful woman of a determined rectitude of mind and manner. It was impossible to discourage her, impossible to dampen the optimism that sparkled in her eye or to impede the cliché that leapt from her lips. Yet there was no criticizing her, even to himself; it was obvious to everyone, with the kind of obviousness that made them immediately want to impart their awareness of it to him, that Mrs. Dilworth, say what one might, was an admirable woman. She was admirably aware, too, of how difficult a hand she had to play, and her efforts to play it sportingly were valiant.

"Well, did you have an interesting day, George?" she would greet him in the evenings when he came in. "Did you appear in court? Did you argue?"

And she would stand up straight, her head tilted slightly back, her eye fixed on him with a strained attention as though to defy him to tell her any legal problem, no matter how long or how involved, that she would not hear to the end, just as she was, without twitching a muscle. "I may not be able to give you the comprehension that you're accustomed to," the bright bird's eye of the poor old lady seemed to flash at him, "but if bodily discipline is any substitute, it's yours, it's all I've got. See how straight I am!"

She was as good with the children as could be expected. In the first weeks of Eloise's absence Peggy and Jo had rather enjoyed the novelty of their motherless situation and found the company of their kindly and easily beguiled grandmother a pleasant change from the old regime. Boredom, however, had soon filled the void left by novelty. Mrs. Dilworth not only had a tendency to repeat herself, but she insisted on reading them pleasant stories about nice boys and girls which she had brought with her in faded volumes dating from their father's childhood. They decided that it was time their mother returned. When they went to George to tell him this, however, they were astonished at what happened. He immediately assumed a very grave expression and took them out to buy ice cream sodas and then to the movies. This was gratifying enough, but the next time they tried it they were simply given a long, serious talk about how Mummy would like them to be good girls whether or not she came back. This produced such tears and screams that old Mrs. Dilworth had to be called in and they were promised that they would be taken to see their mother in a few weeks' time if they were good. Peggy at this point began to sulk and to cry at night, and a remark made to her at school about her mother being "bad" caused such an emotional upheaval that she had to be kept home for a week. Jo, less sensitive, nonetheless saw the value of scenes and was quick to perceive that one made about Mummy would always go unpunished. Sometimes at breakfast, when Peggy would come in red-eyed and sniveling and Mrs. Dilworth would start indefatigably the daily task of cheering her up, Jo would suddenly stamp both fists on the table and shriek at the top of her lungs:

"I want my mummy! I want my mummy!"

When George left the apartment after one of these breakfasts and went down to the new offices of Dilworth and Hamilton it was not, alas, to find an atmosphere more tranquil. He and Harry had rented an imposing suite of rooms with an even better view of New York Harbor than they had had at Hunt & Livermore, and they had already hired eight associate lawyers and a staff, but everything from the decoration of the reception hall to the arrangement of the files was still in a state of chaos, and Harry, who loathed administration and organization, who had been accustomed all his legal life to having such details handled by the lay employees of a large firm, was constantly storming into George's office with his hands in the air and screeching about each new "abomination" of which some subordinate, usually so instructed by George, had been guilty. New clients were coming in satisfactorily, it was true, but George did not fool himself. He and Harry had taken a considerable drop in the opinion of the bar, and the woebegone look in Harry's large watery eyes was sad to see. But it was not until George read in the evening papers that Arthur Irwin and Irene had been married that morning in the chambers of a supreme court justice that he realized that the last and largest item had been appended to the bill of his self-indulgence. As he looked out his window over the wintry harbor to the raised arm of the Statue of Liberty he reflected with a dull placidity that there was indeed no justice.

When he got home that evening his mother met him in the hall. The bright look in her eyes was even shinier than usual, but it was the shine, as he immediately knew, of alarm.

"George, Peggy's sick."

"What does she have?"

"The doctor's been here, and he says it's nothing but flu, but her temperature's up to a hundred and two, and she keeps asking for Eloise. He told me we ought to get her. He said she'd only make herself sicker if Eloise didn't come."

George put his briefcase down in a corner. It was heavy with papers that he had meant to read that night, and as he straightened up he knew that he had surrendered. It was so simple, so inevitable. Almost as inevitable as saying to Gerald the things that he had said in their final interview.

"All right, Mother," he said calmly. "Will you call her? She's still at the Stafford."

His mother stepped up to him and gave him a quick kiss. It told worlds of what she had been going through. Then she hurried off to make her call. He went on down the corridor and into Peggy's dramatically darkened room.

"Your mother will be over in just a bit," he said, sitting on the bedside and rumpling her hair. "We thought she'd better see you. How are you, Peg?"

She sat up and threw her arms around him.

"Oh, Daddy! And will she stay? Will she stay with us now?"

He heard steps behind him, and Jo came bounding in.

"Is Mummy coming?"

"Jo, you know you're not allowed in here!" Peggy reproved her. "I'm contagious," she added self-importantly. "And besides, Mummy's coming to see *me*. I'm sick."

"Will she stay, Daddy?" Jo demanded, looking up at him.

"Well I don't know if she'll exactly stay," George said, getting up. "But we'll fix up something, don't worry. Come, Jo, we've got to get out of here. We don't want to be sick ourselves, do we?"

He was alone in his study later, after dinner, when he heard his mother talking to someone in the hall, and knew that Eloise had arrived. He abandoned all thought of work and paced slowly up and down the room, wondering with a rather blank detachment what had become of his resentment. He even asked himself if she might not be interested, simply as an intellectual matter, to discuss with him the enormity of what had happened to them both. They had always, at least so it had seemed to him, tried to face things rationally. He started when he felt his mother's hand on his arm.

"She'll be going in a minute, George," she whispered theatrically, as if Eloise, at the other end of the apartment, could hear. "I thought I'd tell you, so you wouldn't be caught in the hall."

"Don't be ridiculous, Mother," he said sharply. "Please tell her that I would appreciate it very much if she would see me before she goes."

"Oh." Mrs. Dilworth's expression was suspended as she sought his mood, to know what to conform to. "Oh, George," she whispered again, "do you thnik you could ask her to come again? Do you, George? The children love it so. I know it's hard for you, dear, nobody knows that better than I do, but—"

"I must do as I see best, Mother," he said impatiently, angered to have her take credit for a greater sympathy for the little girls than his own. "Please give her my message."

He stood near the door a few minutes later, tensely listening to the voices in the hall. His mother was still speaking in that irritating whisper, but he heard Eloise say: "George does?" and "Really?" and then he stepped quickly away from the door as he heard her steps.

"Did you want to see me, George?"

Her tone was as matter-of-fact as her expression. She looked calm and well.

"Please. Won't you sit down?"

She sat in the chair in front of his desk, and he in the one behind it. It was like an interview in his office. But that, it occurred to him, was perhaps just what it was.

"How did you find Peg?"

"She'll be all right. It's nothing, really."

"I hope you will come and see her tomorrow."

There was a slight pause.

"Very well," she said. "Can I come in the evening again? I'm working now, you know."

"Certainly."

In the silence that followed he realized that it was up to him to provide the openings. There was nothing, after all, for her to say. Unless, of course, she said she was sorry for what she had done to him. But he knew she wouldn't do that. This was implicit in the firm, mildly interested expression that she now turned to him.

"I don't just mean tomorrow, Eloise," he said in his lawyer's voice, "or the day after that. Or just when the girls are sick. I want to share them, the way you originally suggested. Of course, you'll have to get an apartment that's big enough, but we can work that out later. There won't be any trouble about the money."

He looked straight at her as he said this, but his directness was a pose, his professional pose. Behind it he was as excited as a small boy, hiding behind the dining-room curtain to see what the reaction will be to the birthday present that he has put on his mother's plate. Eloise, however, did not looked pleased, as a parent might have. Her expression was one of simple astonishment.

"You mean you went through all that trial for nothing?"

"Apparently."

"But why, George?" Her voice for the first time showed feeling. "Why? Was it just for revenge?"

"I can't swing it, Eloise. Mother. The children. The whole deal's too much for me."

She stared. "You haven't tried long."

"Long enough." He paused and then looked down at

the blotter on his desk. I'll send one of my boys to see Chapin in the morning. Don't worry, I won't send Harry. They can draw up a new agreement."

She put her fingers to her temples and rubbed them slowly.

"Well—well, yes," she said. "God knows it isn't that I don't want the children. But it's all—it's all so bewildering."

"I don't blame you for being bewildered, Eloise. Would you like a drink?"

"Thanks. I guess I need it."

Relieved at the interruption, he got up and went to the bar and poured whiskey into two glasses.

"It's pretty simple, really," he said, his back to her. "When you're spent, you're spent. Jealousy is like a disease that has to run its course. And then it leaves you, feeling flat as a pancake. But cured."

"And you mean all that hate," she protested, almost as if the waste was too much for her to contemplate, "all that break-up of the firm—"

"Has been for nothing," he finished for her, turning and handing her a drink. "As you said. For nothing at all."

There was a certain satisfaction in the superiority of being able to admit it, of being able to face the fact that he was a man who was seized from time to time by gusts of passion that it was fruitless to resist. What could he do but bow his head before the tempest and then go slowly and philosophically about the reconstruction of his life?

"But you take it so calmly, George. I don't understand."

"How else can I take it?" he said, pleased. "I face myself."

"Yes, I suppose you do." She nodded reflectively. "I suppose you always have, really. When you lose your

243

temper, you face it. It's a part of you, I suppose. You give it leash."

But he wanted some reaction besides the intellectual, something less detached, more appreciative.

"I won't be able to give you as large an allowance as before," he said, "but I'll do what I can."

She shook her head, as if this were a detail.

"I won't need it. I like my job, and I intend to keep it. The girls are in school all day."

"I don't want you to feel you have to work."

"And as for the apartment," she continued, ignoring this, "Irene's will do for me. She's moving out now, and Arthur's paid the rent for the rest of the year."

He felt suddenly deflated. Arthur Irwin, of course, with his inexhaustible fortune, would stand forever between him and his generosity.

"It's funny to think of Irene being in a position to help out," he said bitterly. "I don't know if I quite like the idea of your being supported by Arthur Irwin."

"You have hardly put yourself in a position recently, George, to complain about who supports me."

"Oh, it's all right, I guess," he said gloomily. "For the past, anyway. But I'd like to look after the bills in the future, if you don't mind."

"You can pay for Peggy and Jo," she agreed. "That's your right and obligation. But as for me, I don't intend to be supported by you *or* Arthur. I intend to look after myself. Anything you give me by a legal agreement must come to me on behalf of the girls. I shall keep a strict accounting."

George looked at her sadly. The gift that he had laid so hopefully at her place had been critically opened, examined and accepted without exclamation. His last act of possession had failed.

"Eloise," he said, swallowing hard.

"Yes, George?"

He saw by the sudden, startled expression in her eyes that she knew what was coming.

"Do you think that you and I could ever—do you think we could ever make a go of it again?"

"Never." The word was definite, unsentimental. "Never," she repeated, shaking her head soberly. "Let me make that very clear. Do you really think, George, after what's happened, that you and I could ever be happy together again?"

"Perhaps not," he conceded reluctantly, for he didn't really see why. "I thought you might have some feeling left. In spite of everything. I know I do."

This, anyway, seemed to crack the hard casing of her mood.

"I don't believe it!" she exclaimed heatedly. "If you'd done what you've done to me out of jealousy, George, I could understand it. There wouldn't really be anything to forgive. But it wasn't that. You went wild at the idea that you were losing something, something that you owned. You're a miser, George! Once you get your hands on a person, you'll *never* let go!"

"It's Landik," he said stubbornly. "You're going to marry him. That's it."

She stood up.

"I'm not going to marry anyone, George," she said firmly. "Inconceivable as that may seem to you. I want to find out first what I am. I want to learn to live with myself. I want to be satisfied with myself as a human being and not only as a daughter or a niece or a wife. I want to go back to where I was when I graduated from college and first met you."

"It would be a fine thing, wouldn't it, if everyone did that?" he retorted. "If every wife walked out on her husband and concentrated on her own development?"

She stared at him.

"Do you really think I walked out on you, George?"

she asked, almost curiously. "Have you really forgotten the door that you slammed in my face?"

"But think what you'd done, Eloise!"

"And you threw me out," she answered dryly. "That was it, wasn't it? Very well, I'm staying out. That's all. I'm piecing together what's left of my life in my own way. And I don't need your help, George. I'm going to wake up in the morning and enjoy the simple fact that I'm Eloise Dilworth."

"You'll be lonely. Just with Eloise Dilworth."

"I'll have friends, I hope. New friends. And now, thanks to your decision, I'll have my children."

He smiled ruefully. He knew when he was beaten.

"Well, I wish you luck, Eloise," he said, holding out his hand. "If you're going to have new friends, perhaps I might be one of them."

For a bad moment he thought she was going to break down. The defiance had faded from her eyes, and her lower lip trembled.

"I don't want you to think, George, that I don't know what this whole wretched thing has cost you," she said with feeling. "I know all about the firm, and if Uncle Gerald had only let me I'd have begged him not to do it. But you'll build it all up again, I know that. And I'm sure you'll marry again, too, but before you do, please, George, come and tell me about it. I think I could give you some advice. And you take advice, too, George. It was one of my faults that I offered so little."

"I'll come," he said smiling. "When we're friends. I'll like that."

"Thank you," she said, taking his hand. "I think that's perhaps the nicest thing you've ever said to me."

There were things, too many things, that he could have said to this. He only nodded, however, and led her out to the hall to help her into her coat.

10

HILDA IN MEXICO had inattentive eyes for the ruins of the Mayan world. In Yucatan she gazed at the line of temples against the setting sun with only a vague curiosity, very different from the specific, well-instructed melancholy that she liked to conjure up when confronted with historical remnants of the vast and gone. But out of her detachment a decision of surprising definiteness was formed, and with its formation her spirits slowly improved. In fact her traveling companion, a former roommate at Vassar, to whom she had confided nothing, but who, like everyone else, knew all about Bobbie, observed that she had become almost cheerful. Yet the decision itself was a simple one. When she returned to New York she would go straight to Eloise and simply tell her that she had changed sides. She would impart the same information to her father and grandmother and proceed to work, in whatever way she could, for an amelioration of the harsh terms of the court's decree. Very likely they would *all* turn on her. It could not be helped. She would only be doing what she had to do.

When she got back to New York, however, it was to find a situation radically changed from the one she had left. Her grandmother had already returned to New Hampshire, and Eloise now visited the little girls every afternoon from five to seven. On weekends Peggy and Jo stayed with her at the Stafford. Her father, entirely preoccupied with the development of his new law firm, seemed to have put completely out of his mind the jealousies and animosities of the preceding months. There was nothing for Hilda to do but move quietly back to her own apartment in the Village, feeling as unwanted and foolish as a crusader of the age of chivalry returning from the Holy Land to find his friends taken up with the small and crass details of a commerce that he had never learned.

There was no excuse now to call up Bobbie or even to write him. Instead of arriving in his cheerless camp, as she had planned, with unexpected reinforcements, she would now be coming, late and unbidden, to the celebration of his victory. Gloomily she turned her attention to looking for a job. She wanted one, if possible, that would send her abroad.

She was coming out of an office building in Radio City, where she had been interviewed by an importer, when she ran into Bobbie's roommate, Larry Weavers. She did not immediately recognize his round and friendly features, so smooth and bland and well cared for, rising above his expensive tweeds like a tulip above its stem, but as she watched him coming towards her, smiling and waving, she had a sudden warm feeling of association, and then, just as he called out her name, she remembered him.

"Hilda!"

"Larry!"

"But I thought you were in Mexico! How have you been? Why, you look like a million dollars, baby. Does Bobbie know you're back?"

She glanced down at the pavement.

"I don't know why he should."

"I don't know why he shouldn't! We're having a party this evening. How about it? Can we count on you?"

"But do you think Bobbie will want me?" she protested. "You can't just assume that, you know. Not after what's happened."

"If he doesn't, to hell with him. *I* want you. Now, then, is it okay?"

She hesitated for a moment and then found herself nodding her head.

"That's my girl. About six?"

She had no more interviews that day. She walked in the park and then sat for two hours at a movie until it was time to dress for the party. Her heart was so filled with excitement that she almost didn't care whether or not Bobbie would be glad to see her. She was going, that was the thing. And if nothing happened, if he was simply polite and sarcastic or even engaged to another girl, at least the turmoil in herself was over.

When she arrived at their apartment a little before seven, having made herself stay away till that hour so as not to seem too anxious, she found the room full of people. Larry came up to her and steered her around.

"Bobbie's in the kitchen," he said. "He'll be right out."

Two men came up to talk to her, but she couldn't seem to concentrate on what they were saying. She drank her cocktail quickly and asked for another. She had almost finished her second before she saw Bobbie emerge from the kitchen with two shakers of different kinds of cocktails. His eyes fell directly on her, and he started. Then he looked around at Larry. Without a word he went over and put both shakers in his hands. Then he turned and came straight to her, taking her by the elbow and guiding her to the window seat.

"So this was Larry's surprise," he said. "He was right. It *is* a surprise."

His blue eyes, perfectly serious, were fixed on her. He was not smiling.

"I hoped you wouldn't mind."

"Mind? Why should I mind? You were the one who

was always doing the minding. When did you change your mind about cocktail parties?"

"A little while back."

He looked down at her almost empty glass.

"And you're drinking, too," he observed. "Perhaps you want another cocktail?"

"I'd love one, thank you."

He waved at Larry who was watching them and came over to fill her glass.

"Mexico does strange things, Larry," he said. "Here's Hilda just back and hitting the bottle."

"That's not Mexico," Larry retorted, winking at her. "That's me. Isn't it, Hilda? She'll always drink with a real guy. And I happen to be the one who asked her to this party. Don't forget that, Chapin. Me. Not you."

"I see," Bobbie said dryly, as Larry moved off, laughing boisterously. "Well, don't overdo it. Or maybe I shouldn't say that. Maybe, as Larry implies, it's only with me that you disapprove of drinking."

She took a sip of her cocktail. She was beginning to feel the gin.

"Maybe."

"Frankly, I'm surprised you speak to me at all."

"You are? Why?"

"Why do you think?"

"Oh, that." She thought vaguely of the divorce and then slowly shrugged her shoulders. "That's all over now, anyway."

He frowned in astonishment.

"You mean you don't *care?*"

"I did. I cared very much." She tried to concentrate on what it was she had cared about. "But I thought you were so good to do that for Eloise."

"For Eloise? Hilda, are you drunk?"

"That's not polite."

"To hell with politeness! Are you?"

She considered this.

"Maybe a little. But not that much. Must you be so stuffy, Bobbie?"

"Stuffy? Me? My God!"

Some people came up and stood before them, chatting with Bobbie. Hilda finished her cocktail without saying a word. From time to time she smiled up, rather fatuously, at them. The happiness inside her kept growing and growing, and she wondered if it wouldn't burst out over her skin like a rash. Bobbie was being rather abrupt with the people, and eventually, they moved off. He turned again to her immediately.

"So you were on Eloise's side?"

She nodded.

"Why didn't you write me or tell me? Didn't you know I'd care?"

For a moment she plucked at one of the buttons in the upholstery of the window seat.

"Not after the way I behaved at the Herberts'," she said.

"But you were upset. I realized afterwards that you knew then about Eloise."

"Yes."

"You weren't on her side then, were you?"

"No."

"What changed your mind?"

"Oh, I don't know." She continued to pluck at the button. "Seeing you in court, I guess."

"In court! And I thought all the time you were sitting there, hating me."

"Oh no, Bobbie!"

He looked at her with almost comic gravity, and she nearly smiled. Quickly she stiffened her lips.

"What does this mean, Hilda?"

"What do you think it means?" she exclaimed. "What would it be apt to mean?" She wondered in an odd distant way if the amazement in his eyes meant that he was glad. It hardly seemed to matter as long as he would sit there, looking at her and let her go on saying unbelievable things like that. "I'm glad I said that," she continued, looking out the window, down into the dark street. "I never thought I'd be able to say anything like that." She paused. "I like your party," she said, changing the subject abruptly and turning from the window to look around the room, "I think I even like your friends. And I *know* I like your cocktails. I'm not at all sure that I'm not going to have another."

"Oh no, you're not!"

"You said once that I'd have to learn to put up with your drinking," she protested. "I don't see why you shouldn't learn to put up with mine."

"Come with me," he said, getting up.

"Where?"

"In the kitchen. I want to talk to you."

She followed him across the room and down the little corridor to the kitchen where a colored man was mixing drinks.

"Go, see who needs what, will you, Tom?"

When he had gone, Bobbie closed the door firmly and came over to her. He took her in his arms and kissed her, pressing his hands into her shoulder blades.

"Sober up, kid, will you?" he said.

"You don't have to do this, you know," she protested, pulling away from him. "You don't have to be nice to me."

"I just have to marry you, is that it?"

"Oh, Bobbie, I hate you!"

She felt the quick tears in her eyes.

"I know what I have to do and what I don't," he said. "I'm a lawyer, you know."

"You're free as air!" she insisted heatedly.

"I was. Till you had that third cocktail."

He pulled her back in his arms just as the door opened. It was Larry with an empty shaker.

"Oops! Sorry."

He was backing out, but Bobbie caught the door handle.

"Come in, lug. Don't you ever knock? I was just taking something out of Miss Dilworth's eye."

"I see." Larry came in, leering at them. "It all goes to show I must have a dirty mind." He made a ceremonious little bow to Hilda. "I'm glad to see that Bobbie has cast out the beam in his own eye, Hilda. Otherwise he might have had competition. By the way, Bobbie," he continued, turning to his friend. "I told you I had a surprise guest. You didn't mention that you had one."

Bobbie looked blank.

"Oh God," he groaned suddenly. "Not Elaine?"

"No, not Elaine. Not a girl at all, as a matter of fact. Quite the reverse."

Bobbie slapped his forehead.

"Oh, *him!*" he exclaimed. "I forgot all about *him!*"

"Well, he's in there right now, surrounded by the girls. They're hoping he'll drop one of his famous four-letter words. You'd better slip out with Hilda."

"No," Bobbie paused, thinking quickly. "You stay here a minute with Hilda, and I'll go in and get him a drink and then tell him there's been a mix-up and that Hilda's here. He'll go. He's got tact."

Hilda opened her mouth, but he was gone, and she was left staring at Larry.

"It's Landik, isn't it?" she said breathlessly.

He nodded.

"Bobbie must have asked him before he knew you were coming," he explained.

Her heart was beating wildly. Everything in her that could hold back was holding back again, suddenly, sickeningly. She had a sense of happiness draining out of her, through her pores, leaving her in a single minute depleted and dry.

"You think I ought to go in and meet him, don't you?" she challenged him.

He shrugged his shoulders.

"I think it would mean a lot to Bobbie," he said.

"But, Larry, I *couldn't!*"

"Well, don't then."

She looked at him miserably, pleading against his neutrality.

"But you think I should?" she persisted.

She was afraid he would shrug his shoulders again, and he almost did, but then he nodded.

"I should?" she repeated.

And it came over her with a rush that, of course, she should, not only should but wanted to, and at the same time she stood there quite still, electrified with the wonderful realization that it was not too late. It was like a dream, it was not too late, not yet anyway, but soon it would be, any moment, while she stood there—

"Well, hurry!" Larry exclaimed.

She ran out of the kitchen and almost collided with Bobbie and a short, dark-haired young man as they were walking towards the front door. She took Carl's hand impulsively and shook it while she stared into his astonished eyes.

"I'm Hilda Dilworth," she said excitedly, "and I'm sorry to embarrass you. But I want you to know that I don't have any feeling any more about you or about Eloise, or about—well, anything."

She felt Bobbie's arm then around her shoulders, and her heart pounded at the thought that she might not have done it. Carl was blushing furiously, of course, but it was all right.

"I certainly thank you for saying that, Miss Dilworth," he stammered. "I'm sure—well I'm sure it was a hard thing to say."

"Come on back in, Carl," Bobbie was saying. "Now we're all friends we'll have a drink on it. All except

Hilda, that is. Hilda, I think, has had enough for tonight."

And Hilda, standing beside them as they drank their cocktails and talked about basketball, tongue-tied as only one can be who has said her piece and said all, reflected how strange it was to feel at once so embarrassed and still so utterly at ease.